WHO DO, VOODOO?

ROCHELLE STAAB

BERKLEY PRIME CRIME, NEW YORK

THE BERKLEY PUBLISHING GROUP
Published by the Penguin Group
Penguin Group (USA) Inc.
375 Hudson Street, New York, New York 10014, USA

Penguin Group (Canada), 90 Eglinton Avenue East, Suite 700, Toronto, Ontario M4P 2Y3, Canada
(a division of Pearson Penguin Canada Inc.)
Penguin Books Ltd., 80 Strand, London WC2R 0RL, England
Penguin Group Ireland, 25 St. Stephen's Green, Dublin 2, Ireland (a division of Penguin Books Ltd.)
Penguin Group (Australia), 250 Camberwell Road, Camberwell, Victoria 3124, Australia
(a division of Pearson Australia Group Pty. Ltd.)
Penguin Books India Pvt. Ltd., 11 Community Centre, Panchsheel Park, New Delhi—110 017, India
Penguin Group (NZ), 67 Apollo Drive, Rosedale, Auckland 0632, New Zealand
(a division of Pearson New Zealand Ltd.)
Penguin Books (South Africa) (Pty.) Ltd., 24 Sturdee Avenue, Rosebank, Johannesburg 2196,
South Africa

Penguin Books Ltd., Registered Offices: 80 Strand, London WC2R 0RL, England

This is a work of fiction. Names, characters, places, and incidents either are the product of the author's imagination or are used fictitiously, and any resemblance to actual persons, living or dead, business establishments, events, or locales is entirely coincidental. The publisher does not have any control over and does not assume any responsibility for author or third-party websites or their content.

WHO DO, VOODOO?

A Berkley Prime Crime Book / published by arrangement with the author

PRINTING HISTORY
Berkley Prime Crime mass-market edition / November 2011

Copyright © 2011 by Rochelle Staab.
Cover illustration by Blake Morrow.
Cover design by Diana Kolsky.
Interior text design by Laura K. Corless.

ISBN: 978-0-425-24459-3

BERKLEY® PRIME CRIME
Berkley Prime Crime Books are published by The Berkley Publishing Group,
a division of Penguin Group (USA) Inc.,
375 Hudson Street, New York, New York 10014.
BERKLEY® PRIME CRIME and the PRIME CRIME logo are trademarks of Penguin Group
(USA) Inc.

PRINTED IN THE UNITED STATES OF AMERICA

10 9 8 7 6 5 4 3 2

A chill of anticipation washed through me . . .

Madame Iyå rocked back and forth, shaking a small brass rattle. "We humbly ask you to send the spirit of our beloved Sophie to join us." A full minute passed, then Madame Iyå spoke again. "Sophie is here."

A candle popped. Shadows flickered on the walls outside of the circle. A draft swept across the floor and flickered the flames of the candles. I thought I saw a shadow move behind Jimmy and Tawny. I brushed away the sensation that someone else was in the room with us. I tensed up.

"Nola. Sophie wants you to publish her spell book." Madame Iyå let out a deep sigh. "She wants me to help you complete it."

Linda's body went rigid. She clenched her hand over mine and began to rock. She spoke in a deep and insistent voice— a voice I didn't recognize. "No. I don't want that. My secrets have to be protected. There will be danger. No."

"What are you talking about, Linda?" Nola said.

Linda stared across the room. "Linda's not here, my treasure."

"Who are you?" Nola's words came unsteady, searching. "Sophie?"

"Not Sophie. I'm Callia."

The back of my neck tingled. Who was Callia? Linda gazed around the circle. She stopped when she got to me. Her face had changed: the softness drained from her features. She looked tired, older. Her eyes were vacant. A small terror edged my rational mind aside. I had a fleeting sensation that someone else's eyes were staring at me from Linda's face.

"You have to keep my secrets safe and with my family. Your question is answered inside." She held her eyes on mine. "Promise me."

I nodded warily, not knowing what she meant. "I promise."

A door down the hall slammed shut with a force so hard it rattled the windows. Tawny screamed. I jumped.

For the little girl on the front steps

ACKNOWLEDGMENTS

My warmest gratitude to Lynn Sheene and V. R. Barkowski, gifted writers in their own right and the best critique partners a girl could ask for. Thank you both for every read, every e-mail, every comment, and your unflagging support. Your friendship is a gift.

I'm deeply indebted to my editor, Michelle Vega, for seeing something special that day in San Diego and for helping me to make this book the best it can be. And a grateful bow to my tireless agent, Christine Witthohn.

My heartfelt thanks goes to the UCLA Writers Program, especially Jessica Barksdale Inclan, Jerrilynn Farmer, Lynn Hightower, and Caroline Leavitt; and to my homegirl Lesley Kagen for showing me the ropes and cheering me on. Special thanks to Berkley Prime Crime's Rita Frangie, Diana Kolsky, and Blake Morrow for creating an amazing cover, and to Eloise L. Kinney for dotting my i's and crossing my t's. And finally, a big shout-out to those noteworthy folks who answered my crazy/complicated questions, opened doors, lent their support, or guided me along the path: Holly Adams, JoAn Brown,

ACKNOWLEDGMENTS

Suzanne Bank, Richard Cates, Cleo Coyle, Jeff Gelb, Captain Eric Davis—LAPD, Detective John Shafia—LAPD, Sergeant AJ Kirby—LAPD, the real Kris Bage—LAFD, Nick Light, Joelle McClure, Ed Nuhfer, Jeanne Robson, Hank Phillippi Ryan, ZS, Marty Suran, Renee Vogel, and Pat Sadowski. Group hug.

Chapter One

"Wait until the third date to fool around? Is that another one of your superstitions? What if there is no third date?" I turned my car north off Ventura Boulevard toward Robin's house.

"You have to make a man desire you, Liz. The longer you make him wait, the more he wants you." Robin folded her arms. Point made.

"That's just a game. If a man didn't want me, why would he be dating me?" I said.

"Your stellar personality? Wait a minute." Robin leaned forward from the passenger seat, eyebrows up with anticipation. "Is there a guy? Did someone ask you out?"

"Hell no. Purely hypothetical. Where would I meet him? I spend my social time with you. Although I love you dearly and your homemade brownies *are* orgasmic, I wouldn't mind a little first-date fun with a real live man again."

1

"Let me know how that works out for you, Liz. Josh and I waited, and we . . ."

I looked over at her. A tear tumbled down her cheek. My heart sank. The first-date discussion was my attempt to lighten the emotional heaviness on our trip back from Forest Lawn Cemetery. Despite my psychological training, I had struggled for words to console Robin as we mourned the two-year anniversary of her husband Josh's death. Easy to remain detached when counseling a client—complicated when comforting my best friend in crisis.

I parked the car in front of her Sherman Oaks bungalow and handed her a clean tissue. A soft October breeze swept leaves across her front yard. We locked arms and strolled in silence up the path to her house.

Robin Bloom and I met in front of the sign-up sheet for fifth-grade pep squad at Encino Elementary. She was the perky blonde who couldn't do a cartwheel. I was the plain brunette with athletic skills. We teamed up to make the team. I taught Robin the art of sideways handsprings. She taught me how to dance, put on makeup, and use hot rollers. Twenty-seven years later, we remained best friends, a bond built on loyalty, shopping, trust, tears, brownies, and being there for each other despite the distance. Between us we'd survived two marriages—hers destroyed by tragedy, mine by my husband's infidelity. Robin raised a gorgeous daughter; I earned a PhD. No matter what, we wouldn't lie to each other and didn't judge—especially if the shoes didn't match the outfit.

We stopped short under her porch light, staring. A tarot card was tacked to her front door. On the card's black background, a beige skeletal rib cage encased a bloody heart pierced with three daggers. "AACEEHHRT" was stenciled beneath. I pulled the card down. Please let it be some stupid advertisement. No one could be that cruel.

"The Three of Swords," Robin said. "It's an omen, Liz."

I knew what the card meant before I deciphered the anagram—*heartache*. The Three of Swords was part of the tarot reading my mother did for Josh the night before he died.

"It's a prank." I flipped it over, hoping to read "You're invited to a Halloween party." The back was blank. I tore the card in half and shoved it into my coat pocket. "Let's go inside."

I followed Robin through the house to the kitchen and tossed the halves into the trash. Robin set a plate of brownies on the table. I poured two glasses of milk and sat down, my mind on the night Josh sat at the head of this table and laughed at my mother's predictions.

Mom had offered to read the cards for Josh's fortieth birthday. When the layout forecast anguish and loss, Josh was certain it meant the water shortage in Los Angeles would ruin his landscaping business. He even joked about the crow—the forewarning of death—that lingered on their front lawn when we left. The next day, Josh died in a head-on collision.

Robin fell into a deep depression, obsessed with omens and the occult. Soon after, my mother stopped carrying her tarot deck around for entertainment. My distrust of the occult, ripened by a lifetime of Mom's ridiculous predictions, turned into disgust.

I took a brownie from the plate Robin slid in front of me and broke off a piece. Baked goods were less fattening when divided into small portions. "When did you make these?"

"Last night. I couldn't sleep." Robin's eyes drifted to Josh's chair.

"We need to talk about the tarot card on the door. I'm not leaving you tonight until we do. What are you feeling?"

Robin usually teased me when I slipped into psychologist mode. But, occasionally, my emotional digging helped, and she knew it. She folded her arms and rocked. "So alone. Unprotected. Since Orchid left for college, I come home every night to this empty house and wonder if it will always be this way. That tarot card is a warning about the future, Liz. I feel something coming, and I'm scared."

"What if you decide that the message reflects what already happened? Today, at the cemetery, we mourned the heartache of Josh's death." I took her hand. "You're not alone. You have friends who love you and care about you. A random tarot card left by some clueless twit as a joke can't control your future."

"But why tonight? And, even if it was a prank, why that card on my door? I don't believe in coincidence. I know it's a sign." Robin looked to the clock above the stove. "Damn. I forgot to call Sam. Will you excuse me for a sec?"

She dialed the phone on the kitchen wall. "Sam? Me. I'm sorry I'm late. Is she still there?" Pause. "The swallows are coming back from Capistrano."

I stopped chewing and listened while Robin talked to her boss, Sam Collins. "What was that about?" I said when she hung up.

"The swallows?" Robin chuckled. "Nonsense I recite when Sam needs an excuse to get someone out of his house. He translates the call into whatever story suits him at the time. He just told me to meet him at the office tomorrow to

4

work on the merger contract with him, alone. I hate keeping this secret from the staff."

"Who else knows he's selling half of the agency?"

"Just the owners of Artists Incorporated, Sam, you and me."

We talked into the night until yawns punctuated our sentences.

Robin called early the next morning. "The phone rang at midnight. When I answered, no one was there. Another warning from the beyond."

"The beyond doesn't telephone," I said. "Did you piss off someone?"

Finally, a laugh. "I'm the pillar of diplomacy," she said. "No one."

"Okay, then you're dating someone else's man?"

"Really? When would that happen? As you know, you're my only date lately," she said. "The widow and the divorcée, doing the town one dinner or bad movie at a time."

When she got home Saturday from the office, Robin found another tarot card tacked on her door. "The Five of Cups." Her voice trembled over the phone. "Who's doing this to me?"

The Five of Cups was the second card in my mother's reading for Josh.

"Call the police," I said. "The hang-up and those cards are harassment."

Robin phoned back later to tell me the Van Nuys desk officer agreed to put in an extra-patrol request. She spent the evening at home, decorating cupcakes. Sunday afternoon, she baked a five-cheese macaroni casserole and invited my mother and me to dinner.

Sunday at seven, with my mother, Vivian, chattering at

my side, I turned onto Robin's block. The quiet Sherman Oaks neighborhood was settled in for the evening.

"Since your father retired, he spends more time on the golf course with his old LAPD buddies than he did when they were working homicide together," she said.

"I'm glad for him, Mom. He looked so rested and happy tonight."

"Well, he always brightens up when he sees you, dear. He favors you. I don't think I'd ever see any of you if you would have, God forbid, joined the force like your brother, Dave, did." She pointed a finger at me. "Which reminds me. You know, your brother, Dave, arrested a gang of cultists last year. Maybe the tarot cards on Robin's door are part of another cult-initiation rite, training runaways to harass without getting caught. Or worse. Liz, there are spookeries and secret cults all over the Valley," my mother said.

I took a deep breath and gripped the steering wheel until my knuckles went white. I rolled my eyes at the initiation-rite theory. And Mom always said *your brother, Dave*, like I didn't remember I had a brother or his name was Dave.

"I know about the cult arrest, Mom. I was here. Remember?"

"Of course I remember," she said, checking her soft-pink lipstick in the visor mirror and brushing back a strand of white hair. "But you were so upset by the divorce—you were distracted."

"I wasn't distracted and I wasn't upset. I was clear-headed for the first time in fifteen years. You were the one who was upset."

"You broke Jarret's heart. I wish you two would talk."

6

"I broke his heart? As if he had a heart to break."

My cheating, drinking ex-husband knew every button to push in my mother's celebrity-loving psyche. He still worked her like he worked rookie batters who faced him on the mound at Dodger Stadium.

"Forget about Jarret," I said. "I'm concerned about Robin. Please don't get her all stirred up about the meaning of those cards tonight. She's vulnerable and scared."

"Dear, please don't make dinner a therapy session. I want to see the cards. Robin told me it's an unusual deck. Maybe I'll recognize it."

I slowed near Robin's house, vowing we'd find the identity of the card-tacking delinquent before I ate my way up a size.

"Park there." My mother pointed at the only space on the block.

When we got out of the car, I saw another tarot card on Robin's door. My fists clenched with anger. We walked toward the two-bedroom bungalow, stopping under the porch light to stare at the picture of a skeleton, hands cupped over empty eye sockets, howling off the black background, with blood spurting through the finger bones. Five sword blades pointed up from beneath.

Mom threw her hand to her chest. "Oh dear Lord. The Five of Swords."

Robin opened the door, but her smile dropped as she followed our gaze to the card. She darted inside and returned with a baseball bat in her hand. I pulled the tarot card off the door.

"I'M WATCHING YOU" was scrawled across the back.

Robin elbowed past us toward the sidewalk. She looked up and down the street, then turned to me, her voice harsh. "Did you see anyone when you pulled up?"

"Not a soul." Crap—bad choice of words.

The three of us searched behind the bushes landscaping the front of the house. A crow cawed from the corner of the yard.

Robin swung the bat at the bird. "Get. The. Hell. Out of here."

I took her arm. "Take it easy. Let's go back inside."

"I'm getting your brother, Dave, over here." My mother took out her phone.

"Call the Van Nuys police. They're closer," I said.

Robin looked toward the street. "They're not going to help. They said they'd send a patrol. Do you see a patrol? No. Me either. Nothing. I'm going to find this jerk and whack some sense into him."

The Sunday *Los Angeles Times* sat on the lawn, untouched.

"Did you go out at all today?" I said to Robin.

"No."

"The card could have been on the door overnight?"

"Maybe." She dropped the bat to her side.

"Any hang-ups today?"

"Not yet."

"Come on. We've looked enough." I slipped the bat from Robin's fist and led her inside.

The living room fireplace blazed. The scent of vanilla drifted from the candles burning on side tables. I hung my navy pea coat and my mother's cashmere wrap on the rack near the door and plopped down on one of the chairs in front of the fire. I kicked off my shoes and tucked my legs beneath me as I studied the tarot card.

The card was the same construction as the others—a laminated three-by-five. I glanced at the anagram on the front of the card: "AEGIINTTVY." *Negativity*. Then I read the back again. "I'M WATCHING YOU." The handwritten message worried me. Whoever was leaving the cards was getting bolder, more personal. The next incident could be face-to-face.

"Do you recognize this deck?" I looked up at my mother, standing over me.

She nodded. "It's the Five of Swords. Nobody wins."

"The deck, Mother. Do you recognize it?"

"No, dear. I don't." She looked over to Robin. "Where's your computer? I'll check my sites."

"Over here." Robin flipped open the laptop on the dining room table. Mom put on her reading glasses and started typing.

I showed Robin the back of the card. "Do you recognize the handwriting?"

"No."

A tiny trademark and a name—S. Johnson—were printed in the margin. "Mom, Google 'tarot cards' and 'tarot S. Johnson.' "

She scanned sites with hundreds of variations of tarot decks, but nothing she found resembled the cards on the table or linked to an S. Johnson.

Thirty minutes later, my mother shrugged and followed us into the kitchen to eat. "I think it's a specialized deck made by a death cult," she said. "Do you have any new neighbors? Anyone missing pets? Those cults do animal sacrifices, you know."

9

I slid into the chair next to her and jammed my elbow into her ribs.

"Ouch," she said. "I was just—"

"Robin," I said. "Think hard. Someone knew the first two cards were meaningful to you. Only the four of us were there that night. Who else did you tell about the predictions before Josh died?"

"Everyone." Robin set the hot casserole on the table and sat down. "Our friends, everyone at my office."

"Could there be someone at work who carries a resentment toward you?" I ignored the salad and scooped a heap of mac and cheese onto my plate.

"Why would anyone resent me for doing my job? They all know how impossible Sam can be."

"Someone could be jealous of the power you have as his assistant," I said.

"That's what I was getting to. A grudge. That's what the Manson murders were about." Mom covered her plate with salad, then dropped a spoonful of mac and cheese on the side.

Robin's eyes widened. "You really think it's a cult, Vivian? Have you heard of this before?"

"Yes, I have. Just last year, when Liz's brother, Dave, broke up a cult that was sacrificing—"

"Slow down, Mom. You're forgetting about the hang-up. This is probably someone who knows Robin." I looked across the table. "Did you talk to the neighbors?"

The food on Robin's plate sat untouched. "I asked around yesterday afternoon after I called the police. The next-door neighbors didn't see anyone unusual come near my house. Neither did Leonard, the man across the street. According to him, the only people coming and going are John, the mailman; FedEx drivers; and people delivering packages from my office."

"Leonard has to sleep sometime," I said. "I assume the last card was left late last night."

"Exactly." My mother pointed a carrot stick at me. "Cults do their rituals after midnight."

I stacked my fork with macaroni and ignored her. "Robin, what else did the police say?"

"They told me to keep the doors locked. There's nothing they can do until someone commits a crime."

"So, I guess 'I'm watching you' wouldn't be enough for them. I hate that," I said. "It's obvious harassment. Can you get your alarm company to install a camera on the front porch?"

"Spirits don't appear on camera," my mother said.

The phone rang.

"Oh, that must be Orchid." Robin picked up the wall phone with a cheery "Hello," then slammed it into the cradle. "Another hang-up."

We cleared the table in silence. Robin brought out dessert.

When I finished the last sip of coffee and the last bite of my buttercream-frosted cupcake, my jeans were one breath away from uncomfortable. We listed the names and addresses of everyone Robin knew in the neighborhood, followed by the names of her coworkers at Collins Talent. We ended with Sam Collins.

"No way," Robin said. "Sam doesn't know anything about the occult. The only deck he handles is a poker deck."

We went over every step of Robin's week. Name by name, no one stood out to her. Everyone in Robin's world couldn't be above suspicion. Could they?

"Maybe you should stay with Liz until they give up and move on to another victim," said my helpful mother, starting to clear the dishes. "Whoever is trying to frighten you would have to give up if you're not here."

"I am not going to be run out of my home." Robin marched to the sink, bumping a glass from the counter, which shattered into pieces on the floor. She crumpled into tears. "This house is part of my family. Orchid grew up here. Josh planted every tree in the yard. I'm not leaving. And I know I can't hide from an omen—it'll follow me."

"Robin." I moved her away from the broken glass and sat her down at the table. "I'll move in here with you for a while."

"You don't have to," she said. "Orchid's driving down from school tonight and staying through Tuesday."

My mother swept the pieces of glass onto a dustpan. "I don't know if that's a good idea after this last message. The three of you alone?"

"There's an alarm system in place, and we'll get them to come in the morning and install a camera," I said.

"The message the Five of Swords carries is nothing to play around with. It means loss."

I glared at my mother. "Stop. We'll be fine."

"Don't worry, Vivian," Robin said. "This time I won't ignore the signs. I learned my lesson about omens with Josh."

Mom held up a finger. "I have an idea. Nick Garfield will know where this tarot deck came from."

"Who's Nick Garfield?" Robin said.

"My son Dave's friend since college. Liz knows him. He helped Dave solve a cult case for the LAPD last year. Nick will know if these cards are tied to a sect."

I closed my eyes and shook my head. "Nick Garfield

would burst into laughter if I called him out of the blue to find a tarot deck. Really, Mom, what are you thinking?"

"I'm thinking that someone who studies the occult for a living would be an ideal person to help you now. We need to talk to him."

We?

Robin started stacking plates in the dishwasher. "Tell me more about this Nick person, Vivian."

"He's a religious philosophy professor at NoHo Community College in North Hollywood. He teaches and writes about alternative beliefs. Every summer he travels around the world, studying exotic religions. He's written four books on the occult."

"How do you know so much about him?" I said.

"If you came to my barbeques more often, you would, too." Her smile dared me to argue.

"Do you really think Nick could help me somehow?" Robin dried her hands on a dishrag and switched off the light above the table.

"Of course he can, dear. Liz—call your brother and get Nick's number. You live near NoHo. Take the cards over there to show him."

"Nick will think I'm out of my mind," I said, following them into the living room. "I'd rather get the camera set up on the porch as soon as possible. That way we can catch whoever's leaving the cards."

An engine started outside. Robin raced to the front door, reaching for the bat. I opened the door. A sedan backed out of the neighbor's drive, and the couple inside waved as the car pulled onto the street. No tarot card on the door, nothing on the landing.

Robin trembled as I led her back to the sofa.

"When Orchid gets here, I'll drop off my mother and come back. I'm staying over," I said. "I'll sleep on the couch. If someone shows up again tonight, one of us will hear it."

"And you'll call Nick." My mother smiled.

"I really don't think he can do much," I said. "Nick's just a professor. The cards might interest him, but then what?"

"But Liz, he might recognize something that could help me figure out who's leaving the cards." Robin peered through the shutters. "I'll go with you."

"Good." Mom stood over us, arms crossed, feet set. "Do it all—stay with Robin, set up the camera in the morning, but for heaven's sake—call your brother and find Nick now."

I knew she wouldn't budge until I agreed with her. And I wasn't about to spend the night with my mother camped out in a sleeping bag on the floor next to me. Calling Nick wasn't a horrible idea. He might add a grain of sanity to this puzzle.

I got my cell phone and auto-dialed Dave. I told him about the harassment, gave him hell about the Van Nuys patrol, and then made him promise to call his friend at the Van Nuys precinct to up their awareness of Robin's house. Once I had Dave on the defensive, I told him Mom's idea and asked for Nick's number.

"Come over tomorrow night and bring the cards. Nick will be here watching the Rams game with me," Dave said. "Make sure you double-lock Robin's doors and windows tonight. And Liz? When you and Robin are over here, don't talk during the game. Commercial breaks only."

"I know the rules. I'll tell her. Don't worry." I hung up.

At least Dave would be there to assure Nick that this was Mom's idea, not mine. Nonetheless, we had the start of a plan.

"When the camera is installed, it'll capture the jerk on film," I said to Robin. "And if the police won't do anything about it, we'll post it on YouTube."

Chapter Two

Dave called at noon on Monday to relay that Nick's car was in the shop. "I told Nick you could pick him up at the college. You and Robin can talk to him on the ride over," he said.

Robin called ten minutes later. Sam needed her to stay late at the agency for a client meeting. "I'll meet you at your brother's place later. Do you mind? I'll messenger the tarot cards over to you so Nick can study them before I get there."

At five that afternoon, I walked into Nick Garfield's classroom at NoHo Community College alone. A cool autumn breeze wafted through the open windows across the large room. The lights of the North Hollywood Arts District twinkled in the settling dusk, while inside fluorescent bulbs bounced a bluish glare off the empty desks.

Nick faced the blackboard, eraser in hand. On the panel

in front of him, "Religion forms on the fringe of society" was printed out in chalk. He turned as my pumps clicked across the linoleum floor. Our eyes met. I felt the familiar bond of affection reserved for old friends.

He flashed a broad smile and walked over to hug me. "It's good to see you, Liz. You look stunning."

"Thanks." I felt my cheeks flush as I grinned back. "It's been a while."

"Three years, I think. Dave invited me to a barbeque at your parents' home the summer I moved to L.A. You had just set up your practice."

Nick's memory was better than mine. If we had talked back then, it couldn't have been for long—I was still married, and even though Jarret knew Nick and Dave from back in college, Jarret yawned through any conversation that didn't center on him.

"Let me finish up, and we'll get out of here," Nick said.

I slid into an empty desk in the front row. Tugging at my hem, I wondered what possessed me this morning when I donned a tight skirt and T-shirt instead of my usual gabardine slacks and wool sweater. I set my purse on the next chair and watched Nick erase the blackboard.

Age suited him. He was tan and fit, and the flecks of gray budding at his temples added a distinguished touch. Nick still carried himself with the same self-confident air he had back at the University of Illinois when I was a freshman and he and Dave were juniors.

"You didn't have to do this. I would have called a cab," Nick said, pulling me out of my thoughts and into his interesting brown eyes.

"No one takes a cab in L.A. except to the airport. I don't mind. I thought it would be fun for us to catch up. Plus, I have an agenda." I smiled up at him.

"Everyone has an agenda." He folded his arms on the podium in front of the blackboard and grinned. "What's yours?"

Might as well get his amusement at my request over with. I reached into my purse, pulled out the three tarot cards, and laid them across the laminated desktop. "These."

Nick laughed out loud as he glanced at the layout in front of me. "You committed to driving me all the way to Dave's apartment so I would read tarot cards for you? Isn't that your mother's specialty?"

"I don't want you to read them." I tried to shake off indignation. I expected him to be amused, but he didn't have to make it personal. How arrogant of him to assume I was asking for a tarot reading. "Someone used these cards to harass my friend Robin. We thought you might know where a deck like this would be sold. We've searched online and couldn't find it."

Laid out side by side, the beige skeletons on the tarot cards came to life. The bleeding heart with daggers over the caption: "AACEEHHRT." The second sobbed bloody tears above "OORRSW." The last was the card we found last night: howling with blood spurting through the finger bones. I showed him the note scrawled on the back.

"They were tacked to her front door over the past few days," I said. "We can't figure out who left them or why. The Van Nuys police couldn't tell her anything. And Dave said the LAPD Robbery-Homicide Division downtown doesn't chase mystic pranksters in the San Fernando Valley."

"So, you came to me."

"I hear you're the expert on the occult now," I said.

"I am."

I shifted in the hard desk chair. "So, do you recognize the deck?" *Just let him look at the cards and give me an easy, dime-store explanation.*

"They're not widespread commercial. That helps to narrow down the shops. A bit sophomoric, but the drawing is clever enough. Voodoo-type images, but neither Haitian nor New Orleans style." He put on brown-rimmed glasses and tapped his index finger on each card. "That's the Three of Swords, that's the Five of Cups, and that's the Five of Swords. Why is the Three of Swords taped together? Was it left on her door in halves? That could mean something."

"I ripped it in half when we found it. Robin dug it out of the trash and taped it together for you to see," I said. "I was certain the first card was a prank."

A blast of air swept across the room and blew the cards off the desk, slamming the door shut. I started and threw my hand to my chest.

Nick touched my shoulder. "Damn cross draft. Happens all the time. Sorry about that. I should have closed the door when you came in." He moved his hand, then stood back. "And what did you think when she found the other two?"

"That some ass is trying to scare her." I said, recovering my breath and swallowing. I leaned out of the chair to pick up the cards and nearly knocked heads with Nick when he bent to do the same. We mumbled apologies to each other.

He gathered the cards, then stood, studying the threat on the back of the last one. "I agree. This note alone is intimidating, but coupled with the captions, the whole message is unnerving. A literal hell of a deck."

"You don't have to bother analyzing them," I said. "We just want to know where they were purchased. If the deck is from a specialty shop, maybe someone there would have a record of who bought copies."

Nick furrowed his brow. "You don't want to know how these cards read together?"

"Not unless it'll help us find who left them, and I doubt that it would."

"I wonder why the artist used anagrams. What a lazy way to appear mysterious."

No kidding. "I'm more interested in the possible threat to Robin," I said.

"The choice of these anagrams still guides the tarot interpretation. I don't see a lot of decks that print interpretation on the minor arcana. The first card reads *heartache*, the second *sorrow*, and the last one *negativity*. There's a strong autohypnosis factor to mysticism. And if your friend . . . What's her name?"

"Robin."

"If Robin is open to believing, then these would have an effect on her whether or not she could decipher them on her own. The willing mind is the most important factor in interpretation. Just the threat of images like this can snake into someone's head and turn a sane person into an irrational wreck," Nick said.

So far, Nick was a master of the obvious.

"It's worse than that. The first two cards turned up in a tarot reading my mother did for Robin's husband the day before he died. That's why I want to track down the deck— to stop whoever is doing this from causing Robin any more

20

heartache." I slid the cards into my purse. "Do you have an idea where cards like these would be sold?"

Nick cocked his head toward the clock above the door. "The game is starting soon—can we talk in the car?"

I nodded, wondering if the game was that important or if Nick didn't have the answer to my question. He slid a textbook and the papers from the podium into a worn brown briefcase. We left the building, crossed the small campus plaza, and got into my Lexus. The streets were already jammed with traffic crawling from light to light through the North Hollywood Arts District. We drove down Lankersheim Boulevard, past coffeehouses, neon-lit theaters, restaurants, and gas stations.

"Fascinating that you're teaching religion," I said when the silence got too loud to ignore.

"Teaching the three major religions subsidizes my study of the occult. That's far more interesting and important to me."

I looked at him. "You're a philosopher, Nick. Why the interest in hocus-pocus?"

"You don't believe."

"I can't see a rational basis or use for it."

"But you're a psychologist. I'd think you'd see how the occult has everything to do with emotional exploration." Nick fiddled with the seat to accommodate his long legs.

"It's an excuse for avoiding feelings," I said. "An attempt to move control and assign the blame to a source outside the self."

"Or see deeper inside the self," he said. "Reading the tarot could be viewed like a Rorschach test—a projection of the subconscious."

"Without the assistance of a trained analyst? Nice try. I don't think so."

"It must bother you that your mother reads the cards," Nick said.

"I'm not my mother's therapist. She knows how I feel."

"What do you think about the major religions?"

"I believe that people need something to believe in," I said, easing into the right lane. "But major religions don't use spells, tarot cards, or crystal balls to forecast or change the future."

"What about prayer?"

"Positive affirmation."

I couldn't tell if his chuckle was an approval or a smug dismissal. We drove two blocks before Nick spoke. "How are your parents doing? I was in Costa Rica and missed their Labor Day pool party."

"They just celebrated their fortieth wedding anniversary. It's us kids who couldn't stay married, and my mother won't let us forget it. She swears we were cursed when we started a fight during the vows at Aunt Minnie's first wedding. Dave was five. I was three."

"How does it feel to be single again?" Nick said.

I asked for that, me and my big let's-talk-about-marriage mouth.

"I'm so busy with my practice that I don't think about it. I guess it feels about the same. Jarret was gone most of the time anyway." I turned left onto Dave's street with ten minutes to spare. I wanted to get Nick's attention away from me and back to the tarot before we went inside. "If you can help us find the shop where the cards were sold, maybe it will lead us to her harasser. What do you think?"

Nick hesitated. Damn. I bit my lip, worried that my attitude about the occult insulted him. He looked out the window. Was he thinking about how to back out gracefully?

He grinned at me. "If that deck was bought in L.A., the shop or shops are simple to find. If someone made them at home, impossible. But the occult community is fairly close-knit, even in a city this big. We can ask around. Tell Robin I'll help." He looked at his watch. "Now park the car. The Bears could lose if we miss the kickoff."

Chapter Three

Dave greeted us at his apartment door, his eyes darting inside to the television. The new flat-screen TV on the wall was the only thing that had changed since he moved in after his divorce five years ago.

"You're late," he said. "The game started."

Dave took a beer from the cooler next to his armchair and sat down. A pizza, a large bag of pretzels, and a bowl of jelly beans sat on the coffee table. I really must start eating at home again. Nick dropped onto a corner of the sofa.

I stood in the middle of the living room, rubbing my arms. I could almost see my breath in the glare of the television. "It's freezing here. What are you trying to do—duplicate the weather in Chicago?"

"Quiet. The Rams are lining up," Dave said.

"I'm getting a sweatshirt." I walked to the small open kitchen, dropped my purse onto the counter, and went down the hall to the bedroom. I glanced at Dave's clothing, thrown over chairs and the bedpost. I took the sweatshirt folded on top of the laundry basket on the bed and put it on. As I checked my hair in the bathroom mirror, Dave's angry shouts drew me back into the living room.

"What happened?" I curled up on one end of the couch and nestled under the throw to keep warm while my damned skirt rode wherever it wanted to.

"The Rams' quarterback fumbled on third down," Nick said.

"Was it forced or did he stumble over his own feet?" I said.

Nick raised an eyebrow at me. "Forced."

I raised my eyebrows and smiled. "No protection."

While the game was on, we followed the rule my dad and brother had drilled into me since childhood: no talk about anything but the game until the game is over. Funny how much I learned about sports because of that rule.

When the Bears' three-point victory was posted as the final, I turned to Nick. "So much for your superstition about missing kickoff."

Dave was still slouched in his leather easy chair. Pretzel crumbs littered the belly of his vintage Los Angeles Rams sweatshirt. "The Bears got lucky. But the Rams will take the conference."

"The Rams couldn't move the ball down the field," I said. "Their front line more or less stood aside and invited the Bears' defense to a quarterback sack party. They didn't even try to run the ball." I grinned, waiting for Dave to snap back. Taunting him was a pastime I never tired of.

"Liz has a point," Nick said, laughing.

Dave's face went red. "I don't have to defend a Super Bowl–caliber team to either one of you. Where's your friend, Liz? I thought she was supposed to be here."

I checked my watch. He was right. Robin should have arrived by now. "I don't know. I'll call her." I stood up a little too fast. The throw dropped and exposed my thighs. From the corner of my eye, I caught Nick looking at them. Men. I wiggled my skirt into place and went to get my phone.

Nick got up and followed me into the kitchen with the pizza carton. He took out the last cold slice of pepperoni and cheese, looking over the counter into the living room. "What do you think, Dave? The tarot cards Liz showed me were clearly meant to shake up her friend. Can't the police do anything?"

"She filed a report, right?" Dave shouted from the living room.

Nick turned to me, questioning.

"Yes," I said.

"That's all you can do," Dave said.

"That's not good enough." I took my phone from my purse and dialed Robin's cell number. It rang twice.

"I was just going to call you," she said. "I'll be there in fifteen minutes."

"Where are you?"

"Turning into my driveway. I just need to . . ." The sentence was clipped by her gasp. "There's something on my door."

"Another tarot card?" I said. Nick stopped eating and looked at me.

"No. Bigger. A sheet of paper," she said. I heard her open the car door. "Wait. I'm walking to the . . ."

"Robin? Talk to me. What is it?"

"It's a photo," she said in a whisper. "Of me. With snakes drawn on my face."

"Get inside the house and lock the door." I covered the mouthpiece and said to Nick, "There's a photo of Robin with snakes drawn on her face, hanging on her front door."

"What does it look like?"

"I just told you. Photo. Snakes."

"Hmm," Nick said. "Snakes represent Kundalini energy, fertility or rebirth in some cultures. But in left-handed voodoo, snakes invite chaos, even death."

"What's left-handed voodoo?"

"Black magic."

"Robin, wait there for us," I said into the phone. "We're coming over."

I hung up and looked at Nick. "Let's go."

"Go where?" Dave came into the kitchen, brushing crumbs off his shirt as he walked.

"We're going to Robin's," I said. "The harasser left a photo of her on the door."

"How do you know it was the harasser?" Dave said.

"It had snakes on it."

Dave shrugged.

"What?" I said. "A marked-up photo following three tarot cards doesn't strike you as threatening?"

"It strikes me as neighborhood kids playing a prank," Dave said.

"I want to see it," said Nick.

I pulled off Dave's sweatshirt, put on my coat, and pointed them toward the door. "Dave, you're coming, too. You're a cop."

"Detective. Come on, Liz. You don't need me for this,"

Dave said. "There's no law against leaving photos on some-one's front door."

"Damn it, she's my friend."

"Hey, I worked all weekend. I'm tired. Nick can take a look at it."

I crossed my arms and glared at him. "Thanks for the help. What's the LAPD motto? 'Protect and serve'? Sure, at your leisure."

Chapter Four

Nick and I pulled up in front of Robin's house ten minutes later. I saw the black-and-white photo from the street. As we got closer, the heavy black symbols became clearer. The artwork was crude—two snakes curved in S shapes, spitting venom and coiled around each side of an unfocused shot of Robin's face. Large and small arrows were drawn over the background, pointing at her head and her eyes. Small hollow boxes were outlined in each of the four corners.

Robin came outside on the porch with us. We gaped at the image while I made a quick introduction to Nick.

"When is this going to stop?" Robin pressed her fist against her mouth.

Nick touched her shoulder, stopping her as she reached for the photo. "Would you two go inside? I want to look around out here alone."

"What do the symbols mean?" I said.

"I'll tell you inside. I want to check something, but I need you to clear the porch."

I followed Robin into the living room. "Where's Orchid?"

"Out with her friends. She's been gone all day," she said.

Robin and I watched at the window as Nick crouched down to study the doormat. He rose, pulled what looked like a key chain flashlight out of his pocket, and swept the small beam across the lawn closest to the porch. He looked up at the sky. When he came back inside, the photo was in his hand.

"Well?" I said.

Nick shot me a glance, shaking his head. "Let's sit down somewhere."

"Yes, of course," Robin said. "In the kitchen."

Nick set the photo in the center of the table, sat down, and put on his glasses.

"We're listening," I said. "Explain what the symbolism means."

"It's a black-magic hex. The two snakes represent powerful and dangerous voodoo spirits, or, more properly, Iwa. The arrows are there to direct the magic to Robin's face. The boxes in the corners are to encase the evil around the likeness so it doesn't flow to the creator or the viewer."

Robin closed her eyes. "I can't take this."

"Does the imaging correspond with the tarot cards we found?" I said.

"Not really. The voodoo I saw in the tarot cards you showed me was generic. The veves on the photo are specific to New Orleans' black magic. This imagery connects to the Petro Iwa."

"Petro Iwa? Veves? Please translate." I leaned in to look at the photo under the kitchen light.

"Iwa are the voodoo spirits," Nick said. "Petro Iwa are

the violent spirits. The veve is the symbolism used to summon spirit into action."

Robin's eyes widened with each description.

"What were you looking for outside?" I said. "Footprints?"

"Water- or bloodstains on the threshold. Signs of fresh digging in the yard," he said. "An authentic voodoo practitioner would have sealed the hex with animal blood or buried something personal close to the house."

"And in the sky? Checking the stars?" I couldn't resist. None of it sounded rational.

Nick smiled. "I was checking the moon phase. Spirit activity increases two to three days before a full moon. Looks like the full moon will hit tomorrow night. Whoever is spooking you knows voodoo."

"Fortunately you have the harasser on film," I said to Robin. "The alarm company came today, right?"

Robin shook her head. "Tomorrow."

I buried my face in my hands. "Do you have anything to drink? I could use a glass of wine."

When Robin went to the pantry for the wine, I whispered to Nick across the table. "Enough with the voodoo academic speak. I need you to help us figure out who's doing this, not scare her to death."

She came back with a bottle of wine and three glasses.

Nick took the corkscrew and, as he opened the bottle, said, "Do you know anyone who practices voodoo?"

"No."

"We know whoever it is takes a lot of chances and doesn't seem to be worried about getting caught. It's someone who's familiar with your schedule," I said, filling my glass. "Do you recognize the photo? Would you know who took it?"

Robin picked up the picture. "Not at all. I can't even tell where I'm standing."

I thought of stories my clients confessed over the years. Jealous women who wanted revenge on cheating boyfriends, girls angry with perceived rivals. Some were furious enough to act out with anonymous hang-ups in the night; others sought out psychics or used makeshift magic spells before coming in for real counseling. They used the occult to channel their uncontrollable anger. None of the clients had magical powers, but they all had one thing in common.

I looked across the table at Nick. "Whoever she is, she wants Robin off balance for some reason."

"She?" Nick and Robin said in unison.

"Women are more likely to use the occult as a tool than men are," I said. "Just a thought."

"Show me the tarot cards again," Nick said.

I pulled them out of my purse and laid them on the table next to the photo.

He picked up the Three of Swords and flicked the edge. "It's laminated, probably a copy of a prototype. New. No wear on the edges. If S. Johnson is part of the L.A. voodoo community, there's a chance we can locate him or her."

"I'll try anything to find the person who's doing this to me." Robin drained her wineglass and poured another. By the time we finished the wine, Orchid had come home, and Nick and I got up to leave.

As we walked down the path outside to my car, I looked at Nick. "What do you think?"

"The only thing those tarot cards and the symbolism on the photograph have in common is an attempt at voodoo.

And the threat implied on Robin's photo was much more serious than the cards."

"The cards are all we have to track down this asshole before Robin breaks down," I said, pulling the keys out of my pocket. "I'm worried about her. She's not a drinker, and she downed three glasses of wine tonight."

"Leave the tarot cards with me," Nick said. "I know someone who might recognize them. I don't have class until late afternoon. I can show him the cards in the morning."

"You don't have a car, and I don't have clients tomorrow," I said. "I'll take you."

Chapter Five

The next morning I knocked on the door to Nick's brown-shingled, one-story Craftsman home in North Hollywood, jockeying two cups of coffee and a plan. An hour of Internet research the night before gave me a good list of occult shops in the Valley and even a few in Hollywood.

Nick came to the door in khaki slacks, white T-shirt, and a navy V-necked sweater. His hair was wet, and he smelled like soap.

I thrust one of the paper cups at him. "Here. I brought coffee to wake you up."

"I've been up for hours. Went for a run, then called the garage and had them bring my car over." He tasted the coffee with a wince. "No sugar."

"I didn't know how you took your coffee."

"Two spoonfuls of sugar. It's always two."

I giggled. Giggled? It was so early-morning-out-of-context

for me. Nick was the first wet-haired man I'd encountered since Jarret and I split up. I forgot how yummy men could be when they're all fresh and polished. I followed him through the book-strewn living room. A long counter separated it from the jade-green kitchen lined with stainless-steel appliances. Three tall chrome and red-vinyl stools stood next to the counter.

"You have your car back?"

"Yep. I'm mobile again," Nick said.

"But we're still going to hunt for the tarot deck, aren't we? I made a list of shops." I scooted onto a stool.

Nick took a spoon from a drawer and scooped two heaping teaspoons of sugar into his cup. Tasting the coffee, he smiled at me. "You're cute. Do you know that?"

"Excuse me?"

"You're cute. You made a list. I don't need a list."

"Don't call me cute. I'll accept *competent*. What do you mean we don't need a list?"

"We're going to Osaze," Nick said.

"Where is that?"

Nick took his keys from the counter, poured the coffee into the sink, and tossed the cup into the overflowing trash container in the corner. "Not where. Who. Osaze is a voodoo king and an occult expert, perhaps the most knowledgeable in the United States. Let's go. I'll drive."

I hooked the strap of my tote over my shoulder and followed him out to his car, curious. "Is Osaze a professor, too?"

"You'll see."

Nick drove to the 101 Freeway, toward Hollywood. I turned on the radio. Nick turned it off.

"You're competent and beautiful," he said.

My nose was cold, but I could feel my cheeks flare hot pink. I crossed my arms to ward off the morning chill. Or to deflect the compliment. "Thank you," I said. We drove past the Capitol Tower into the heart of Hollywood. "How far are we going?"

"Osaze lives just off Santa Monica Boulevard. Liz, I was thinking about Robin during my run this morning. Combining Haitian Vodou symbols with the tarot strikes me as odd, even if the drawings on the deck are meant to portray voodoo. The two devices don't mix. It made me wonder how serious Robin's harasser was about mystic consequences or hoodoo."

"Mystic consequences? They're trying to scare her. Period," I said.

He stopped at a light and looked at me. "Why do you so readily discard mysticism?"

I shrugged my shoulders. "I'm a realist, not a magical thinker."

"Well, I've seen things that would change your mind."

"Oh, I dare you to show me, Nick. But all I care about today is finding those cards and tracking down the person who's after Robin. Why do you say the alleged hex on the photo and tarot don't mix?"

"Well, tarot is a European form of divination, and black magic is New Orleans hoodoo."

"Hoodoo?" I said.

"You do."

"Do what?"

"Remind me of a man." Nick laughed.

"What? What are you talking about?"

He grinned and quoted dialogue as he drove on. " 'You

remind me of a man. What man? Man with the power. What power? Power of hoodoo. Hoodoo? You do. Do what? Remind me of a man.' Come on, Liz. *The Bachelor and the Bobby-Soxer*? Cary Grant? Old black-and-white film? 1947? RKO?"

"Sure," I lied. "I remember. So, what's the difference between hoodoo and voodoo?"

"Hoodoo is black magic. Vodou, v-o-d-o-u, is an Afro-Haitian religion. The commercial forms of voodoo, v-o-o-d-o-o, are associated with New Orleans. The uninitiated tend to mix them up."

"Well, I'm confused."

"Don't be. Let's start with the tarot deck and see where it leads us. Osaze is a mystic master at the heart of the occult collective in Los Angeles. If that particular tarot deck is anything special, he will recognize it."

Nick drove deep into Hollywood and parked on a side street off Santa Monica Boulevard in front of a two-story wood-frame home with a well-kept yard and golden-yellow dahlias blossoming in front of the porch. A small taupe kitten chased two black kittens down the steps, disappearing into the flower bed and under the house. We rang the bell. The front door opened to reveal a magnificent black man in his midsixties standing tall, slender, and dignified in a long triangular robe of gold, rust, and black diamond print.

A huge smile spread across his face. "Nicholas." They embraced and patted each other's backs. "It is good to see you, old friend."

"It's been too long." Nick gestured toward me. "Osaze, this is Elizabeth Cooper. Liz, this is my good friend Osaze Moon."

I smiled and offered my hand. "Hello. It's nice to meet you."

Osaze's grip was warm. He bowed slightly, then looked into my eyes. "It's my delight, Elizabeth. I see the spirits have blessed you generously with beauty and love. Please." He stepped aside to let us in. "Come with me to the sanctuary."

We walked through the house, out to a small yard, and across to a guesthouse. Once inside, I stifled a gasp. The windows were painted over and blocked with cloth. Through the dim light, I saw every inch of wall space covered with skulls, animal skeletons, and statues of saints and gods. Rolled-up money protruded from every open orifice. Dollars poked out of the eyes, ears, and nostrils and from between every tooth of the skulls or jutted out of the genital cavities of the dried-out skeletons. Plates were filled with coins, and beads were draped over the shoulders of the statues. Mirrors and boxes were stacked on shelves and stands. A maroon velvet throne sat at the end of the room.

Osaze caught me staring. "They are offerings to the spirits from those seeking help and blessings. I take no money. This room and all of its contents belong to the gods and the spirits."

I felt Nick's hand on my shoulder. The warmth of his touch drew me out of my awe. He faced Osaze, taking a tarot card out of his pocket. "We came with a question. Do you know this card?"

Osaze took it and, to my surprise, snorted. "Of course I know it. Madame Iyå. How do you have this chicanery? You do not take it seriously, do you?"

"It was unusual enough to make me wonder where it came from," Nick said. "It was left on someone's door, obviously to frighten her, and we're trying to track down the person responsible. Who is Madame Iyå?"

"Sheila Johnson."

I looked at Nick and smiled. S. Johnson was the trademark on the cards.

Osaze sat on the throne and leaned forward. "As Madame Iyå, she runs a shop in Hollywood called Botanica Mystica. She reads palms and sells incense and baubles to tourists. She and her worthless son, Jimmy, tried to publish this deck a few months ago to sell to the legitimate shops and stores in town. None will buy, of course, because there's no tradition or dignity behind it. She came to me for my blessing and I refused." He threw the card down, agitated. "It's not tarot, and it's not wisdom divinity. Madame Iyå made the deck herself in the spirit of opportunism. It's an insult to our authentic mystical systems. She's not legitimate in my community. And now she brags of a book."

Nick picked up the card and put it back in his pocket. "I think we found our answer. Osaze, we're grateful for your help, and I apologize for coming here and upsetting you. Is there anything else you can tell me before we go?"

"Yes, my friend. Madame Iyå and her son are charlatans. Do not believe anything they tell you. Be careful."

Chapter Six

"Now to find Botanica Mystica." Nick slid into the driver's seat beside me and started to dial his cell phone.

"I know where it is." I dug into my tote for my list of shops. "It's the sixty-seven-hundred block on Hollywood Boulevard. I thought you knew where all the occult specialty shops are."

"My haunts don't include tourist traps," he said, starting the car. "What prompted you to add Botanica Mystica to your list?"

"The name jumped out at me."

"Ah, so the spirit guided you." Nick grinned.

"Not likely."

He drove north and turned onto Hollywood Boulevard, cruising past the Wax Museum and the tourists strolling over the stars cemented on the Walk of Fame.

"Botanica Mystica should be somewhere across the street, on the north side," I said as we neared McCadden Place.

I craned my neck around him, looking for the shop, when a yellow Mini Cooper convertible with temporary Beverly Hills dealer plates jerked out of a parking space in front of us, barely clearing the front of Nick's car.

He hit the brakes hard. We lurched to a stop. "Damn," he said. "Are you okay?"

I caught my breath. "Yes, thanks. That was close."

The yellow sports car sped up the street, zigzagging through traffic. Nick pulled into the empty space in front of the Egyptian Theater.

I hesitated before opening the car door. "What's our angle here? How do we get Madame Iyå to show us the deck and tell us how many she sold, and to whom?"

"I have an idea. Let me take the lead."

We crossed Hollywood Boulevard and headed up the block. Just past Ritchie Valens's gold star, an alley of shops named Artisans Patio was tucked between an African jewelry store and a souvenir shop.

"I think it's down this way," I said, taking Nick's arm.

A double row of small storefronts lined a clean, bricked walkway. Toward the end of the alley, past a bead shop and an artist's studio, the sign for Botanica Mystica hung in a window filled with multicolored glass jars, sparkling in the late morning sun. I stopped in front of the shop and pointed at the huge cardboard drawing of a hand hanging beneath the shop sign.

"The hand of fortune," Nick said. "Like Osaze said—she's a palm reader, too."

As I peered into the window, a loud female voice came through Botanica Mystica's closed shop door. "You better apologize to her tonight, Jimmy. And if you can't be smart about it, then just be quiet."

41

Bells jangled and the door opened.

"I know what I'm doing." A young man stormed out of the shop and headed down the alley without looking back.

Nick caught the door before it shut, and we entered the small shop. The air inside was thick with the scent of sandalwood. Books, candles, jars, and figurines lined the shelves from floor to ceiling. In the center of the room, a long wooden table was stocked with colored candles in round and phallic shapes. In the far corner, near the back wall, a lamp with a finger bone base shed a circle of light on a glass counter. Next to the counter was a small, cloth-covered table with two iron chairs.

I picked up the book displayed on the counter, *Hexes and Witchcraft for the Modern Woman*. The title made me chuckle. If this is what modern women are reading, I'll stick to the rational old days.

"You here for a palm reading, honey?" An older woman with orange-red hair settled onto a stool behind the counter. Her cheeks were rouged. Thick-mascaraed lashes weighted wrinkled lids, and bright coral lipstick lined her thin mouth. A purple shawl hung over large shoulders. Layers of gold necklaces circled her fleshy neck.

"Oh, no, I'm here with . . ." I turned. Where the hell was Nick?

He came up beside me and said to the woman, "Hello. Are you the owner?"

"I am Madame Iyå." She tilted her head back and looked him over.

"I'm pleased to meet you." He offered his hand. "I'm Dr. Nicholas Garfield. My girlfriend and I are over at the Renaissance Hotel this week for a conference. I'm meeting with colleagues from across the country on the latest philosophical theories in mysticism. Tomorrow I'm giving a talk on the tarot. Unfortunately, I forgot my sample decks for the presentation. I heard about your shop and thought you might be able to help me."

I glanced at Nick. What part of his plan to woo Madame Iyå cast me as his girlfriend?

Madame Iyå aimed a ringed finger toward the bookcases on the wall. "The tarot decks are on the second and third shelves and on the table."

Nick walked to the bookcase, reaching for the boxes of cards. "Yes, these are fine, but I also wanted some decks new to market. Do you have the Witches Tarot?"

"Over there."

"And the Egyptian deck?"

"Next to it."

He studied the front and back of each box with care. "I also heard about a new voodoo deck from New Orleans. My lecture is about mixed interpretations of the tarot, using voodoo woven into the readings. I'm looking for the unusual, something new I can talk about. Do you have anything like that? Anything out of the ordinary?"

Madame Iyå's eyebrows shot up. A smile formed on her lips. She shifted her frame on the stool and leaned on the counter toward Nick. "You say you're a doctor of mysticism?"

"Professor of religious and mystical philosophy."

"I have a deck you've never seen. A deck I was inspired and guided to design by the spirits unleashed by Hurricane Katrina. It will be published soon. Right now it's only for readings with my special clients."

Nick returned the other decks to the shelf. "May I see it?"

Madame Iyå reached into the bottom of the glass case, brought out a wooden box, and fanned the deck inside across the counter. "If you want your talk to be about something unique, take a look at this."

A full deck of skeleton cards, in black, tan, and bloody red, spread across the counter for us to see. All three of the cards left on Robin's door were there.

Nick made a grand gesture of studying each card. "Very unusual. Very detailed. Yes, these are amazing, fascinating. You designed them?"

"Yes, of course. With the spirits guiding my hand and teaching me the language."

Teaching her anagrams? Sure. I covered my mouth to conceal a smirk.

"Congratulations. Very well-done," Nick said. "May I see the manual?"

"Of course." Madame Iyå took a spiral notebook from under a stack of papers behind her. "It will be bound in leather when the deck goes on sale."

I looked up at her. "These cards aren't for sale?"

"Not yet."

"It's only this one copy, then?" Nick leaned in closer.

"I made two prototype decks," Madame Iyå said. "This is the original."

"I'll buy the other deck," Nick said.

"Sorry. It's not available."

"Then sell me this one."

Madame Iyå shook her head. "I can't let it leave the shop."

"That's disappointing. Your illustrations and captions are ingenious. Your publisher must be very excited. It's a shame I can't preview your deck at my conference. It would draw a lot of attention." Nick slid a card out of the spread on the counter. "AEKMORTW," an anagram of *teamwork*, was written across the top, and three skeletons danced beneath three coins. "We'd make a good team."

"The Three of Pentacles is an interesting selection, Dr. Garfield," Madame Iyå said, smiling through yellowed teeth. "But I already have a partner."

"Are you sure you won't let me buy or even borrow the other copy?" Nick said. "I'd pay you well to be able to take the deck to my meeting tomorrow."

She hesitated. "It's not here. My partner has it."

Nick leaned in, flashing a smile. "Can we call your partner? As I said, I'll pay for the use of the copy. I'll even go over and pick it up."

"She's not home. I just talked to her. She's out for the day."

"If you give me her name and number, I'll call her later. Surely she'd understand how much the conference publicity would mean to future sales."

Madame Iyå wavered, clearly torn. "I can't give you her name. It's confidential."

"Your partner sounds very mysterious," I said.

"She's marvelous." Madame Iyå turned back to Nick. "I've been practicing voodoo for forty years. I really shouldn't be telling you this, but my partner is a voodoo princess. We're publishing a book together on voodoo soon. She's contributing spells her grandmother taught her in New Orleans."

"I'd like to meet her," he said.

"I'm sorry," Madame Iyå said. "She insisted on privacy. I have to honor that."

Nick was getting nowhere. I decided to test her. "I think we should try some other shops, darling," I said, hooking my arm into his. "We'll find another interesting tarot deck to buy. The reporter interviewing you from the *Times* won't know the difference."

"You're right." He looked back at Madame Iyå as we turned to leave. "It's too bad. But thanks for your time. Good luck to you and your partner with your tarot deck and book."

Madame Iyå came around the counter. "Wait. When is your lecture?"

"Tomorrow afternoon," Nick said.

"I'm seeing my partner tonight. I'll ask to borrow her copy for your lecture. But I need a security deposit and a fee from you to show good faith. The deck isn't copyrighted yet."

"Are you sure she'll comply? Otherwise, we'll look elsewhere," Nick said.

"If she doesn't, I'll rent you my original. But it will cost you," Madame Iyå said.

"I'm happy to leave whatever you ask on delivery," Nick said. "I'll come back tomorrow morning with cash."

"I open at ten." She touched my arm and whispered in my ear. "You come back, too. I'll make you gris-gris to release your erotic powers on your professor."

I gave her a skeptical smile and then followed Nick out to the alley. As we crossed Hollywood Boulevard, I said, "Mystic academics, seriously?"

"Seriously. Great group. You'd love them."

I brushed away the thought of me at a paranormal convention. "Now what? We still don't have the name of this princess."

"First, you talk to Robin. We know for certain that it's a woman, we know it's someone who practices voodoo, and we know the shop the cards came from. If Robin still can't guess who it could be, I'll come back in the morning and try to warm up Madame Iyå a little more."

"And pay for the second deck? How does that give us a name?"

"I won't have to pay. We already know the second tarot deck is short three cards, rendering it useless for a conference. And if I'm alone with Madame Iyå long enough, I know I can coax the voodoo princess's name out of her."

"Does Madame Iyå interest you?" I said.

"The way a carnival act does."

We got into the car, and Nick turned the key in the ignition. "Osaze is right. Madame Iyå and her shop are as bogus as a movie set. I was waiting for Sidney Redlitch to appear from the back room with Pyewacket."

I wrinkled my forehead. "More witchcraft friends of yours?"

"*Bell, Book and Candle*, 1958. Ernie Kovacs played Redlitch, a fake witch expert who was writing a book. Pyewacket was the cat in the movie." He pulled into the street.

"Oh, of course." I didn't have any idea what he was talking about. I dug into my purse, pulled out my cell phone, and dialed.

"Collins Talent, this is Robin."

"Robin, it's Liz. Do you have time to talk?"

"Not this sec. Sam's leaving for sound check in an hour, and the phones won't stop. But I'm dying to hear if you and Nick found the tarot deck."

"Yes, we did," I said. "What if I come by the office and tell you what we learned? I just have to pick up my car."

"Perfect. We can go out for coffee after Sam is gone."

Robin stopped. "Hey, I just had a thought. Do you like Steve Weller?"

"That's a joke, right? You know I do."

"He's our client, and he's playing the Greek tonight. Would you and Nick come to the concert as a thank-you for helping me out? There's a party afterward. I'll introduce you to Steve."

"Are you serious?" When I was nineteen and singing along to his albums in my dorm room, if someone had told me that I would end up meeting Steve Weller backstage at a concert, I would have screamed out loud. Today I pumped a fist and mouthed a silent *yes*.

I said to Nick, "Want to go to Steve Weller's concert at the Greek tonight and meet him?"

"Absolutely." Nick turned onto the freeway entrance toward North Hollywood, smiling.

"Nick and I are in," I said to Robin. "And coffee's on me this afternoon."

Chapter Seven

After Nick dropped me off at my car, I drove to Beverly Hills and pulled into one of the Collins Talent guest parking spaces beneath their Camden Drive office building. I took the elevator to the fifth floor. A girl with spiked black hair, wearing a black leather miniskirt and a silver metallic tube top, greeted me in front of the huge "COLLINS TALENT" sign. I gave her my name.

"Hi, Liz. I don't think we've met. I'm Lulu, the receptionist," she said without pausing. "I started here a year ago. Robin's expecting you. You know where Sam's and Robin's offices are, right?"

"Yes, thanks, I do." I pointed down the hall.

"Cool, then. Can I get you something to drink?"

"No, thanks. I'm fine."

I walked down the eggshell-colored hall, lined with framed black-and-white photographs of movie and music stars—all clients of the agency Sam Collins founded almost twenty years ago. Potted fig trees, flourishing from the light off the windows at each end, were set between rows of simple beige file cabinets on beige carpeting. Steve Weller's album played in the background. At the end of the hall, I entered the familiar door to Sam Collins's suite.

Robin came around her pine desk to hug me. She held me tight. When I pulled back to look at her, I saw the dark circles framing her eyes. I settled into one of the guest chairs and adjusted my skirt down to protect my legs from the scratchy tweed upholstery.

"Are you holding up okay?" I said.

"I'm trying." She took a deep breath. "You came at a good time. I'm ready for a break."

"I finally met your new receptionist," I said. "Chatty."

Robin laughed. "Lulu? I'm sorry. She talks everyone's ear off, convinced that each new friend could be her ticket to stardom. The clients love her, though." She glanced toward the closed door to her right. "We can be out of here in no time. I'm anxious to hear what you found out. Sam is in his office with Buzzy Lacowsky, our independent publicist. They're finishing up a call, and then Sam's leaving to meet Steve."

"Steve?" I said.

"Weller. They're going to sound check."

I laughed. "Oh, yes, him."

"I'm so happy you're coming tonight."

"Me, too. And Nick asked me to thank you for the invite. We're both excited," I said. "Will Orchid be at the show?"

"Yes. I'm making her drive back to school afterward. I don't want her alone in the house in case there are any more threats."

"Did you get the camera installed?"

"Yep. This morning. But I still don't want her coming home to . . ."

An auburn-haired whirlwind in a purple paisley mini-dress and a Prada tote on her shoulder blew in holding a paper cup. She headed toward Sam's closed office.

As the girl reached for the doorknob, Robin darted out of her chair and blocked the door. "Sam and Buzzy are on the phone with a client, Sophie. I can't let you go in right now. Sorry."

Sophie stopped short, clicked her tongue, and then dropped into the chair next to me. She set the coffee cup on the corner of Robin's desk, crossed her legs, and sighed.

"Liz, this is Sam's girlfriend, Sophie Darcantel," said Robin. "Sophie, this is my friend Liz Cooper."

Sam's girlfriend? Sophie looked more like Sam's daughter than his lover.

"Hi." Sophie glanced at me, then began to rummage in her tote bag. She took out a large envelope and dug deep into the bag until she came up with a phone. She began texting, then said to Robin, "I need three more names on the guest list and a parking pass for myself tonight."

"Give the names to Lulu," Robin said. "Why do you need a parking pass? Aren't you riding with Sam?"

"No. I'm going home to change after the sound check. Sam likes to sit behind the board during the show, and it's too boring for me to hang out through another whole concert of old-people music. I already saw the show in San Diego and Phoenix. I don't want to sit through it again. I'll come back at the end for the party."

"Suit yourself," Robin said as she typed on her keyboard. "Lulu has all the passes."

Sophie left the room as fast as she entered it.

"Old-people music?" I frowned. "When did that happen?"

Robin laughed and held up a hand. "You don't even know. I'll tell you later."

"I'm going to freshen up while we're waiting for Sam to leave," I said, standing.

Out in the hall, Sophie was bent over Lulu's desk. A delivery man came out of the elevator and walked toward her, his eyes fixed on either the carpet or Sophie's legs. From the smile on his face, it wasn't hard to guess which one. I, and the young agent walking in the hall ahead of me, had a full view of her cleavage. Both men kept their heads turned to Sophie until they collided at the side of the reception desk. I laughed.

Sophie said to Lulu, "You're sure all my friends will get their passes at the gate?"

"Positive," Lulu said with a vigorous nod. "I'll be there myself. Just call me if there's a problem."

I headed to the ladies' room. When I returned to Robin's office, Sophie was standing behind the computer, reading the screen. She looked up at me, walked around the desk, took a hand mirror and a small wand out of her purse, and dabbed gloss on her lips.

The inner door to Sam's office opened. Robin came out with two men. The first was in his midthirties, dark haired and balding. He cracked a smile at Sophie.

"Hey, gorgeous," he said to her, reaching his arms out wide. "Come here and give Buzzy a big hug."

Sophie let him hold her briefly while he whispered something in her ear that made her giggle.

Sam Collins, slim, pale, and handsome, brushed past

them. He nodded at me, and then turned to Robin. "Is the driver here yet with the car?"

"Yes, he's waiting for you in front of the building," Robin said.

He took Sophie's arm. "Let's go," he said, and headed for the door with Buzzy following.

Robin called after them. "Sam, I'm going out for a little while. Lulu will watch the phones. Call my cell if you need anything." She came back in and pulled her purse from the drawer. "Let's go. I need some fresh air."

I noticed the envelope sitting on the edge of Robin's desk. "I think Sophie left this behind."

"Will you grab it?" Robin said, walking out. "We'll catch them at the elevator."

But by the time we got to the end of the hall, Sam and Sophie were gone.

Lulu stopped Robin. "Sophie gave me three more names for backstage tonight. That makes ten of her friends on the list. Is that approved?"

"Just put them on," Robin said.

We got onto the elevator, and I said, "Ten friends? Sophie acts like she owns the place. Sam lets her get away with that?"

"She's harmless," Robin said. "And not as important to him as she'd like to believe. Want to walk to the coffeehouse on Beverly? It's only three blocks."

"Sounds good. Can we stop at my car for my sweater? And what should I do with this?" I held up Sophie's envelope.

"Oh, damn. My purse is too small for that thing. I hate to go all the way back upstairs. Do you mind carrying it along in your tote? I'll take it back to the office with me later."

Inside the garage, a yellow Mini Cooper convertible with temporary Beverly Hills dealer plates was parked next to my car. "I saw that car earlier," I said.

"The Mini Cooper? They're cute, aren't they? Sam just gave that car to Sophie as his breakup gift. But she doesn't know that yet," Robin said. "He'll probably tell her it's over after the concert tonight."

"Girls get cars for breakup gifts in Beverly Hills? I live in the wrong neighborhood," I said.

Robin smiled. "Don't call your real estate agent. It's unique to Sam."

"That car with those dealer plates was parked in Hollywood near the shop that sold the tarot deck," I said, pulling my sweater from the backseat of my car. "Quite a coincidence, isn't it? Do you think Sophie could be your harasser?"

Robin's mouth dropped open. "Sophie? Are you certain it was that car?"

The afternoon sun warmed our backs as we walked through Beverly Hills. I described Osaze and his sanctuary, his loathing for Madame Iyå, and our trip to Botanica Mystica. "Madame Iyå told us a voodoo princess has the only other copy of the tarot deck, confirming my suspicion that a woman left the tarot cards at your door. Why didn't you bring up Sophie when we talked possibilities?"

"You didn't tell me to list significant others," Robin said in a matter-of-fact tone.

"We were going over everyone you knew," I said. "Sophie never came to mind?"

She didn't answer. I followed her into the coffeehouse, jammed with customers on Blackberries or cell phones. We settled with our drinks at a small table near the door.

I stirred a packet of sugar into my mocha and said, "Come on, Robin. What's going on? Why aren't you all over the fact that a car identical to Sophie's was on the street outside Madame Iyå's shop? You can't ignore the connection."

"Sophie doesn't know where I live." Robin stared at the foam on her latte.

"That's all you can come up with? Anyone who knows where you keep your purse could go into your desk drawer and find your driver's license. You can't tell me that today was the first time you left Sophie alone near your desk. And she didn't look too thrilled when you blocked her out of Sam's office."

"It's complicated."

I snapped my wooden stirrer in half. "Too complicated to bring her up the other night? Too complicated to mention before Nick and I spent our morning tracking down the tarot cards for you?"

Robin started to reply, then shook her head. "I'm sorry. Maybe it is Sophie. But why would she go after me?"

"Let's talk it out. Tell me what you know about her."

"Sam's been dating her since last spring," Robin said. "The first few months, she and I were friendly. Nothing special, just chitchat. Then she began to ask personal questions about Sam. I either changed the subject or pretended I was too busy to talk. When Sam began working on the agency merger a few weeks ago, he warned me about discussing it in front of Sophie. The busier he got, the nosier she got, and the less I talked to her."

"So Sam looks like a good guy by giving her a car, and you, by his instruction, stopped being chummy with her and shut her out." I sat back in my chair. "It sounds like Sam set you up to be the bad guy."

"Sophie has nothing to gain by threatening me."

"She may think that if you wigged out and quit, his next assistant would be nicer to her and easier to manipulate."

"If that's her plan, she loses. He'll probably break it off with her tonight." Robin's face became red. "How could she be so brazen as to go to my house? I better warn Sam to be careful."

"Let's talk to her first. We're not positive yet. Her car in front of Botanica Mystica is a big red flag. It's significant but . . ." I remembered something Madame Iyå had said. "Is Sophie from New Orleans?"

"Yes. How did you know that?"

"I didn't. But I do know that the voodoo princess with the tarot deck is from New Orleans. I have an idea. Tonight I'll ask Sophie if that was her car I saw parked near Botanica Mystica today. There's no reason for her to lie about it. She either knows the shop or she doesn't. If she admits it, all the pieces fall together."

"No, don't." Robin stood up. "I'll talk to her myself."

We tossed our cups and walked back to Collins Talent. Robin gave the window displays in the shops more attention than usual. Her silence made me wonder if she was holding something back.

"I want to be there when you talk to Sophie," I said. "The tarot cards and the photo were scary enough to alert the police and increase your security. I don't think it's a good idea for you to approach her alone. The handwritten threat and the symbolism on your photo worry me. They reveal an almost unhinged anger and spite over something you may have done without even realizing it."

"She'd lie if you were there," Robin said.

"She could also lie if the two of you are alone," I said as we climbed the steps to the front of the office building. I stopped. "I'm worried about you. I can't figure out why you're cavalier about this. Yesterday you were freaked out."

"Yesterday I didn't know who the bully was. Today I do. I can handle this myself." Robin took a packet out of her purse. "Here are your tickets for the concert. I'll give you your backstage passes at the show. The Greek gets chilly at night so dress warm and stay close to your man."

"My man?"

"Excuse me? You spent the day with Nick. Didn't he ask you out?"

"No, of course not." I noticed that the subject of Sophie was closed.

"He will," Robin said. "I saw the way he looked at you last night. His eyes followed you everywhere."

"You're so wrong. Nick's just a friend."

"I think you're missing something. Dress sexy for him and warm for the cool night air." She got on the waiting elevator.

Annoyed, I took the steps down to the garage. What was she up to with Sophie? And what the hell was she thinking about Nick and me?

Chapter Eight

Late-afternoon traffic crawled as I drove from Beverly Hills into Studio City. Meanwhile, my mind raced back over the day. I pulled into my townhouse garage with just enough time to shower and dress for the concert.

The scent of pumpkin wafting from the autumn potpourri on the kitchen counter reminded me how hungry I was. I stopped at the refrigerator and found a cheese stick to munch on and wandered into the living room. I flicked on the lamp next to the fireplace, closed the front curtains, and headed upstairs.

The message light was blinking on the phone in the office loft.

"Liz Bear, it's me, babe. I'm pitching in the play-offs tonight in Houston and ESPN's televising the game. I hope you'll be watching." Ex-husband. Delete.

"Where are you, darling? It's Mom. I'm waiting for you to call me and tell me what Nick . . ." Delete.

"Hi, Liz. It's Nick. I'll pick you up at seven fifteen. Don't forget the tickets." Replay. *It doesn't sound like he's flirting with me.* Replay. *I like his voice.* Delete.

I padded across the hall into the bedroom and dropped my tote on the chair next to my dresser. The tip of Sophie's envelope peeked out. *Damn. I'll take it to Robin tonight.* I started the water for a shower, stripped, and glanced at myself in the mirror on the sliding closet door. Not bad. I stepped into the tub, shampooed, and scrubbed my skin with a brown sugar and honey paste. As water pounded on my face and ran over my breasts, I wondered what Nick looked like naked. I shook my head. *Snap out of it. We're friends.* I had to get dressed or I'd be greeting him at the door in a towel.

After I dried my hair, I slathered rose-scented lotion over my body. I slid into jeans from the back of my closet, pulled on socks, and zipped up my boots. A heavy black pullover covered a long-sleeved cotton T-shirt. I brushed on blush and mascara and finished with amber lipstick. Good enough. I took my wallet from the tote and slipped it into a small shoulder bag. The phone rang. I knew who it was without looking.

I went downstairs to answer, taking the cordless into the living room, and sank into the white Camden chair next to the fireplace. "Hi, Mom."

"Did you just get home? Why didn't you call me? Well?" My mother's voice was at full high pitch. "Did you find the tarot cards?"

"We did." I told her about Madame Iyå's shop but left out the visit to Osaze. Knowing my mother, she'd be inviting not only Nick, but also all of his occult friends to the next family barbeque.

"Did Madame Iyå tell you who bought them?" she said.

Although the details about a mysterious voodoo princess would make my mother's night, I didn't have time to get into it. "She didn't give us a name, but Robin and I think it might be Sam Collins's girlfriend."

"I knew Nick Garfield would guide you to the right place," she said. "I did a reading about Robin today and drew the Chariot. Victory after adversity."

She talked on about her genius idea to involve Nick and her opinion of Sam's conniving girlfriend until the doorbell rang and I interrupted her.

"Gotta go, Mom."

I opened the front door. Nick smiled and examined me, head to toe. "Is that what you're wearing?"

"Yes, this is what I'm wearing." I looked down at my tight jeans and heavy sweater, then back up at him, hurt. "What's wrong with it?"

"Nothing at all—you look great. Just want to be sure you're warm enough."

I already felt flushed. I grabbed my purse, and we headed out the door. On the way to the concert, I told him about Sam, Sophie, and the Mini Cooper in the lot.

The Greek Theater was nestled under the starlit sky in a hillside in Griffith Park, just northeast of Hollywood. We took our seats in the tenth row on the aisle. The chatter of the crowd and the smell of pine filled the air. Before the concert began, Nick went to the concession stand and returned with a box of hot dogs and drinks. Robin and Orchid followed behind him.

Orchid gave me a hug and a kiss. "We're sitting together. I'm so excited."

"You look as adorable as a snow bunny," I said, admiring the white parka and jeans that complemented her light-blonde hair.

Robin was still in the same sweater and boots she wore at work. Three laminated passes—"Access All Areas," "Crew," "Steven Weller World Tour Staff"—dangled from black cords that hung from her neck. "I'll be running around, but I'll try to come back and visit." She handed each of us a "Steven Weller World Tour" pass. "These will get you into the hospitality suite. If we lose each other, I'll meet you there after the show. Orchid knows where it is."

"Go do your job. Don't worry about us," I said.

She pointed to the huge balloon of a moon, rising over the theater in the eastern sky above. "Remember what Nick said about the full moon last night? The spirits are restless." Robin's phone rang. She answered and walked away as the opening act took the stage.

Chapter Nine

Nick slipped his hand around mine during Steve Weller's encore. We swayed shoulder-to-shoulder amid five thousand fans, singing along beneath a shower of fireworks. The theater lights blinked on as the final ovation ended. Orchid led us up the aisle and out to an open area near the concession stand. A security guard kept bystanders away while a woman checked names off a clipboard, allowing listed guests through the door to the hospitality suite and the party inside. We showed our passes, and she nodded us through.

The party was mobbed with a hundred or so guests, chatting and drinking. The closeness of the crowd warmed the air. Waiters wove through with trays of champagne flutes and hors d'oeuvres. Two girls near the entrance eyed Nick and smiled. I caught their eyes, smiling back. Yes, I had the best-looking date in the room. Correction, he wasn't my date. He was just a pal, albeit a very handsome pal, who just happened to have his arm around my shoulder.

Lulu, in black leather from chin to toe and bright fuchsia lipstick on her lips, came over. "If you want a drink, there are two bars outside, one on each deck. And the buffet table is across the room."

As Nick and I mingled our way across the room, I recognized some of the faces from the *Celebrity Circuit* magazine my mother clipped for her this-would-look-great-on-you fashion tips. Four men surrounded a notorious blonde socialite. We brushed past the morning weather girl from Channel 11, chatting with a man who was staring at her breasts. Nearby, Steve Weller's drummer shook hands and posed for pictures with a line of middle-aged men and women.

I scanned the crowd for Robin but didn't see her. Off to the side, Sophie, in a strapless purple dress, was swapping her empty champagne flute for a full one. The two girls facing her downed their champagne, then walked away.

Nick plucked a mini crab cake from a passing waiter's tray. I tugged at his sleeve. "There's Sophie."

He swallowed the snack and bent down to hear me over the din. "Who?"

"Sophie. Sam's girlfriend. The one with the car that almost hit us outside Madame Iyå's."

"Let's go over and ask her if she's been tormenting Robin with tarot cards." Nick gave me a playful wink.

"I don't think so," I said. "Robin wants to take on that mission alone."

" 'Fasten your seat belts, it's going to be a bumpy night.' "

I took a flute from a passing tray and toasted him. "Bette Davis, *All About Eve*. Even I know that one."

"Finally. I almost gave up on you and movie trivia." Nick scanned the room. "Let's find the bar. I want a real drink."

"Go ahead, I'll meet you there," I said. "I want to stop at the ladies' room."

A waitress pointed me toward a corridor. I elbowed my way through the crowd and entered the ladies' room. Voices came from the two occupied stalls.

"She thinks Sam's going to propose, maybe in San Francisco."

"Too exciting," the other girl said. "I wonder what the ring will look like?"

Sam's name put me on alert. I went into the third stall and locked the door to the sound of simultaneous flushes. Faucets ran and paper towels were pulled. I listened.

"I have to tell you how she sealed the deal. She brought him coffee every day."

"Coffee? You think that's why he'd marry her? Come on, Nola."

"Maybe she served it on her knees," Nola said with a snort. "But I know for a fact she laced the coffee with her urine. A friendly little voodoo recipe for hooking a man."

"Ugh. That's sickening," the other girl said. "Sophie could charm any man she wants. Why would she resort to using the occult?"

"She likes the insurance, Linda," Nola said, laughing.

The bathroom door opened, and they left. I thought about the cup of coffee Sophie brought into the office earlier and nearly gagged. Voodoo recipe. I couldn't wait to tell Robin.

Back in the main room, I wove through the crowd, searching for Robin or Nick. Paper lanterns, hanging from tree branches outside sliding glass doors, drew me to a large open deck where a smaller group was congregated. White twinkle lights roped around railings set under a canopy of green pine. Nick was with Orchid at the base of wooden steps leading to another deck above. Sophie was at the other side of the deck under a tree, flipping her hair and talking to a man. I waved at Nick and stopped at the bar. It was three deep with people ordering drinks. The line shifted. A woman with a shock of familiar orange-red hair backed into me.

Madame Iyå swung around in a jangle of gold bracelets and sloshed her cup of wine over her hand. We both danced back to miss the splash. She brushed her gold muumuu with the other hand and scrutinized me through black-framed glasses. "Don't I know you?"

"I was in your shop today with Professor Garfield," I said.

"I remember now. You're the one who needs a bag of my erotic gris-gris," she said.

I plastered on my most agreeable smile. Sure. Carnal help from Madame Iyå was just what I needed. "That's right. That's me."

"You're coming back tomorrow?"

"Yes, of course. It's good to see you again. Did you bring your voodoo-princess friend?"

She gulped what was left of her wine. "Will you excuse me? I need to find my son." At that, she whirled around and lumbered away in a swish of lamé, straight toward Sophie.

Nick waved at me to come over. I gave him an in-a-minute nod and circled the room the long way to trail Madame Iyå. When she got to Sophie, I slipped behind a tree near them.

"I told you this morning—leave me alone. No deal." Sophie backed away, unsteady. "I have to go. My fiancé is waiting for me."

Madame Iyå boxed Sophie in. "Oh no, we have a deal, honey. You made a promise. We're partners. Don't worry—you'll get half of everything. Jimmy, tell her."

The young man we saw leaving Botanica Mystica this morning stroked Sophie's arm. "Come on, baby. We're your people. Who takes care of you?"

Sophie shook him off. "Stop it, Jimmy. I told you it's not like that anymore. I'm with Sam now."

"Until he dumps you, you stupid little whore."

Madame Iyå pulled Jimmy back. "Watch your mouth. Sophie is family."

Sophie took another flute of champagne from a passing waiter. "I'm not your family. I don't need your piss-ass money. Go back to your souvenir shop and leave me alone." She downed the champagne and walked away.

Madame Iyå grabbed her son's arm. "I told you to watch your mouth. Now go after her and apologize."

Jimmy left through the crowd.

"What was that about?" Nick's voice, whispering in my ear, made me jump.

I backed him away from the tree, out of Madame Iyå's earshot. "I'm not sure what the argument was about, maybe the tarot cards, but our two voodoo women are not happy with each other," I said, moving toward the buffet table. "Have you seen Robin?"

"Nope," Nick said.

Bowls of whipped cream and brown sugar surrounded mounds of fresh strawberries on the buffet and beckoned for my attention. I heaped whipped cream onto my plate and threw on a few strawberries for color. Nick opted for Brie and crackers, and we settled at a table.

Between bites of berries and cream, I told Nick everything I heard—from the ladies' room to Madame Iyå, Sophie, and Jimmy.

"Interesting," Nick said. "We solved that mystery fast."

"Solved?" I poked him hard in the arm. "If hearsay from bathroom stalls and tidbits from behind trees equal facts, they're merely more reason for Robin to talk to Sophie. But nothing I heard explains why Sophie left the cards."

"We were looking for who, not why," Nick said.

"I want to find out why," I said. "Don't you?"

"Only because I like watching how curiosity makes your eyes sparkle."

"What old movie is that from?"

"None." He handed me a napkin.

"Am I dribbling excess sparkle?" I said.

"Whipped cream."

I wiped my mouth. Nick decided he wanted another drink. I went into the main room to look for Robin. Where was everyone? Robin, Sam, Orchid, Buzzy, and Lulu were nowhere in sight. I circled back outside to check the upper deck. As I made my way toward the stairs, shouts came from the deck above me. I looked up.

At the top of the stairs, Sophie shrieked at Robin. "I'll have you fired, you dried-up old bag. You can't talk to me like this. You're crazy, you freak. Wait until I tell Sam."

My foot was on the first step and my eyes were on Robin. She grabbed for Sophie's arm. Sophie twisted away and rushed down the steps, stumbling past me. Robin was behind her. I followed them into the main room. Lulu appeared and joined in the dash across the room. They stopped at a door marked "Private."

Robin took Sophie's arm, holding her back. "Sophie, wait. Don't go in there. Leave him alone."

Sophie shoved her away, went in, and slammed the door in Robin's face.

Robin turned and saw Lulu. "Where the hell were you? You're supposed to be watching the door."

"I went to get a drink," Lulu said, backing away. "What's wrong?"

"Sophie's out of control," Robin said. "You could have helped me keep her out of there until she calmed down."

"I'm sorry. I was only gone a few minutes. On my way to the bar, I had to stop at the ladies' room. Then I met a girl I knew from a photo shoot I went to last week, and she asked me if I could get her inside to meet Steve. Then I had to explain to her that . . ."

Robin held up a hand. "I don't need every damn detail from you. You don't leave your post unless you ask me first."

"You weren't around, and I had to pee. What was I supposed to do?" Lulu said.

"You get a security guard to take your place, for God's sake."

I eased next to Robin and lowered my voice. "What the hell happened?"

"I bumped into Sophie upstairs, told her we needed to talk," Robin said. "She turned her back on me. I snapped. I'd had it with her. I told her I knew she left the tarot cards and the photo on my door."

"Did she admit it?" I said.

"She laughed. She denied leaving the cards but said I deserved to be hexed and called me an interfering bitch. Told me Sam didn't want me in his life, that I should get the message and quit. I told her she was a drunken tramp."

Robin glanced behind her, her forehead creased. "I have to get in there."

The door opened. Sam Collins came out with Sophie in tow and Buzzy Lacowsky following behind. Sam said to Buzzy, "She's drunk. Get her out of here."

Buzzy took Sophie by the upper arm. Her eyes flashed when she saw Robin. Sophie spit out her words, pleading and hateful, to Sam: "That bitch tried to push me down the stairs, baby."

"Sam, you know I wouldn't do something like that," Robin said.

He looked between the two women in front of him, expressionless. "Robin, you and I will discuss this another time. Please, get in there"—he thumbed his fist to the door at his back—"and distract Steve from this bullshit. I don't care what you do—just make him forget the scene she just made."

He said to Buzzy, "Get Sophie out of my sight and off the premises."

"Don't make me go." Sophie rubbed tears away, smearing mascara onto her cheekbones. "Please? Please, baby. It's not my fault. I don't want to leave."

"Go home." Sam turned his back to her. He pulled a cell phone from the inside pocket of his coat and walked away.

Buzzy pulled at Sophie while she looked back at Robin, Lulu, and me at the door. "You'll be damned sorry you opened your mouth," Sophie said. "A curse on you. Your luck has just changed, bitch."

Robin went inside. I watched Buzzy edge Sophie through the crowd. Her girlfriends came to her side, offering tissues. Madame Iyå and her son followed. I lost sight of all of them at the exit. Then I took a deep breath.

Nick sidled up beside me. "Your parties are far more interesting than any of mine."

"Where were you?" I said.

"Outside at the bar. The bartender is one of my students." He draped an arm over my shoulder and we leaned on the wall, watching the crowd until the door behind us opened.

"Come in," Robin said. "It's quieter inside. Will you wait while I walk Orchid to her car? I'll be back in a few minutes and then I'll introduce you to Steve Weller."

About ten people were scattered inside the small artist lounge. A few sat on couches, watching TV, while others chatted and drank in small groups. At the far end of the room, Steve Weller was sprawled on a sofa, his arm around the young woman nuzzling his neck. Nick and I headed to the bar to wait for Robin. I told him about the fight.

"If Sophie had it out for Robin before, she must be on the warpath by now," Nick said.

"Robin can handle herself," I said. "She's more capable than she appears. But I'm worried that Sophie might go to Robin's house again."

"Should I call Dave and have him alert the Van Nuys patrol?"

"Not yet. Let's follow Robin home," I said. "And figure out the rest when we get there."

A drink and a half later, Robin came back and introduced us to Steve Weller. "These are my friends Liz Cooper and Nick Garfield."

Steve reached out his free hand to us and smiled. We said our hellos, and I told him how much I loved the concert. Nick asked about the rest of his tour. Robin went across the room to Sam, and they whispered their way back to us.

Steve laughed as Sam approached. "Did you fix your little problem?"

"My problem?" Sam was relaxed and smiling. "I thought that was a groupie that I had to rescue you from."

"Liar. Wasn't she ranting about Robin trying to off her? Robin, are you still knocking off Sam's doll collection one by one?" Steve looked over to us. "Did you know that Robin was Sam's secret hit man? She does all the dirty work in the organization. Actually, I think she might be the real boss."

Sam laughed. "Steve, you're the boss. We're just here to entertain you. The problem is solved. The girl had too much champagne and was looking for attention. She decided to go home. Now listen, if I can't coax you out of this room and back to the hotel, your pilot will fly to San Francisco in the morning without you. Call time is six a.m."

Steve looked up to us, his face resigned. "My life is not my own. My cruel handlers won't even let me enjoy this beauty beside me for the evening." He nuzzled the girl curled up next to him. "Shall we finish what you just started?" He pulled her closer, put his free hand on her breast, and kissed her. She responded like they were the only two people in the room.

I averted my eyes from the kiss. Nick grinned. Robin coughed, then looked at her boss. "Sam, this is Liz's friend Nick."

"Thank you for coming," he said, shaking Nick's hand. Sam turned to Robin, cocking his head toward the couple on the couch. "I have to get Steve out of here so he doesn't miss his flight in the morning. Find the driver and tell him we'll be out of here in twenty minutes. Have him pull the car to the back door. And find out what Buzzy did with Sophie. I don't want her showing up at my house tonight."

"I will," Robin said. "Sam, we need to talk. She's a problem."

"I told you, tomorrow. And I want you to talk to Lulu about doing her job. She was supposed to be watching the door. She'll be lucky if I wake up in a good mood because right now I'm ready to fire her. Someone should have pulled me out instead of letting Sophie fly in here in a rage."

Sam slid onto the couch next to Steve, who now had his leg over the brunette, and touched his shoulder. "Come on, buddy. Time to say good-night."

I tapped Robin. "We don't want you to go home alone. We'll follow you."

"No, don't," Robin said. "I have to stay for at least another hour and do the settlement. I'll be fine. The security system at home is armed, and the camera is set. I'm not worried. Go. One of us should get some rest."

"Want to have lunch tomorrow and recap? We have a lot to talk about," I said.

"I'd love that. Thanks for coming." She kissed my cheek, then turned to Nick. "You were right about the full moon stirring things up."

"You didn't have to take it so literally," he said, laughing.

Chapter Ten

It was past midnight when Nick and I left the party. The main room was empty except for the waiters and waitresses, picking crumpled napkins out of plant pots, mopping watermelon chunks off the floor, and tossing paper plates with cigarettes squashed in avocado dip. Bartenders piled empty bottles of Krug into cardboard boxes. Lulu was across the room, talking to a waiter with a bag of garbage in his hand. She gave me a wave good-bye as we went out the door. Just one small group of guests lingered, finishing the last cigarettes of the night.

We wandered in silence through the exit gate and across the street to the wooded picnic area where his car was parked. The full moon illuminated our way to Nick's car, one of three under the trees near the hill. Wind rustled through the leaves overhead. The caw of a crow came from the woods ahead of us. The late-night air in Griffith

Park made me shiver, and I rubbed my arms to shake off the cold.

Nick took off his jacket and put it over my shoulders. "What do you think Robin's going to do about Sophie now?"

"She still has to explain everything to Sam," I said. "I don't know what she'll do about Sophie."

Nick looked up at the moon. "I wonder if Sophie considered the Rule of Three when she decided to spook Robin?"

"What's the Rule of Three?"

"Everything you do to others comes back to you threefold."

"That's odd." My eyes were drawn to the flash of yellow under the trees.

"Not really. A lot of practitioners believe in it and—"

"Not that, Nick. Look." I pointed across the grass to the base of the wooded hill. The yellow Mini Cooper with dealer plates was parked nose in at the trunk of a large evergreen. "That's Sophie's car over there."

"Maybe she left it here and went with her friends," Nick said.

"Except the driver's door is open," I said. "And she left the party over an hour ago."

"Let's go take a look," Nick said.

No light or movement came from the car. I saw a form alongside the open door. I grabbed Nick's arm and tugged him. "There's someone on the ground."

I raced ahead with Nick close behind. My throat tightened. A dark smear streaked the driver's door window.

Sophie was slumped on the ground. Her back leaned at a sharp angle against the door hinges, one knee up and the other bent open. Her head tilted against the car door. A gash on her left temple oozed blood over her face.

"Shit," Nick said. "Call 911. Tell them to hurry."

I yanked my phone out and called Emergency Services, while Nick gently eased Sophie onto her back. I looked down at her. Outrage flooded through me. I took off Nick's jacket to cover her and keep her warm.

He touched the side of her neck. "I can barely feel her pulse. Her skull looks fractured," he said. "Stay with us, Sophie. We're here to help you."

"I'll wait on the street for the ambulance." I dashed across the lawn and flagged the security guards outside the theater. Then I called Robin. Sam needed to know Sophie was hurt.

"Sophie was attacked in the parking lot. It's bad," I said to her. "Tell Sam the ambulance is on the way."

"Oh God," Robin said, her voice more irritated than upset. "Where are you? We'll be right out."

Within minutes, sirens wailed up the hill toward the Greek. A limousine pulled out of the backstage driveway and sped down the hill as the flashing red lights of an LAPD black-and-white, followed by the red LAFD ambulance, appeared. I stood in the street and directed them toward Nick, waiting at Sophie's car.

Robin walked across the street toward me. "Where is she?"

"Back there, at her car." I pointed through the trees. "The ambulance just got here. Where's Sam?"

"He left with Steve." Robin glanced over her shoulder, down the street. "We didn't want Steve to get held up. Sam told me to make sure she's okay and to let her know he'd call her tomorrow."

"His girlfriend was attacked, and all he could think about was getting Steve away?"

"You don't understand. His priorities are . . ."

"Really messed up," I said, irritated and angry at their callousness. "She's hurt. Bad. He should have come over here to be with her."

Robin's voice rose. "How could Sam know whether or not she was pulling a stunt for attention?"

"Because I called you and told you," I said, raising my voice to match hers. "What's wrong with you, Robin? You're acting like Sophie isn't hurt at all."

"I'll go over there and talk to her." She started toward the picnic area. "Can she drive home?"

"She's unconscious," I said. "Someone needs to go to the hospital with her."

Robin stopped. "I'll get Lulu. I need to go back to do the settlement."

"I can't believe you're being so casual about this," I said.

"I'm sorry Sophie's hurt. Lulu will ride to the hospital with her. But there's no one left at the theater to do the box office. Sam's already angry with me about the argument. I'm not going to do anything else to put my job in jeopardy. I'm sure Sophie will be okay."

"You didn't see her, Robin. She's not okay."

An LAPD patrolman came through the trees toward us. "Ladies, I need you to back away from this area. Did one of you call 911?"

"I did," I said to the young officer.

"And were you together when you found the victim?" he said, looking at Robin.

"No," she said. "I just walked over here from the theater."

"I was with that man over there," I said, pointing over to Nick.

Nick left the EMT crew working on Sophie and walked toward us. Patrolmen cordoned off the park and kept Sophie's car isolated. The picnic area was filled with police and emergency crews. A small crowd of people formed on the sidewalk.

"She's dead," Nick said quietly.

"Dead?" Robin stepped back, her hand to her mouth.

The patrolman said to Nick and me, "Can you wait for the detective to arrive to give your statement?"

We both nodded.

"I have to call Sam," Robin said.

"Here," I said, pulling out my cell phone.

"No. I have to get back to the ticket office. They're waiting for me." Robin started to cross the street.

I stopped her. "That's it? You're going back to work? Robin, she's dead."

"I'm sorry," Robin said. "But there's nothing I can do out here. I don't know Sophie's family—Sam will know who to contact. I'll be of more help on the phone inside than here on the street."

I was on the sidewalk, watching Robin walk toward the theater. Nick stood there with me. Two more squad cars joined the two already parked outside the small, gated area. A short-haired woman, maybe forty, in glasses and a heavy black coat arrived fifteen minutes later and introduced herself to us as Detective Carla Pratt. Nick and I sat at a picnic table in the moonlight and described to her how we found Sophie.

"Did you know the victim?" Detective Pratt took notes as we talked.

"Not really." I explained that Sophie dated Sam Collins, my friend's boss.

A patrolman pulled Pratt aside. His voice carried through the still night air. "It doesn't look like a mugging. Her purse and wallet are in the car, and she has on jewelry."

"Sexual assault, a thrill kill, or someone she knew attacked her," Pratt said. She came back to Nick and me. "Are you sure you didn't see anyone else in the lot?"

"No, no one," Nick said.

"Did you see her leave the theater?"

I described how I saw Sophie leave with Buzzy Lacowsky and her friends, then lost sight of them at the door. By the time we finished our statements, it was after two a.m.

Nick drove through the Valley toward my house. "What a bizarre coincidence. This morning Sophie pulls out of a parking space in front of us, and tonight we find her near her car, dying."

"And you're saying there's a connection?" I lowered the window a crack. If Nick was going to begin theorizing, I needed air.

"Everything in the universe is connected," he said.

"It's all random, Nick."

"I don't agree." He turned the car heater on. "Think about this—if you didn't recognize her car at Collins Talent today, then Sophie and Robin might not have fought over the tarot cards, and Sophie might not have left the party when she did."

"No causal connection," I said. "*Might* is the operative word in your logic. Sophie very well could have left the party at the same time, despite whatever happened earlier. And if someone she knew planned to kill her, it wouldn't matter what time she left."

"Why do you insist on being so logical?" he said.

"Why are you so abstruse?"

Nick looked over to me. "That's a fifty-dollar word."

"Want me to break it into tens?"

"You can't deny that our fate is linked with Sophie," Nick said.

"Our fate?" I said. "I can't wait to hear this."

Nick turned left onto Carpenter and drove up the hill. "If Sophie hadn't left the tarot cards on Robin's door, you and I wouldn't be together right now."

I stared out the car window and grinned. Nick parked in front of my townhouse and got out to open the door for me.

"You don't have to walk me," I said. "I'm fine."

"I want to be certain you make it in safe." He followed me up the steps.

I took out my key and turned to say good-night. Nick put a finger under my chin, tilted my head back, and kissed me lightly. Then he brushed the hair out of my eyes. "Get some rest, Liz. I'll call you tomorrow."

Chapter Eleven

I woke with less than three hours of sleep behind me. I showered and dressed by rote. I had one goal—a double shot of espresso before I met my first client.

The aroma of coffee brewing inside the Caffeine Café prodded my senses. The veil of tiredness, clouding my mind and aching my body, was about to be lifted. I got in line to order and glanced at the TV above the condiment station. A headline flashed across the bottom of the screen: "Breaking News: Murder at the Greek."

A female reporter stood in front of the Greek Theater marquee. "Police are investigating the death of a young woman found in the parking lot of the Greek Theater last night. Sources who attended a private function at the theater after singer Steve Weller's concert disclosed the victim engaged in an argument at that party."

I gave the barista my order and dialed Robin.

"I was just going to call you," she said after my hello. "I hope we're still on for lunch in Beverly Hills. I know I acted like an ass last night, and I'm sorry. I was upset."

"We're on. My last client is at eleven. Meat-loaf sandwiches?"

"Great idea."

"Did you see the news this morning?" I said, picking up my steaming espresso from the counter. Ouch. I set it down and reached for a cup sleeve.

"Not yet. Did they say something about Sophie?"

"They talked about the murder but didn't identify her by name. But they knew about the argument at the party. I'm sure the police will want a statement from you," I said.

"They'll probably want the guest list, too," Robin said. "Liz, do you think someone from the party attacked Sophie?"

I walked to my car, set my cup on the roof, and unlocked the door. "I know Madame Iyå and her son followed Sophie out. But killing Sophie over a deck of tarot cards doesn't make any sense. And I didn't know anyone else there. What do you think?"

"I don't know. Maybe I'm not the only person she harassed," Robin said. "The girl was evil."

"She didn't deserve to die."

"No, you're right. She didn't," she said.

"Maybe the guest list will help the police. Listen, I need to get to the office to meet a client," I said. "I'll call you when I'm on my way to lunch."

I downed the espresso and drove toward the courtyard of offices on Ventura Boulevard where I rented a one-room suite for my therapy practice. I parked in the back and hurried past the purple and yellow pansies along the walkway.

Jillian Maine, forty and looking as tired as I felt, waited on the iron settee outside.

She got up, her arms folded. "You're late."

I checked my watch. It was seven fifty-five. "Our appointment is at eight, isn't it?"

"But you're always here when I get here," she said.

"I was delayed this morning," I said, opening the door. "We can get started now. I'm happy to see you."

Jillian sat on the sofa. I poured a glass of water, set out the box of tissues on the side table, and sat in my chair. Her anxiety about my arrival was a good opening for our session. Unlike my mother, who masked her anxiety by attempting to control everything, Jillian employed confrontation. However, unlike my mercurial mother, Jillian sought therapy to unravel her issues. My mother's therapy was to draw tarot cards.

After the fifty-minute session ended, I saw two more clients and then called Collins Talent.

"Robin's with . . . She's in a meeting," Lulu said. "Can I take a message or have her call you?"

"No—please tell her I'll be there by noon. She'll know," I said. Call waiting beeped, and I clicked through to answer.

"Dr. Cooper? This is Detective Carla Pratt, LAPD. I have some follow-up questions and would like to meet with you at the Northeast Division later this afternoon. Would that be convenient? Or should I come out and talk to you?"

"I can come to you," I said. "How about two o'clock?"

"Yes, thank you." She gave me the address. "I'll see you then."

I hung up, knowing that Pratt would ask about the argument at the party. Why the face-burning guilt for not telling her last night? Thirty minutes after I left my office, I parked my car and rode the elevator up to Collins Talent.

Lulu stared at me wide-eyed as I approached her desk. She beckoned to me to lean closer. "The police are here," she said in a whisper.

I looked around. Why the secrecy? We were the only people in the hall. "Where's Robin?"

"She's in her office. Sorry, they told me not to disturb them. Oh. My. God. Can you believe it? Sophie? Murdered? Dead? She was just right there, standing where you're standing, just yesterday. Miss Thing with her attitude and purple nails. And acting all like a princess at the concert last night with her entourage following her around. And now she's dead. Dead. I can't believe it. Can you believe it?" Lulu exaggerated each word by blinking her eyes and bobbing her head.

I couldn't believe that motormouth of hers didn't tell me on the phone that the cops were here. She could have saved me a trip over the hill. "No," I said, glancing down the hall, eager to find Robin. "I can't."

Lulu ran her hand through her short black hair. "It's been insane here all morning. One detective was waiting on the couch for Sam when I got in. Another one just showed up. I had to keep the whole place together all by myself, what with lawyers coming, the press calling, and clients asking questions while everyone was all huddled up behind closed doors. I've been here almost a year so I know exactly what to do, but it was so crazy that I haven't had a minute to deal with my own emotions, you know? I talked to Sophie a lot when she would call for Sam. And I know her roommate, too."

I was half listening to Lulu and half wondering if I should leave. But Lulu being friends with Sophie's roommate caught my attention. "You know her friends?" I said.

"Well, kind of. Yes. We go to the same gym every morning. Linda didn't show up today. I'm sure because of the . . . murder."

"I wonder if I saw her at the party. Was she there?"

"Yeah. Linda's tall, like five-seven, with blonde hair chopped in layers. Good body. Not as pretty as Sophie. At the gym she wears her hair pulled back in a ponytail, and I almost didn't recognize her because last night she wore it down. She had on a red dress and Jimmy Choo knockoffs laced up her calves. She was with a girl named Nola. Nola has straight black hair and wore a green satin dress. Nola wasn't at class this morning, either. You know, I guess, because of the . . . murder."

The names I overheard in the ladies' room at the Greek, the same girls who followed Sophie when she left the party. How close to Sophie were these friends? And did they walk her to her car?

"So the three of you were friends?" I said.

Lulu's eyes darted up. "Not friends. I work out with them at Hissy Fit."

The phone rang. As Lulu answered, I looked toward Robin's office. To my surprise, my brother, Dave, came out, head down, talking on his cell phone. Why would the LAPD Robbery-Homicide Division send Dave to investigate a parking-lot murder? RHD was a specialized task force. I strode down the hall and tapped him on the shoulder.

He closed his phone and looked up. I grinned. Detective

Pratt walked out of Robin's office. She looked at me, then at Dave.

"Detective Pratt, this is my sister, Liz," said Dave.

"We've met," Pratt said. "Dr. Cooper found the victim last night. I didn't realize she was your sister."

Dave pinched the bridge of his nose and sighed. "Will you excuse us for a minute?" He pulled me down the hall.

We said in simultaneous whispers, "What are you doing here?"

"You first," I said.

"No," he said. "You first."

"I'm here to have lunch with my friend Robin. Your turn."

"Sam Collins got the deputy chief out of bed at dawn with a request for RHD to monitor the investigation of his girlfriend's murder. The press is sensationalizing the connection between the victim and Steve Weller. The chief asked me to meet Pratt here and show Collins we're on it."

"Sam Collins and the chief are friends?" I said.

"No, Liz, the whole damn city has his phone number. Yes, they're friends," Dave said. "I'm here, aren't I?"

"Is Sam a suspect? Doesn't the husband or boyfriend always top the list?"

"You know I can't answer that," Dave said. "Maybe you should tell me what you know. Why the hell didn't you call and tell me about it last night?"

"First of all, I got home late, then spent the morning with clients," I said. "It didn't occur to me to call you. Second, for God's sake, Nick and I just found her."

"Nick?" Dave stood back. "Why were you with Nick?"

"Didn't you read the police report? Nick and I were at

the concert together and found Sophie when we left. Why are you grilling me about my social life? Shouldn't you be holding a press conference or searching for Sophie's killer?"

"Not funny, Liz. This complicates everything," Dave said.

"Why?" I said. "Because I found Sophie's body or because I was with Nick?"

"I can't go into it right now," Dave said. "Pratt's waiting for me."

I glanced at Pratt, watching us from outside Robin's door. "She asked me to meet her at the Northeast station this afternoon," I said. "Will you be there?"

"I doubt it."

He left to talk to Pratt. I brushed past them and entered Sam and Robin's suite. Robin's outer office was empty. Hearing voices beyond Sam's open door, I peered inside.

Sam was behind a wide glass tabletop desk; the view behind him spanned the city to the ocean. Gold records and framed photographs of him with celebrities covered the walls. The scent of baked goods drifted past the door. Off to the side, Buzzy Lacowsky idled near a glass conference table cluttered with bagels, donuts, and a half-eaten coffee cake. Robin waved me in while the group inside continued talking.

Two men in business suits sat facing Sam's desk. The younger one said, "She shouldn't go to the station without counsel."

Sam looked at Robin. "Call Ralph Barnes. Tell him I want him to meet you there. And don't say anything until he arrives."

"I don't need a lawyer," Robin said.

"Just call him," Sam said.

I said to Robin, "Why do they want you to go there instead of questioning you here?"

"I don't know. I didn't ask." Robin turned to the men in front of Sam. "Guys, this is my friend Liz Cooper. She found Sophie last night. Liz, meet Paul Dunbar, our chief litigator. Next to him is Mike Gold, our contract attorney, and that's Buzzy Lacowsky, who I think you've met already."

"Hello," I said. Two lawyers and a publicist. Someone had called in the troops. I looked past them, at Sam. "I'm very sorry for your loss."

"Thank you," he said.

The older man, Paul Dunbar, said to Robin, "Don't offer the police any information about Sam. He's not involved in this."

"I know," Robin said. "I assume they want to hear what happened at the party."

"You two must have had one hell of a fight," Buzzy said, forking a bite of coffee cake. "I'm sorry I missed it. Sophie made a spectacular scene of herself when she broke into the artist's lounge, screaming that you were after her."

My stomach went sour. Would Buzzy repeat the same thing to the police? Did he? Was that why Pratt wanted to question Robin at the station?

"I think it may be wise for Robin to take a few days off and work from home until the police clear this up," Paul Dunbar said. "Let's keep this distanced from the agency."

Sam nodded. "Good idea. The press won't be able to ambush her."

Buzzy shuffled behind Robin and draped his arm around her shoulder. "You could use a few days at the spa and some leisurely shopping, couldn't you, lovey?"

Robin brushed him off and looked at Sam. "I'll do whatever you want me to do, but I want you to be sure of one thing: I didn't do anything wrong."

"I know," Sam said. "You can work from home. Lulu will answer the phones here and refer the press to Buzzy. We'll stay in touch. Nothing will change. Find out when Sophie's funeral will be and send flowers."

"From you?" Robin said.

"From the agency."

"Are you going?" Robin said.

"No. Sophie knew how I felt about funerals. I'll grieve on my own."

Detective Pratt appeared at the door. "Mrs. Bloom? Are you ready?"

I followed Robin to her office. Pratt went out in the hall, talking on her cell phone. Dave must have left. I didn't see him.

"I'm sorry about lunch," Robin said to me. "I'll call you this afternoon."

"No problem." I lowered my voice. "Sam's so composed. I thought you said he was frantic about Sophie."

"That was last night when I called him," Robin said, quietly. "This morning after the press started hounding him and the police and the lawyers showed up, his priority became keeping scandal away from the merger."

Sam walked out of his office and said to Robin. "You know none of this is personal. I believe you and trust you more than anyone. This will blow over, and we'll get back to normal in a few days. If there's anything I can do to help . . ."

"I know, Sam. Don't worry." Robin watched him go back inside and close the door. She said to me, "Normal? Sophie puts a curse on me, and here I am, leaving my job like she wanted, for who knows how long."

"You don't believe that," I said.

"I don't? Sam thinks I need a lawyer. This is out of control." Robin took her briefcase from behind her desk and packed it with papers.

"They can't force you to go to the station," I said. "You're not a criminal."

"I know. Paul Dunbar told me to cooperate, so I agreed. And your brother was very nice about the request."

I shook my head and held up a hand. "No. Don't be taken in so easily. Dave's nice to everyone, including criminals, when he needs them to cooperate. And Paul Dunbar's job is to protect the agency, not you. You do everything else Sam tells you to do. Please don't let this be the one time you don't. Call the lawyer."

"Okay, okay," she said, shrugging her shoulders. "I'll call him on my way across town." She shut the briefcase and pulled her purse from the drawer.

"Mrs. Bloom?" Detective Pratt was at the door again.

"Sorry. I'm coming."

I followed Pratt and Robin to the lobby, where Dave sat on the couch waiting.

Lulu was at her desk, on the phone. "I gotta call you back," she said. "I have to talk to my boss."

Robin gave Lulu instructions and then got onto the elevator with Pratt and Dave.

"Where did you say that exercise class was that you like so much? I might try it," I said to Lulu.

"Hissy Fitness on La Cienega," she said. "The morning class is at six. You have to come. It's amazing. You'll love it. Getting into shape for that hunky guy you were with last night?"

"He's just a friend," I said, walking toward the elevator to avoid more questions. "I need to work off the junk food I've been eating for the past week."

As the elevator closed in front of me, I smiled. Lulu was right about Nick.

Chapter Twelve

I wanted, no, needed the meat-loaf sandwich. Outside on Camden Drive, I walked toward the burgundy awnings of the Brighton Coffee Shop, the oldest coffee shop in Beverly Hills. I sat on a stool at the end of the counter and ordered the special on sourdough bread with an order of fries.

I pictured Robin at the police station, explaining why she and Sophie quarreled. Robin would tell the truth, no matter how odd an argument over tarot cards sounded. Robin was the worst liar I knew. Back in high school, when the freshmen set off the fire alarm before our chemistry final, Robin blabbed to the first teacher who confronted us.

A half sandwich filled me up, but the fries were too perfect to leave—well-done and crunchy. I was dipping the last one in ketchup when I heard him.

"Hey." The word came out in a long, nasal tone and

dragged into two syllables. Buzzy Lacowsky slipped onto the stool next to me, grinning.

I grinned back.

He set his cell phone on the counter. "Eating alone or waiting for someone?"

"I was supposed to have lunch with Robin," I said.

"Too bad for her," Buzzy said. "I hear the food in jail is crap."

"Not funny," I said.

"Not joking. They're going to try and arrest her. The police asked me three times if Robin followed me and Sophie out to the parking lot or if I saw her when I came back to the party." He patted my hand. "She's lucky I didn't tell them e-ver-y-thing. Sophie hated Robin. I hope Robin didn't follow Sophie into the parking lot."

I pulled back. "What are you saying? For God's sake, Robin didn't kill Sophie. You were the one who left the party with Sophie. What happened when you got her outside?"

The waitress stopped for his order and brought him a soda.

He took a long draw through the soda straw. "Like I told the cops: I left Sophie at the curb with her girlfriends. She was pissed as all hell, rambling all kinds of drunken shit. And she called Robin a thief. She said she took her spell book."

I stared at him. "Spell book?"

He smirked. "You really don't know?"

"Tell me," I said.

"Our little Sophie sold spells on the side from her granny's voodoo book. Five hundred bucks a pop and guaranteed to work."

"How do you know that?" I said.

He finished his drink and signaled the waitress for a refill. "I knew Sophie before she met Sam. She and her friend Nola were regulars on the party circuit. There was always talk about her voodoo vibe."

"What's a voodoo vibe?"

"Sophie put on an esoteric air. Liked to hint about her secrets. She came off as the New Orleans chick who knew stuff. One night, a few weeks ago, I asked her. She swore me to secrecy, then sold me a voodoo money spell."

I snickered.

"Oh, don't laugh, honey. The spell worked like a charm. I picked up three new clients." He muffled a burp with his hand and smiled like a Cheshire cat.

"Did you tell Sam?"

Buzzy swept his eyes around the crowded restaurant like a spy worried about eavesdroppers. His words came out slow. "Sophie told me not to. If I told on her, she swore I'd be cursed." Then he sat back and grinned. "Besides, I'd never talk to Sam about shit like that. But now that Sophie's dead, I don't see any harm in bragging a little. So, do you think our friend Robin took the spell book?"

"Of course not. Why would she do that? She didn't know Sophie sold spells," I said. "Five hundred dollars is a lot of money. What happened if the so-called spells didn't work? Do you get your money back?"

"I just told you—they did work," Buzzy said. "Sophie told me another one of her friends bought a love spell and met a guy on the Internet a week later."

"So she said." I rolled my eyes. Nice scam.

Buzzy sat back, folding his arms in front of him. "You don't believe."

"No, I don't. But it doesn't matter what I believe. Who do you think killed Sophie?" I said to him.

"An ex-boyfriend? A mugger? Robin? How should I know?" He shrugged and picked up his ringing cell phone.

I paid the waitress and left. I had just enough time to drive all the way across Hollywood to the station for my meeting with Detective Pratt. As I turned my car east on Santa Monica, my cell phone rang. It was Nick. Was that a little thrill I felt at the sound of his voice?

"I just finished my class," he said. "How are you?"

"Right now I'm concerned about Robin. She might be a suspect in Sophie's murder. Detective Pratt called me in for another talk. I'm on my way to the police station now. I have a lot to tell you."

"I want to hear everything." I heard him take a breath. "Will you have dinner with me tonight?"

I thought of his kiss last night and smiled. "Yes, I'd like that."

"Good. Me, too. I'll pick you up at seven. Don't get yourself into any trouble before then."

"Darn," I said. "I was planning on making a huge scene at the station. But, okay, maybe I'll hold back. Because you asked."

"I don't ever want you to hold back. Just make sure you're free for dinner."

When I hung up, the phone rang again.

"Hi, Mom," I said, switching lanes to avoid the bus ahead.

"Did you hear the news? Sam Collins's girlfriend was murdered at the Greek Theater last night," Mom said. "Isn't Sam Collins Robin's boss?"

"Yes." I winced. Did I tell my mother the truth? If I didn't and Dave beat me to it, she'd never forgive me. "Mom, Nick Garfield and I found the body. It was awful."

She gasped. "Oh my Lord. I knew something was wrong. I knew it. I read stress in the cards this morning when I asked if there was a resolution for Robin's trouble. The Eight of Swords appeared. It's fear, Liz. Robin's imprisoned in fear."

Imprisoned wasn't what I wanted to hear. "I don't need a tarot reading to understand that Robin's anxious," I said. "She's at the station, being questioned this afternoon."

"You said you and Nick Garfield found the body," Mom said. "What were you doing with him?"

I find a dead body, and my mother would rather hear about why I was with Nick. I stopped at a traffic light. "We were at the concert together."

"I thought Nick had a girlfriend," Mom said. "What's wrong with you? You shouldn't be dating attached men."

The french fries and meat loaf swelled in my stomach. I felt nauseous. Nick had a girlfriend? He didn't act like he did.

"Our tickets were a thank-you to us from Robin for finding the tarot cards," I said. "Robin and her daughter were at the concert, too. It wasn't a date."

Just like tonight wasn't a date—Nick and I were simply having dinner together.

"Be careful," Mom said. "Nick Garfield gets around."

"Nothing to be careful about. And what makes you think he has a girlfriend? He didn't mention one to me," I said, clenching the wheel.

"A smart, good-looking man like that must have a girlfriend. Your brother, Dave, would have told me if he's gay. By the way, have you talked to Jarret lately?"

I gritted my teeth. "Listen, I have to go. I'm on my way to the police station. They need me to answer more questions."

"You need to tell the police that girl who died was running around town harassing people. I'll bet she was a member of a cult. Tell Robin and her boss to make sure that your brother, Dave, works the case. He'll catch the killer."

I didn't know what was worse, letting her lecture me about Nick or listening to her choreograph the murder investigation. "Calm down, Mom. Dave's already on it."

"Dave didn't tell me," she said.

"Say hi to Daddy for me. How is he?"

"He's fine. Oh—this afternoon I want him to take me to that shop you told me about."

"What shop?"

"The shop where you found the tarot cards," Mom said. "They might have my incense. You know, my favorite brand that I can never find? What was the name of the shop?"

No, no, no. My mother couldn't breeze into Madame Iyå's shop and blow the story Nick and I told her. "I forgot."

"Where is it?"

"Somewhere in Hollywood," I said. "Don't worry, I'll stop there for you and see if she carries your brand."

"Are you sure you know the brand?"

I turned left onto Sunset, then right on Hyperion. "I know exactly what brand."

"Mystic Bouquets," Mom said. "I want two boxes of the Moonlit Blend in the small violet-and-yellow case. Ask her if she carries Raspberry Dawn, too. Oh, and see if she has—"

That was enough for me. "Hello? Mom? Are you there?"

"Yes, honey, I can hear you . . ."

"I think I lost you," I said. "Hello?"

"I'm here."

"If you can hear me, I'm hanging up. Talk to you later."
I clicked "Call End," set the phone on the seat next to me,
and smiled.

Chapter Thirteen

I hated when street names morphed. Hyperion became Glendale Avenue, and when Glendale became Brand Boulevard, I was certain I was about to get lost. Following Detective Pratt's directions, I turned onto San Fernando Road and saw a huge "Police" sign on a pole above a one-story building. Excellent. I parked and entered the LAPD Northeast Division through double glass doors.

A young officer in LAPD blue sat behind the sign-in window to the right. I took a place in line, while a middle-aged, leather-jacketed man asked the officer questions about recovering a stolen car. When he finished, I gave my name, sat down, and waited for Pratt. Thirty minutes later, she appeared and escorted me inside.

The Detective Room was as big as a tennis court and held cubicles grouped in sets of six. A few men and women, on the phone or reading computer screens, sat behind desks.

Feeling self-conscious, I had an urge to explain that I was a willing witness and not a suspect, but no one looked up at us. I followed Pratt through the maze to a section at the far corner. She stopped and opened one of the two interrogation room doors on the back wall.

"We can talk in here," she said.

The fluorescent-lit interrogation room with a metal desk and two chairs was the size of a walk-in closet. The register above us blew out hot air that smelled like burned dust. I swallowed to ease my anxiety. Nothing to worry about; I had nothing to hide.

I sat down. Pratt opened her notepad, then folded her hands on the desk and smiled. Her hair was buzzed above her ears. Sandy-brown bangs covered her forehead and brushed the top of gold-rimmed eyeglasses.

"Thank you again for coming in, Dr. Cooper," she said.

"Please, call me Liz."

"And you can call me Carla. I'm sorry I kept you waiting outside. It's been a busy day," she said. "You must know from your brother how nonstop a murder investigation can be."

"I do. From both my brother and my father. My dad spent twenty years as a detective at Hollywood Homicide. He retired six years ago." Oh God. Carla was trying to put me at ease, and I responded with the family history. Oh well.

"What's your father's name?"

"Walter Gordon. Do you know him?"

"No, don't think I do. I haven't worked Hollywood," Carla said. "I've been at Northeast since I made detective."

I set my purse on the floor next to me. "By the way, did Robin Bloom leave? I didn't see her car out front."

"Mrs. Bloom drove to the station with us. And she's still here, waiting to complete her statement," Carla said.

Waiting? For what? Robin left Beverly Hills with Carla and Dave more than an hour before I did, and I waited in the station lobby for another thirty minutes. Robin must have brought along one hell of a guest list for her interview to go on so long without finishing it.

Carla pulled a pen from her blazer pocket and clicked it open. "Let's talk about last night in more detail. I'd like you to give me the rundown of your evening at the Greek Theater as you remember it."

I settled back into the hard chair. "Nick Garfield and I arrived at the theater about twenty minutes before the show started. Robin and her daughter, Orchid, met us at our seats."

"Did you see Miss Darcantel at the concert?" Carla said.

"No," I said. "She wasn't at the show."

"How do you know?"

I backtracked my story to Robin's office and explained that I heard Sophie say she planned to attend the party and not the show.

"When the concert ended, Nick and I went into the after-show party," I said. "We saw Sophie there."

"What time was that?"

"I think we walked in just after eleven," I said.

"And where was Miss Darcantel the first time you saw her?"

Each answer led to another question. How often did I see Sophie during the course of the night? Did I see her with anyone in particular?

I described Sophie's conversation with Madame Iyå,

Sophie's outburst at Robin, and Sam's demeanor when he led Sophie out of the artist lounge.

"What did Mr. Collins say?"

"He told Buzzy Lacowsky to escort Sophie out of the party. Sophie protested, Sam ignored her, and then Buzzy led her out."

"Where were you when Miss Darcantel left the party?" Carla said.

"Standing with Robin outside the door to the artist lounge," I said.

"Did Miss Darcantel say anything before she left?"

"Sophie cursed Robin," I said.

Carla raised her eyebrows. "Miss Darcantel cursed at Mrs. Bloom? As in *shit* or *damn* or *go to hell?*"

"No. Sophie looked at Robin and said something like, 'Curse you—your luck just changed.' "

"Did Mrs. Bloom respond?"

"No. Robin went into the artist room. Sophie and Buzzy left," I said.

"Miss Darcantel and Mr. Lacowsky left alone?"

"No." The temperature in the interrogation room had to be eighty degrees. I pulled at the neckline of my cashmere sweater, fanning myself as I explained how Linda, Nola, Madame Iyå, and Jimmy paraded after Sophie and Buzzy.

Carla took notes, then said, "What did you do after Miss Darcantel left the party?"

"Robin invited Nick and I into the artist lounge."

"Who else was inside?"

As I tried to picture the group, every face was a blur except Nick's. "I know Steve Weller was there. Honestly, I didn't know anyone except Nick, Sam, and Robin."

"Sam Collins?" Carla said.

"Yes."

"Mrs. Bloom was there, too?"

"Yes, I thought I just said that."

Carla set her pen down. "Mrs. Bloom never left the artist lounge before you and Mr. Garfield departed?"

She waited for my answer, her eyes locked on mine. It was a question I didn't anticipate. My pulse quickened.

"Robin left for a few minutes to walk her daughter to her car," I said.

"What time was that?"

"I couldn't say. It was soon after we went in." I straightened to release the tension in my back.

"How long was Mrs. Bloom gone?"

I looked down at the desk. I knew damned well that Robin was gone long enough for me to finish a full glass of wine and start another. "I'm not sure," I said.

"Take a minute to think about it, Liz. Ten minutes? Twenty? Thirty?"

"Honestly, I couldn't say. Nick and I were talking at the bar. I didn't see when Robin walked back in. She could have been inside awhile before she took us to meet Steve Weller," I said.

"Then how long were you in the artist lounge before Mrs. Bloom collected you and Mr. Garfield for the introduction?" Carla said.

"Twenty minutes or so?"

"Or so?"

"You're trying to make me commit to a time frame I don't remember," I said, growing irritated and uncomfortable.

The air, or Carla's persistence, was stifling. I reached my hand back to sweep my damp hair off my neck.

"Let's go back to the incident between Miss Darcantel and Mrs. Bloom on the steps. Did Mrs. Bloom tell you what the argument was about?"

"Yes." My cell phone rang in my purse. I let it go to voice mail and said to Carla, "Robin asked Sophie about tarot cards that were tacked to Robin's front door."

Carla took off her glasses and set them on the table. "Do you know what Mrs. Bloom meant by that?"

"Yes. Someone left tarot cards on Robin's door to scare her. They were unnerving. 'I'm watching you' was written on the back of one of them. Monday night, a photo of Robin marked with voodoo symbols was tacked on her door. We think Sophie left them."

"What made you and Mrs. Bloom think Miss Darcantel left the cards?"

"We learned that Madame Iyå designed the tarot deck the harasser used. Her copy was intact. Sophie had the only other copy," I said. "It must have been Sophie who left the cards."

"You saw Miss Darcantel with the tarot cards?"

"No."

"Did finding the tarot cards make Mrs. Bloom angry?" Carla said.

"Not angry. She was frightened and curious."

"Why do you think Miss Darcantel would try to frighten Mrs. Bloom?"

I shrugged. "I don't know."

"I understand Miss Darcantel was dating Robin's boss."

I nodded.

"Is that a yes?" Carla said.

"Yes." Was she recording us? I glanced up to the corners of the ceiling, looking for a microphone or camera. I didn't see one.

"How did Mrs. Bloom feel about Miss Darcantel and Mr. Collins's relationship?"

"I don't think Robin cared who Sam dated," I said.

Carla sat back. "Even if Mrs. Bloom and Mr. Collins were lovers, too?"

I cocked my head. "Robin and Sam?"

"Boss and secretary? It happens," Carla said.

"Not with them," I said.

"Are you certain?"

I lived out of town when Robin took the job at Collins Talent. She told me about her sexy new boss over the phone. I remembered teasing her about Sam. She laughed off the joke. Robin and Josh were the happiest couple I knew. But Sam was a player. Could I swear that Robin and Sam never had a fling? Even after Josh died?

"Of course I'm certain." My foot tapped on the floor.

"What other reason would Miss Darcantel have to taunt Robin?"

"I don't know," I said. "What are you getting at?"

"I'm trying to get at the truth."

"You're going in the wrong direction if you suspect Robin."

"I didn't say Mrs. Bloom was a suspect," Carla said.

"Robin wasn't the only person Sophie argued with. I told you, she fought with Madame Iyå, too. Madame Iyå and her son followed Sophie out of the party. From what I overheard, until last night, Madame Iyå and Sophie were partners."

104

"Tell me about the rest of the evening. What did you and Mr. Garfield do after Mrs. Bloom came to introduce you to Mr. Weller?"

When I completed my story up to the moment Nick and I found Sophie in the parking lot, Carla smiled and stood. "Thank you for your help, Liz. I wish we'd had all of these details last night."

"One more thing," I said, ignoring the dig. "Buzzy Lacowsky told me that Sophie was selling voodoo spells. What if a dissatisfied customer attacked Sophie?"

"Thank you for the information. I'll check it out."

"You're welcome," I said.

I picked up my purse and followed Carla out. Her suit pants were dusty; her boots were caked with dirt. She must have been up all night at the theater parking lot and then worked all day. As we passed the other interrogation room, I looked through the open door to see if Robin was inside. It was empty.

"You said Robin was still here," I said. "Where is she?"

"She's being detained."

I staggered, stunned. "What you mean *detained*? I thought you said she wasn't a suspect?"

Carla didn't respond.

"I want to see her," I said. "Right now."

"I'm sorry. Detainees aren't allowed to have visitors," Carla said.

My astonishment spun into a swirling anxiety. "What are the charges?"

"We're waiting for her lawyer to arrive," she said. "That's all I can tell you right now."

I left the station with my head spinning. I leaned against

my car door and let the late afternoon breeze cool me off. I slid into the driver's seat, took out my phone, and picked up my message. It was my mother with the rest of her shopping list for Botanica Mystica. I erased the message and called Dave.

"It's me," I said when he answered. "Where are you?"

"On my way downtown," he said. "What do you need?"

"I need you to tell me what's going on."

"About what?"

"Carla Pratt is detaining Robin at the station," I said. "Can she do that?"

"Yep."

"Based on what?"

"Your friend had blood on her purse when she got into the car with us."

I dropped my head and closed my eyes to ward off the piercing pain that shot into my forehead. "Blood on a purse doesn't mean anything," I said, trying to convince myself as much as him. "It could be anyone's blood. It could be her blood."

"On top of the fight she and the victim had at the party, the blood is enough to detain your friend until they can run the DNA," Dave said.

"That's crazy. I don't believe it," I said. "They can't hold her while they wait for a DNA test. That could take days, weeks."

"Did you forget that your friend's boss called the chief and riled everyone up? We're moving fast. The press is all over this case. Trust me, the DNA test will get done before Pratt has to let your friend go."

Good. The test would come back negative. I said, "What about other suspects? Who else are you questioning?"

"That's all I can tell you," he said. "Pratt is the lead detective on the case. I'm not going to interfere. Ask your friend or her lawyer, okay?"

"Robin. Why are you acting like you don't know her name?" I said. "You have to tell Carla that she's on the wrong track."

"Pratt will follow the leads she has. If you have other information, I hope you gave it to her," he said. "Did you finish your statement?"

"Yes."

"Then let it rest. Let Pratt do her job."

I shouted into the mouthpiece. "Do her job? She's holding Robin. There had to be a hundred people at that party. Why not interview everyone else who was there before jumping to conclusions?"

"I won't talk to you about this anymore. Leave the investigation up to the detectives and the lawyers, Liz. I have to go. I have another call." Dave hung up.

Furious, I pulled out of the lot and drove toward Hollywood. Thanks to my mother, I had an excuse to stop at Botanica Mystica and do my own investigating.

Chapter Fourteen

Daylight faded into dusk as I drove into Hollywood. My anger masked the worry churning inside me: What blood on Robin's purse? Impossible. Even with the god-awful suggestion that Robin might have killed Sophie, Robin wasn't stupid enough to march into the scene at the parking lot last night with a blood-soaked purse on her shoulder. And what criminal carries a bloodstained purse to work the next morning? Was Robin close enough to Sophie's killer last night to brush against blood? Or was it planted?

The blast of air from my car heater dried the perspiration that had dampened my sweater during my interview. I probably smelled like a gym locker and needed a hot shower and change of clothes before dinner with Nick. Maybe I would wear something sexy. Wait. Robin was sitting in a holding cell. Why was I worrying about my evening attire?

I parked in front of the entrance to Artisans Patio and

walked through the sconce-lit alley of shops toward Botanica Mystica. The bells above the door jingled as I entered. Madame Iyå stood in the aisle, stacking books on a shelf.

Her brows arched, she tilted her head and forced a smile. "You came for the tarot deck for the professor?"

Damn. I forgot that Nick told her he was coming back with a check. There goes my incense story. "Oh. No. I came to apologize. Professor Garfield couldn't come in this morning. His lecture on the tarot was this afternoon. He decided to forfeit the display," I said. "We received horrible news about a friend and were up very late. I think you knew her. I saw you talking to her last night—Sophie Darcantel?"

Madame Iyå placed the last book on the shelf and wiped her hands on her black tunic. She studied me. "Yes. You knew Sophie?"

Her stare unsettled me. Fortune-tellers were adept at reading face and body language, and I didn't want her to catch me in a lie. I said, "She dated a friend of a friend. I spoke with her yesterday afternoon, before the concert. So tragic."

Madame Iyå settled on the stool behind the counter and rubbed both hands over her face. "Sophie was like a daughter to me."

I walked over and touched her arm. "I'm so sorry."

"Thank you," she said. "My son and I are still in shock."

"Does this affect the book of spells you were writing with her?"

"Not at all. Sophie gave me her spell book to use." She looked away.

Buzzy told me that Sophie accused Robin of stealing the spell book. Madame Iyå was either lying or she stole the spell book from Sophie.

109

Madame Iyå said, "How did you know Sophie was my partner?"

"You told us yesterday you were writing your book with a voodoo princess from New Orleans. I guessed Sophie was your partner when I saw you together last night. I know someone who bought a spell from her. He claimed she was the real thing." I looked around the shop, fixating on the jars of herbs lined on a shelf. "You were both given the gift so it was a natural assumption."

"Then you believe," she said.

"Yes," I said. Dodging the truth was getting simpler as the day progressed. "I'm curious. How does Sophie's death affect the spells or curses she put in motion while she was alive? What happens to the clients who bought spells from her?"

"Once a spell is put in motion, only the spirits can stop it." Madame Iyå shifted on the stool, the movement jangling the bracelets on her arms.

"What if one of the spells was purchased by her murderer?"

Madame Iyå laughed softly. She looked down at the amulets in the glass case that separated us. "The hoodoo would be stirred up. Sophie's ancestors were powerful voodoo women. Their spirits would ensure the spell turns on the murderer so he or she would pay dearly—in this world, in the afterlife, or in both."

The early evening darkness crept into the nooks of the shop. Small lamps at the end of each counter shed a pool of amber onto the glass. Smoke from the sandalwood incense burning in a bowl circled in the air.

"I wonder what happened to Sophie last night, don't you?" I said.

She crooked her finger for me to lean in. "Maybe Sophie will tell us the answer. Are you a true believer?"

I lowered my voice to punctuate the lie. "Yes, of course."

"Sophie's roommate, Linda, is hosting a séance tomorrow night to summon Sophie's spirit before she crosses over. Familiar faces will be there to send her off. If Sophie knew her killer, maybe her spirit will give us the name."

My pulse thrummed. I took a calming breath to shield my excitement. I couldn't sit and do nothing. My friend was being detained for murder. The séance would be my opportunity to meet Sophie's friends and maybe her clients. And if Madame Iyå was Sophie's killer, the séance might prove telling.

"I'd love to attend," I said. How could I pull off an invite? Sophie's friends exercised with Lulu in the morning. Meeting them at class was a long shot but worth a try. "I'll see Linda at class in the morning. Is she hosting the séance here at the shop?"

"Not here. We're doing it at Sophie's apartment. Linda and my son, Jimmy, will prepare the setting. I need to be surrounded by Sophie's energy," she said.

"Thank you for telling me. I'll try to be there." I forced a smile and hoped that Nick and Osaze would understand.

Madame Iyå bowed her head. "The spirits do all the talking. I'm only the vessel."

"You have a gift." The gift of salesmanship. I couldn't wait to see how Madame Iyå hustled a crowd.

"Yes. I've been an intuitive all of my life."

I'll bet. I glanced at the incense display on the shelf behind her and remembered my mother. "Do you carry Mystic Bouquets Incense?"

"No. I don't know the brand," she said. "I could look it up and order it for you."

"Don't worry about it. I must have mistaken the name," I said.

She reached under the counter and pulled out a blank index card. "Write your name and address on here. I'll put you on my special customer list. I teach classes and do readings. Tell everyone you know."

I filled out the card with my office address and started to leave. "I hope to see you at the séance."

"Wait. Yesterday I told you I'd fix a special gris-gris to drive your professor crazy with lust for you." She reached to the shelf above the incense and set a small bag on the counter in front of me. "Here you go. Guaranteed to work."

"I really don't need it. We're just friends."

Madame Iyå leaned back and stared hard. "You have a broken heart, Liz. You need the help of the spirits to let the professor in."

Sadness surged up from my chest and lodged in my throat. Having a stranger see through me was startling. I took a breath and pushed the feeling back.

"Don't you trust me?" Madame Iyå narrowed her eyes.

Not one bit. But I needed to get out of there and didn't want to argue. "Sure. I'll try it."

"That'll be forty dollars." She smiled and handed me the small bag. "Cash or credit card?"

I fingered the pouch. The inside felt grainy and rough, like it was filled with dried leaves and sand. Reaching into my purse for the cash, I said, "What do I do with it?"

"Sprinkle the gris-gris across your threshold. When the professor walks across it, he will desire only you."

"Thank you."

"Liz? You'll be pleased. It's potent."

I nodded, dropped the velvet bag into my purse, and left. Outside, the neon lights on Hollywood Boulevard bounced off the low ceiling of clouds. The cold evening air smelled damp. As I walked to my car, I imagined Nick scooping me into his arms and carrying me up the stairs to my bed after walking over my magic dirt. Sure.

Chapter Fifteen

If there was a curse in Los Angeles, it was on me, stuck in rush hour traffic. A minor accident on the freeway turned my ten-minute drive to Studio City into a forty-five-minute nightmare. I felt helpless as my car inched along the highway. My unanswered calls to Robin's cell intensified my apprehension that the police were targeting her as Sophie's killer. A pleasant recollection of Nick's kiss last night evolved into a dating anxiety I hadn't felt since high school. Tonight, Nick and I were having dinner. It was dinner, only dinner. His kiss had been to soothe me, not to seduce me. My emotions were out of control, and I didn't like it.

I pulled into my garage with little time to put myself together, whatever that would look like. I darted upstairs to check for messages. Nothing. Not even my mother. I tossed my purse and the black sweater and slacks I wore all day onto the pink-and-white striped chair by the bedroom window, then padded over to the closet in my bra and panties, ready to audition anything that would make me feel pretty. Two days ago I threw Dave's sweatshirt over a crumpled skirt and didn't give a damn what I looked like in front of Nick. Tonight, my heart did a little dance of anticipation as the clock ticked toward his arrival.

I pulled out a white blouse and my gray pencil skirt. Nope—back in the closet. Too businesslike. I know—a paisley wrap dress, black boots. No, too Barbarella-shops-at-Ann-Taylor. Seriously, it was slacks and a T-shirt because I didn't care. Who was I kidding? I did care. I settled for a soft black jersey skirt with a gray silk blouse and black teddy and black silver-clipped pumps. I set aside a black wrap sweater for warmth. I dug out my rarely worn, sexy lingerie from the corner of the drawer. Then I headed for the shower to shave my legs. Not that I wanted or anticipated anything happening. Shaving was simply good grooming.

After the shower, I slathered my body with rose-scented lotion, put on my outfit, and finished my makeup in record time, adding a final touch of Chanel Red to my lips. I threw my head upside down to fluff out my hair. The doorbell rang. Shoes in hand, I trotted downstairs and opened the door. In black pants and a charcoal sport coat over a blue shirt, Nick looked seven feet tall from my five-foot-five barefoot viewpoint.

I tilted back my head and grinned, breathless. "Hi. You're right on time."

"So I am. Are you okay? You're flushed," he said, reaching to touch my cheek.

I ducked his gesture, bending to put on my shoes. Nick leaned against the doorjamb, watching me wobble on one foot, then the other.

"I'm fine. Robin's not." Pumps in place, I stepped aside to let him in. "When I left the station this afternoon, she was still being held for questioning in Sophie's murder."

"Held, arrested, or detained?" he said.

We walked into the living room, his hand on the small of my back, and sat on the sofa.

"Detained. Waiting for her lawyer," I said. "That was over two hours ago, and I haven't heard back from her yet. Detective Pratt wouldn't let me talk to her. She wouldn't answer when I asked about charges. The police know about Robin's argument with Sophie at the party. Dave told me they found blood on Robin's purse. Is that enough to hold her? It sounds shaky to me."

"Slow down." Nick's voice was calm, his face serious. He held his eyes on mine, his mouth in a straight line. "Her lawyer will know what to do. Do you know who's representing her?"

"It's probably Ralph Barnes. That's who Sam told her to call. Should I contact him?"

"I think you should wait. Did Dave tell you anything else?"

"No," I said. "He rushed me off the phone."

"I don't like hearing that." Nick rubbed his chin. "If Robin doesn't call you tonight, maybe I can get more information out of Dave tomorrow. It'll be okay, Liz."

How could it be okay? My best friend was suspected of murder. I pinched my lips together, hoping Nick was right. He put his arm around my shoulders. His smooth, strong touch made me feel safe. I noticed a tiny cut on his clean-shaven face.

Suddenly shy, I sat back. "I'm hungry. Are you?"

116

"I am," he said, smiling.

"Let me get my bag." I got up and started upstairs for my purse. Conscious that he might watch my ascent, I swayed my hips ever so slightly and paused to look down over my shoulder. "Where are we going?"

Nick was looking out the window, not at me. "How about Italian?"

"Perfect," I said.

One last look in the bedroom mirror, and I was on my way back down. Nick watched me descend the stairs, without the swerve. The phone rang.

I darted past him through the living room and toward the phone in the kitchen. Relieved, I said over my shoulder: "I bet it's Robin."

When I answered, Orchid's voice was shaking. "Aunt Liz?"

A shiver of dread ran through me. "What's wrong, honey?"

"My mom is in jail. I don't know what to do," she said. "Detectives are coming up here to question me tomorrow. They're going to search Mom's house, too. What's going on? Do you know?"

While my heart thudded in my chest, I urged Orchid to be calm. I related what I knew about Sophie's murder. I assured her that between the lawyer, Sam Collins, and me, Robin would have the support she needed. "Just answer the detectives' questions. They'll want to know what happened when you and your mom walked out to the parking lot last night. Tell them the truth. What did the lawyer say to you?"

"My mom has to stay in jail while the police check out her story and search the house for evidence. They couldn't do it tonight. They didn't get the warrant in time—something about searching only during the day. My mom doesn't want me to worry but I can't help it. I'm totally freaked out. The lawyer said he'd call me tomorrow. Should I come down there?"

"Listen to the lawyer. Was it Ralph Barnes?"

"Yes," Orchid said.

"I'll contact him in the morning and see if I can learn more." Promising Orchid I'd stay in touch, I asked her to do the same. "We'll get through this."

Nick was standing behind me when I hung up with a sigh. I repeated the conversation, and then said, "What should I do?"

"Take the same advice you gave Orchid—call Robin's lawyer in the morning and try not to worry tonight," Nick said. "We can talk about it at the restaurant."

We drove to Vitello's, an Italian restaurant on Tujunga Avenue—a block tucked into the heart of Studio City and lined with quaint coffeehouses, gift shops, yoga studios, and gourmet food shops. Inside, Vitello's décor was classic Italian, from the murals on the beige walls to the terra-cotta floors.

Mario, the maître d', led us to the back room, where a mahogany bar stretched across the wall and ended at an upright piano. I slid into a circular red-leather booth while the pianist played and sang "That Old Black Magic" over the chatter in the full dining room. Nick settled in next to me.

"Good evening, Professor, signora," the waiter said. "Can I get you some wine before I give you the specials?"

"Red," I said, looking up from the menu.

Nick waved hello to the bartender, then said to the waiter, "Tell Joey to pour two glasses of the house red. Thanks, Tommy."

I relaxed into the soft cushion, grateful for the wine that

was about to be served. My palms were damp, and my nerves were jumping. And every time I looked at Nick, I pictured our kiss at my door last night, my first kiss since my divorce. Did he kiss me to calm me down? Assure me? *What about the thrill I feel when I'm with him?* Was I ready for a relationship? Good grief, I was projecting into the future. Probably to keep my mind off Robin's dilemma. *Stay in the moment, Liz.* It was a simple kiss. Certainly something we could discuss. Then I wondered if he'd kiss me tonight.

"You're quiet, Liz," Nick said. "Worried about Robin?"

I took a deep breath, considered my options, and then decided to follow my own counsel. "I am. But I was thinking about what happened later last night."

"I understand. Finding Sophie was horrible. I'm sorry."

"I'm sorry, too—for Sophie. But I was thinking about something else. About what happened at my door, Nick."

Tommy came back and set two glasses of red wine in front of us. I waited for him to leave before I finished.

"You kissed me," I said.

Nick unbuttoned his jacket and started to lean toward me. "Liz."

I didn't see him reach for my hand as I reached out for the wine in front of him. Our hands collided, and in a splash, the glass of red wine toppled out of my hand, and wine spread over the tablecloth toward his lap.

I jumped for a napkin. Nick leaped out of the booth while I scurried to avoid the drip off the table.

"Oh my God. I'm so sorry," I said.

"No worries." His light-blue shirt was spattered with red. He brushed droplets of wine from the front of his trousers. "I'll be right back."

Before Nick was out of sight, the waiter was at the table with a rag. He wiped down the seats, then changed the table-cloth and replaced the settings. He left and came back in a flash with two fresh glasses of red. I took a deep sip to steady my now completely shattered nerves. Breathing deep, I sat back and watched Nick across the room talking to the pianist.

As Nick sat back down next to me, the piano player began to sing "As Time Goes By."

"Liz." Nick put his hand on mine. "I'm glad I kissed you. Was I wrong? Nothing has to change between us unless we want it to."

"But why did you kiss me last night?"

"I was drawn to you," he said. "You were vulnerable, upset."

I pulled my hand away. "And that's how you calm women down? By kissing them?"

"Maybe." Nick grinned. "Does every kiss have to mean something?"

"Every kiss does mean something."

"And it's your job to analyze each one?"

"No, just the kisses I get." I smiled.

"Okay." Nick sat back and folded his arms. "Here's the analysis of last night's kiss. You were irresistible. Despite the bad end to the party, I loved being with you last night and the night before. I knew I wanted to kiss you the moment you walked into my classroom. Does that make you nervous?"

"Yes."

"Then I won't kiss you anymore," he said. "Feel better?"

"No. I liked the kiss," I said.

"Then let's keep kissing for a while."

"Let's." I looked over to the piano player and laughed. "You made him play that silly song for me, didn't you?"

Nick took my hand again and kissed it.

Tommy came to give us the specials. I ordered a dinner salad and eggplant parmigiana. Nick chose sausage and peppers. Our table filled up with bread, butter, and wine. I picked at my food, thinking of Robin in a stuffy interrogation room or a gray-walled cell, eating whatever the cuisine du jour was in jail. As we ate, Nick gave me a recap of his day. He had been called back for questioning also. I told Nick what happened while I was at Collins Talent and about my lunch with Buzzy, leaving out my side trip to Madame Iyå's. I'd tell him about the visit after I got the invite to the séance from Sophie's roommate.

"I know Robin will blame her night in jail on the curse Sophie laid on her," I said. "She already blamed her leave of absence on it."

"Do you believe in curses?" Nick tore a piece of bread and mopped up the last of the red sauce on his plate.

I shook my head. "I think Sophie cursed Robin as a way of coping with her anger. She wanted Robin to suffer. By putting her wish in the form of a curse, she removed her responsibility to act on the anger. Sophie used curses and voodoo as an emotional crutch."

"Be careful, Liz. Some types of voodoo are very serious."

I sat back in the booth. "Okay, Professor. Teach me. Tell me what you know."

"It's a lecture and then some." He laughed. "Let me see if I can oversimplify. Vodou, v-o-d-o-u, is a complex monotheistic religion that reveres spirits—some good, some harmful. Its roots began in West Africa, traveled with slaves to the Caribbean, and flourished in the Haitian mountains for centuries. Haitian Vodou was so secret that its traditions are only passed orally from generation to generation."

He leaned in. His eyes lit up as he spoke. His passion for his work was sexy, and I smiled as he went on.

"Then there's the New Orleans variety, the v-o-o-d-o-o voodoo," he said. "It emphasizes black magic and is practiced pretty much in the open. That's the type of voodoo you see sensationalized in the movies and sold in occult shops. If Sophie used New Orleans voodoo, her curse, if you'll allow me, was a mind trick on Robin, an open and believing victim. But if Sophie practiced true Haitian Vodou, the mystery, and therefore the curse, runs deeper."

"We know Sophie had some kind of a spell book. Buzzy told me she sold voodoo spells," I said.

"Real Vodou isn't written down."

"It's a shame Sophie thought she needed the help of magic. She was a gorgeous young woman with the world open to her." I stared at my wine glass. "One reason I chose to study psychology was to discover what drives people to do what they do and to help them."

Nick nodded. "Spiritual belief systems play a big role in our motives and lives. That's one of the reasons I study religions. We have something in common."

"We agree right up to the part where you take the supernatural seriously and I don't," I said.

Nick waved at Tommy for the check, then put his arm across the back of the booth and turned his attention to me. "There's one thing I haven't told you. Dave called late this afternoon. He asked if I would take on an unofficial, advisory role in the case and look at the occult symbolism and altar in Sophie's bedroom. The police want to know if there could be a connection between whatever she was practicing and her murder."

"What?" My voice pitched up an octave. The waiters and busboys stopped, poised to clean up another spill. "You could have mentioned this earlier."

Nick grinned. "I was distracted, wondering when I could kiss you again."

"Stop it, Nick. Not now. This means the police are either considering other suspects or searching for evidence against Robin. You could help Robin get released. When are you meeting Dave?"

"After my morning class."

"I'm going with you," I said.

"You can't," he said. "You're a witness."

I leaned back and stared. "So are you."

"I didn't hear the argument between Robin and Sophie," Nick said.

"So? You were at the party. You were—"

Nick put his hand on my shoulder. "I'm the only resource on the occult Dave could come up with when Detective Pratt asked. I told you: my going there will be an unofficial visit. If I see something there that connects Sophie to a dangerous group, someone else will have to do the official investigation."

"I'm still going with you," I said.

"You're relentless," Nick said. He sat with his eyes on mine, silent.

I waited until I couldn't bear the quiet. "Well?"

"Actually, I could use your help," he said. "You were savvy enough to recognize that Robin's harasser was a woman the other night. I'd value your perspective. But letting you in the apartment will be up to Detective Pratt. It's her investigation."

"What about Dave? I could ask him," I said.

"Don't. Just come to the apartment. We'll deal with Dave at the scene."

Nick signed the bill. We said good-night to Tommy and Mario, then walked outside. Low clouds blanketed the sky; a crisp breeze blew my hair across my face. I brushed it back, and the flash of neon from the Gelato Bar across the street caught my eye.

Nick followed my gaze. "How about a little dessert?"

I didn't need convincing. Inside the tiny shop, mounds of homemade gelato filled a glass-encased cooler. I chose Dolce Amaro, a creamy custard gelato filled with chocolate-covered pralines. Nick ordered fresh raspberry gelato, and I could still taste it on his lips when he kissed me good-night at my door.

"Want to analyze the kiss before I go?" he said.

"No, it was delicious," I said. "I'll take seconds."

Chapter Sixteen

After Nick left, I leaned against my front door and smiled. Despite two glasses of wine at dinner, I felt clear-headed and optimistic. Nick and I may find something at Sophie's apartment that could steer the investigation away from Robin and toward Sophie's killer. And if that didn't work, there was still the séance and Sophie's friends. I went into the kitchen to check for phone messages. No calls. With a bottle of water from the refrigerator in hand, I turned off the lights and headed upstairs to bed.

If I intended to meet Sophie's roommate at the exercise studio at six to wrangle an invite to the séance, I needed to wake early. I set my alarm on loud for five a.m. and dressed for bed. I tossed my blouse and skirt into the hamper along with the pile of clothing that had been on the chair since yesterday. Then I opened the window a crack to let in some fresh air. Fog draped the streetlights outside. The sound of thunder grumbled in the distance.

"I love my bed." I said it out loud on nights when I appreciated the cozy cocoon of my bedding the most. I was in cotton pajama bottoms and a T-shirt, propped up on pillows, and snuggled under my down comforter. Exhaustion seeped out of my back and neck as I sunk in between the sheets. When I reached across to the nightstand for my novel to lull me to sleep, I glanced at the tote on the chair across the room. It had been buried under the pile of clothing.

There was something about the tote that stopped me. What was I forgetting? The last time I carried it, I met Sophie at Robin's office. I climbed out of bed, trotted over, and pulled it open. Inside was the brown envelope Sophie left behind on Robin's desk.

Curious, I untucked the flap and shook the envelope upside down. A brown-leather eight-by-ten notebook embossed with a delicate gold-leaf border slid out. The worn leather on the cover felt soft and pliable. I carried the notebook back to bed and opened it. The symbol of a palm frond surrounded by an intricate fleur-de-lis pattern was centered on the inside front cover. I leafed through the yellowed pages filled with cramped, black script and stopped on a page at random. The heading, printed in letters across the top, read "To Break a Hex."

A spell. I caught my breath and my pulse began to race with excitement. I had Sophie's spell book. The book Madame Iyå claimed she had; the book Sophie thought was stolen.

Weren't hexes and curses the same thing? Robin was troubled by the curse Sophie hissed before leaving the party. I scanned over the spell, fascinated by how a practiced seer like Sophie might invoke the supernatural and make it appear believable.

The page was laid out like a cookbook: ingredients followed by instructions. The spell called for a sketch of the person who initiated the hex, cinnamon incense, and the recitation of the accompanying incantation. Cut the sketch into eight pieces and burn a piece, along with the incense, for eight consecutive nights while reciting the incantation and envisioning the person disappearing peacefully. On the eighth night, burn the piece that pictured the hexer's eyes. Hex removed. Happy ending.

At the bottom of the page and on the page that followed, names and dates, then initials and dates, were listed alongside dollar amounts. The first date on the page was August 1870; the last entry February 2005. Dollar amounts ranged from one hundred to five hundred.

I turned the pages, fascinated. Would Buzzy Lacowsky's name be somewhere inside, along with the rest of Sophie's recent clients? Was there a clue in here that might lead us to Sophie's killer? Another title stopped me: "To Break a New Lover's Old Relationship."

Nick. What if my mother was right? What if he had a girlfriend? My mother guessed; she didn't know. And where did I get off casting Nick as a cheater like my ex-husband, after only a few days and a few innocent kisses? Dating was about discovery. Whoa. *Stop, Liz.* I rubbed my eyes and took a deep breath to clear my thinking. Was I drunker than I thought? Something Nick said flashed through my mind: *Voodoo can snake into someone's head.*

Well, this voodoo wasn't going to snake into mine. I closed the spell book and opened it again. It fell to the same page.

Weird. Not funny. I could see why Madame Iyå wanted this, I thought, squinting at the book in my hand. It was provocative.

This was Nick's bailiwick. He needed to hear about the spell book—now. I reached for the cordless phone on the bed stand. Lightning flashed outside, followed by an earsplitting crack of thunder. The lights flickered and went out. I picked up the handset from its cradle and pressed a button. Nothing lit up. The line was dead. This was a joke, right?

Sliding out of bed and feeling my way to the window, I opened the shutters. The streetlights were out; my neighborhood was black. Another bolt of lightning flashed in the distance, illuminating the thick, gray-clouded sky. It was a rare Southern California electrical storm.

I padded back to my nightstand and fumbled for the flashlight in the drawer. Clicking it on, I crept downstairs to the kitchen to find my cell phone. I picked it up to dial; the pad didn't light up. I forgot to plug it into the charger. *Really smart, Liz.*

Barefoot and without a robe, I shivered. I rubbed my arms, wondering what to do. A thud on the floor above made me jump. A jolt of nerves shot through me. What the hell? I waited, hearing nothing except thunder rumbling and the wind blowing outside.

I double-checked the locks on both doors and crept upstairs. The flashlight flickered. I smacked the back of it until the light was steady again. I swept the beam across the bedroom floor. Face open on the carpet, next to my bed, was Sophie's spell book. Had it slid off the bed when I got up, or was that the thud I had heard? My hand trembled as I shone the light on the open page and the spell title: "How to Imprison the Mind and Spirit of an Enemy."

Imprison my mind? I kicked the book shut with my toe.

Taking a breath to calm my now-jangled nerves, I rummaged through my closet for sweats and gym shoes. I dressed with the flashlight beam pointed at me from the bed stand and went back downstairs to the kitchen. With my car key in hand, I opened the back door to the garage.

I got in my car, plugged my cell phone charger into the lighter, and turned the ignition to accessory. When I dialed Nick's cell number his voice message answered:

"Leave your number."

"Nick, it's Liz. I . . ." I hesitated. I hadn't expected voice mail. I couldn't just hang up, so I said, "I have something to show you. Call me."

I rested my head on the back of the seat and winced. I had something to show him? What kind of message was that? Why didn't I say Sophie's spell book? Show him? What? My book collection? My breasts? I should call him back. Explain further. I started to dial, then stopped. *Get a grip, Liz. It's only a message.*

I flipped on the car radio to a news station. The announcer confirmed that power was out throughout the San Fernando Valley because of a lightning strike at a power plant. Power-restoration crews were assessing the damage. Stay tuned.

There was nothing to do but wait. I sat in my car like a child, reluctant to go back into the house and nowhere to drive to. The only thing missing was my brother popping up from the backseat to scare the crap out of me like he did when we were kids. Tonight, the bogeyman was the crackpot spell book upstairs. Nope. The rational adult in me could and would go inside and back to bed. I picked up the flashlight and got out of the car. Outside, the wind whipped rain against the garage door.

On my way through the kitchen, I stopped to plug my phone into the charger. The power would return eventually. I took a candle from the drawer and put fresh batteries in the flashlight. I walked through the living room, the flashlight lighting my way. Before I started up the stairs to the bedroom, I hesitated. Nope, keep going. A stupid spell book of complete fiction wasn't going to intimidate me in my own home. No matter what it said.

Setting the flashlight and candle on the bed stand, I picked up my watch and checked the time. Midnight. Of course it was. I put the spell book on my dresser and crawled into bed. The lights came back on. Of course they did.

Chapter Seventeen

The rain pounding on the rooftop lulled me to sleep. At five a.m. a blast of rock music from my clock radio jolted me awake. I fumbled for the off switch and flicked on the light. Sophie's spell book was still where I left it, closed. No overnight messages from the supernatural.

Still in sweatpants and T-shirt, I slid into my workout shoes, went downstairs, and made coffee. If I had to exercise in order to meet Sophie's friends, I needed a jolt of something to wake me up. Fresh air and cold water weren't going to do it. I wondered if Robin got any sleep. The thought of her waking up in a jail cell was stimulus to grab my keys and head for the door.

Dawn broke as I drove through Laurel Canyon to West Hollywood. The streets were shiny from last night's rain; the air was clear and crisp. The neon "Hissy Fitness" sign stood above a two-story building on La Cienega south of

Santa Monica Boulevard. I parked and followed an arrow pointing up a flight of stairs into the combination reception area, fitness shop, and juice bar. The walls were covered with life-size black-and-white posters of Kate Hissenger posed to show off her muscle-cut body. How many classes would I have to take to look like that?

"First-timer?" The girl behind the front desk took my twenty dollars for the single class and directed me to "Studio One," down the hall. "You can leave your things in the back against the wall. Do you need a bottle of water?"

"No, thanks." I was still chilled from the cold morning air, and water was the last thing on my mind. Another hot coffee, maybe.

I entered the huge mirror-lined studio filled with women in workout bras, tanks, running shorts, and leggings that accented their toned frames. No cellulite anywhere in the room except the cache under my sweats. Lulu, in black crops and a "Collins Talent" tank, stood near the front of the mirror, talking with the two women I had seen follow Sophie out of the party.

"Oh, wow," Lulu said, running to hug me. "It's so cool that you came. You're gonna love this class."

"I'm ready," I said. Not really, but how hard could it be? "I see Sophie's friends made it this morning, too."

"Yeah." Lulu looked over to them. "Linda and Nola. I'll introduce you after class. Linda's the blonde in the pink halter and tangerine sweats. Nola's over there in the gray shorts. I was just . . ."

A piercing blast of rock music drowned out Lulu's words. She took a spot in the front row. I picked up a set of five-pound weights and found a space in the back.

WHO DO, VOODOO?

Kate Hissenger, midforties with the lean body of an Olympic swimmer, faced the class. "I'm Hissy," she said into a wireless headset. "For the next ninety minutes, you're mine. Pace yourselves, drink lots of water, and have fun. Let's warm up." She cranked the music louder and began to jog in place.

Sixty minutes later, my five-pound weights felt like twenty; my T-shirt was soaked. Hissy pumped her hand weights and shouted encouragement. I slipped outside to find an open window for a breather.

Linda came out of the ladies' room across the hall and stopped. "First time?"

I nodded, gulping fresh air.

"It gets easier," she said over her shoulder and went back in.

By the time we hit the floor for sit-ups, I was so grateful to be lying down that I could have kissed the sweat-covered rubber mat. After leading us through two sets of abdominal crunches, Hissy finished with a series of stretches, and class was over. We put away our weights and mats and filed through the door into the hall. I fell into a seat at the juice bar in the lobby.

"I'll have a strawberry smoothie, please," I said to the boy behind the counter. Sweat rolled from my forehead into my eye.

Lulu came up behind me, dabbing moisture from the back of her neck. "Did you like the class? Doesn't Hissy have an amazing body?"

Linda followed and ordered a banana smoothie. "Hi, again," she said to me. "I promise you, the first time is the worst."

"Yeah. You'll get used to it," Lulu said. "I thought I was gonna die the first time, but I got over it. Now it's easy. I wish she'd beat us up harder."

Sophie. I gritted my teeth at Lulu's unfortunate choice of words. A pained look flashed across Linda's face. Was she thinking the same thing? I held out my hand. "I'm Liz Cooper."

"Linda Miller." She returned the shake and smiled. "And this is Nola."

Nola had bumped between us and ordered a carrot juice from the bar boy. "Hi," she said to me.

"Liz knows my boss," Lulu said.

"You know Sam?" Linda shook her head. "He must be a wreck. Did you talk to him yesterday?"

"I don't know Sam that well," I said. "His assistant, Robin, is a good friend of mine."

Nola's eyes flashed; her lips curled into a snarl. "Robin? The bitch who killed Sophie? That pig deserves the death penalty for what she did to my cousin."

Her revelation surprised me. I had no idea Nola was Sophie's relative and understood her fury. Taking a step back, I looked to Lulu for support, but she had walked away to answer her cell phone.

"I think whoever killed Sophie deserves to be caught and punished," I said.

"I do, too," Linda said. "And I'll do whatever I can to help the police."

It wasn't much of an opening, but I didn't have a lot of time to get to my point before Linda and Nola left. "I was at the party. I saw you walk out with Sophie. What happened when you got outside?"

Linda dropped her eyes. "Sophie insisted she was okay to drive. Our cars were on opposite sides of the theater. We separated at the curb. Sophie walked to her car alone."

"I'm sorry." If I had left Robin to walk to her car and never saw her again, I'd be devastated. "Did anyone follow her?"

"I didn't look," Linda said. "I wish I had. But I told the police about the fight Robin had with Sophie at the party. We all could see how angry Robin was. Who else would have gone after Sophie?"

"Robin was frustrated at the party, not angry. Robin and Sophie had a misunderstanding. Unfortunately, it escalated into shouting. But Robin and I have been friends for a long time. She's like a sister to me. Robin wouldn't physically attack Sophie. I intend to prove she didn't."

Nola downed her carrot juice and said to me, "Let the police figure it out."

"You must want to know the truth," I said. "The police are trying to pin the murder on Robin. Sophie's real killer will go unpunished. If you were unjustly accused, wouldn't you want your friends to support you? Maybe you can help me find the real killer."

"I know who the killer is: your pal," Nola said. "The witch wanted to break up Sophie and Sam. When Robin found out Sam was going to propose to Sophie that night, she went berserk."

"You're wrong," I said.

Lulu returned and set her bag on an empty stool.

"You think so?" Nola said. "She was probably banging her boss until someone younger and prettier came along. She was jealous. Sophie told us that Robin called Sam's house at night with pathetic stories to get him to make Sophie leave."

"Whoa." I held up both hands. "Sam told Robin to phone.

He even prearranged the time with her. He wanted the interruption as an excuse to send Sophie home. I was at Robin's house for one of those calls. It was business, nothing else."

"Yeah, right." Nola looked away.

"It's true," Lulu said. "One time he even made *me* call his house when Sophie was there. He pulled that phone-emergency trick on all of his girlfriends. Even the one he was dating when I started working there. What was her name? I forget. But I know for sure that Sam didn't like sleepovers at his house. His old girlfriend—what was her name? Ginny, I think—told me the only time she stayed overnight with him was when they were out of town in a hotel." Lulu slapped her hand over her mouth and looked at me. "Sorry. I shouldn't be talking about Sam. He's my boss. Whoops."

"I don't believe it," Linda said. "Sophie adored Sam. She was positive he was going to propose to her. He bought her a car."

I shook my head. "He was going to break up with her. The car was his going-away gift."

"I don't believe that, either," Linda said.

"Lulu, did Ginny mention that Sam gave her a car when they broke up?" I said.

"Oh, yeah, a VW convertible," Lulu said. "Cream-colored."

Linda looked at Nola, then at me. "Sophie was in love. She did everything she could for Sam."

"Everything?" I said.

"She dressed to please him, showed up when he called, dropped everything to meet him. Everything," Linda said.

"Including using voodoo? Sophie was a voodoo princess," I said, lowering my voice.

Nola narrowed her eyes. "Who told you that?"

"Madame Iyå." I turned back to Linda. "It's sad Sophie didn't know about Sam's reputation before they got involved. She had no reason to hate Robin. I wish Sophie could tell us what really happened in the parking lot Tuesday night."

"Her friends think she will," Linda said. "There's a séance tonight. In fact, Madame Iyå is running it. You should come."

Nola threw her gym bag onto her shoulder and edged between us. "Linda, I think we already have enough people. The apartment is small."

"No, I think Liz should be there. She can tell everyone what a rat Sam is."

"I'd like to pay my respects to Sophie," I said.

"Good." Linda smiled and turned. "Lulu? Will you come to the séance tonight, too? You knew Sophie."

"No, I can't. I have rehearsals. I'm playing a gig this weekend. A solo show. Some record label guys might show up. I can't miss rehearsal. It'll be all night. Sorry. I'd like to, but I already made plans. In fact," Lulu said, looking at the clock on the wall, "I have to go home to change. I can't be late for work today. Sam needs me there to handle the calls. I'll see you guys tomorrow." She picked up her things and left.

Nola shrugged. "There are already too many people coming. I thought the séance was only for close friends, not just anyone."

"More people will add more positive energy," Linda said. "We'll have a loving celebration."

"I think the séance is a great idea," I said.

"It was Jimmy's idea—Madame Iyå's son," Linda said. "He called Nola yesterday morning. Jimmy and Sophie dated a little before she met Sam. They were friends."

Interesting. Jimmy was an ex-boyfriend. I doubted the

police had made that connection yet. I needed to pass that tidbit along to Robin's lawyer.

"The séance will be healing for everyone," I said. "It'll help to bring closure."

"Do you know what a séance is?" Nola said to me. "Do you believe?"

"My mind is open," I said.

"And what if Sophie's spirit tells us Robin is guilty?" Nola said. "Can you handle that?"

"What if Sophie's spirit tells you that someone else killed her?" I said.

Nola raised her eyebrows.

I touched Linda's shoulder and said, "Thank you for inviting me. I'd love to come."

Nola, Linda, and I gathered our things and went down the stairs toward the street. Linda's lips were pinched together, her head bowed.

"Talking about Sophie must be difficult for you right now," I said.

"Very. But I want to know what happened. I feel so guilty," Linda said. "We should have walked her to her car. We let her go into that parking lot alone."

Chapter Eighteen

I got home from Hissy Fit a little after eight, too early to call Robin's lawyer. I put on a pot of coffee, then showered and dressed. My first client wasn't until ten so I switched on my computer in the den, found Ralph Barnes's number, and called to introduce myself.

He already knew who I was. "I'm glad you called. I'd like to get a statement from you."

"Whatever I can do," I said. "How's Robin? When will she be released?"

"I'll know more when the DNA results come in." Barnes's tone was flat, matter-of-fact. Not the eager, compassionate advocate I expected.

"When will that be?"

"The test is being rushed. We might hear as early as tomorrow morning. If it comes back positive, Robin could be arraigned on Monday."

"Arraigned?" I sat up straight. "How can that be?"

"I said *could*. Depends on what other evidence the police put together. They're still searching for the murder weapon. They have a warrant to go through her home."

"Does she have to stay in jail while all that's happening?"

"They can hold her for forty-eight hours. Then they have to either arrest or release her. The publicity on the murder is creating pressure for an arrest. The police have witnesses who heard Robin and the victim argue that night. If they come across someone who saw Robin near the victim's car, or if the blood comes back a match, the DA will probably charge her."

My body tensed. "Didn't Robin explain to you what happened? Why they argued?"

"I'm sorry. Please understand that I can't discuss conversations with my client. All I can tell you is that the police intend to keep Robin in custody as long as they can."

"What can I do to help?"

"You were there that night. Tell me what you saw."

I gave him my account, from the tarot cards on the door to finding Sophie's body. "But I want to emphasize again—Robin was relaxed when she came back from walking Orchid to her car. There were no signs that she had just pummeled Sophie to near death."

"What do you mean?"

"Robin and I have been friends since grade school. I know her better than anyone, and I'm a psychologist. I would have noticed an inconsistency in her behavior," I said. "There has to be something we can do to get her released and clear her."

He sighed. "Tell me who murdered Sophie Darcantel. I've been up all night, trying to get Robin released into my custody. I wish she had called me before they took her statement. Now we need the DNA to come back negative or find some evidence, hard evidence, that points toward someone else."

I closed my eyes and shook my head. Robin had promised she'd call Barnes on the way to the station. Leave it to her to decide her innocence would protect her.

"I think Madame Iyå knows something. And her son, Jimmy, used to date Sophie. You should talk to them," I said.

"Did you see Madame Iyå or Jimmy in the parking lot?"

"No."

"Was anyone else in the parking lot when you found the body?"

"No. Only Nick and me. What happens next?" I said.

"We let the police continue to investigate. And hope they uncover another suspect."

"What makes you think they're looking for someone else?" I said. "It seems like the entire investigation involves building a case against Robin. What about Sophie's other friends? Her clients?"

"It's too early to hire an investigator. I want to wait. If Robin is arrested and arraigned, we'll begin our own inquiries," he said.

I decided to wait before telling Barnes about Sophie's spell book. He may be hesitant to search for the killer. I wasn't. That book may give me some names. Why didn't I go through the damn thing more thoroughly last night after the lights came back on?

I looked at my watch. It was nine forty. "When can I call Robin?"

"You can't. But you can visit her. I'll tell her we spoke. If you remember anything else, please call me."

I agreed and hung up. My neck was stiff with tension. After I downed two aspirin with a cup of coffee, I picked up the messages from my answering machine.

My mother had called at seven, Jarret at seven thirty.

"Lizzie Bear. I'm back in town. Call me on my cell. Let's get together." Jarret's voice was casual and friendly.

No, thanks.

The other message was from Nick, apologizing for missing my call last night. He left Sophie's address and said to meet him at one. I gathered my tote and the spell book, locked up the house, and left for the office.

Back-to-back clients kept me busy until noon. Each session was a struggle for my concentration; my mind kept wandering to Robin alone in jail. As I sat at my desk making notes, I decided to cancel my next-day appointments to be fair to my clients—none of whom were in crisis mode like I was—and to clear my calendar to help Robin. I left messages with apologies and then drove over the hill to meet Nick.

Sophie's apartment was in an old stucco building on Orange Street, a few miles east of the Fairfax District and CBS Television City. As I walked up the steps to the two-story Spanish structure, I saw the curtain in the front apartment move aside. At the landing, I found "Darcantel/Miller" on the directory. Before I could ring the bell, an elderly man opened the front door.

He looked me over, and then scanned the street behind me. "You the press?"

"No." I smiled. "I'm here to meet the police in apartment three."

"You have ID?" He blocked the doorway.

WHO DO, VOODOO?

I smiled and pulled a business card from my purse. "Detective Dave Gordon will vouch for me."

After he read my card, he nodded and let me in. "Okay. The police are down the corridor in number three."

The door to the apartment was ajar. I knocked lightly and took a step inside. Across the room, sheer white curtains covered the windows and pooled on the hardwood floor. A white deco couch sat against one of the white-stuccoed walls. Red-and-gold tapestry pillows were stacked in the corner. To the left of the front door, an open counter separated the living room from a small kitchen, where I saw Carla Pratt on the phone. Damn.

She hung up, her brow furrowed. "What are you doing here?"

I pulled my shoulders back and gave her a confident smile. "Hello, Carla. Are Dave and Nick Garfield here?"

"You can't be in here." Carla came around the counter and stopped me before I could walk in farther.

"Actually, I was invited."

Carla didn't blink. "No."

I had nothing to gain by riling her, so I held my smile and said, "Professor Garfield asked me to do a consult."

"He had no right to invite you without clearing it with me beforehand," she said.

"Oh. Sorry. I didn't realize. I would have called you myself, but I assumed you were in Santa Barbara interviewing Robin's daughter."

"Out in the hall." She pointed to the door.

"Did Orchid tell you she was with Robin in the parking lot that night?" I said.

"I can't talk about the case."

I looked past her, down the hallway. If I kept talking, maybe Dave or Nick would hear me and come out. "I wonder—doesn't statistical probability suggest Sophie's killer was likely male and someone she knew?"

"Probabilities aren't facts." Carla edged me toward the door.

Dave's voice came from down the hall. "Nick will be done in the bedroom in about fifteen minutes, Carla. What happened to the manager?"

"He went to answer his phone," she said. "There's someone here to see you."

I waved at Dave. He responded with an angry stare. I knew that old expression. Same look he gave me when he caught me snooping in his room when we were kids.

"I'm here to meet with Nick. Did he tell you?" I said, knowing he didn't.

"I'll be right back," Dave said to Carla while grabbing me by the arm. He pulled me outside into the corridor, toward the back door. "What the hell are you doing here, Liz?"

"I came to look at Sophie's bedroom. Nick thought my input would be valuable." I hiked my purse on my shoulder and brushed lint off my sleeve to avoid his glare.

"Your input? Since when are you Nick Garfield's assistant?"

"I'm not anyone's assistant. But while you and Carla are holding Robin in jail, unjustly I might add, Nick and I are going to find Sophie's killer."

"Not in there, you're not," Dave said, pointing to Sophie's apartment, "and not on the city's dime. I called in Nick for *his* opinion, not yours. And, by the way, I don't want you dating him."

"Excuse me?" I hissed at Dave. "That's it. Enough with the looks and treating me like a delinquent. What is this, high school? Where do you get off telling me who to date?"

"Listen. It's bad enough you showed up here, trying to insert yourself into an investigation. Now you and Nick are suddenly a team? Watch yourself. You could get hurt, Liz. Did he happen to mention the woman in Costa Rica he almost married last summer? Don't make me choose between you two because my choice will always be you. Don't put me in the middle. I don't want to lose my best friend."

Almost married? I drew back, blindsided, and flashed on Sophie's spell book: "To Break a New Lover's Old Relationship." No. I couldn't let Dave sidetrack me.

"Lose your best friend? Quit overreacting. My best friend, Robin, is in jail, Dave. I'm trying to help her," I said.

"You can't go in there. It's against procedure for anyone not on official business to be in there without the occupant's permission. Nick's a consultant. You're not," Dave said. "Wait for him outside."

Dave went into the apartment. Instead of going outside, I decided to sit on the back stairs and wait. I needed to hear Nick's opinion about Sophie's room before I came back for the séance tonight. I didn't relish attending without a clearer sense of who Sophie was or what I was getting into.

After a few minutes, Dave and Carla came out of the apartment. When their voices faded, I peeked down the corridor. They were at the front door. I waited until they went outside, then slipped into Sophie's apartment and found Nick taking photos inside a bedroom.

"Hi," I said, catching my breath.

He looked over his shoulder and smiled. "About time. Give me a minute. I want to finish photographing this altar."

While he clicked off pictures, I looked around. Unlike the airiness of the rest of the apartment, Sophie's room was darker, more seductive. Above the bed, a black, three-foot heart was outlined with lavish flair on the deep-sunflower-gold wall. The center of the heart was checkered, a round dot in the center of each small square. Bold black fleur-de-lis lines flowed from the top, bottom, and sides. Black-metal wall sconces with burnt candles hung on each side.

Next to the door, a mirrored dresser held a wooden statue of the Virgin Mary surrounded by votives. A red-lace scarf draped the shade of a small brass lamp in the corner. Makeup, jewelry, small books, and jars littered the top of the dresser. A violet sweater hung on a drawer pull. The scent of roses permeated the air. I pictured Sophie getting ready for the concert in a rush, leaving a mess behind to clean up later.

Nick set down his camera.

"Find anything interesting?" I said.

He turned, still smiling. "Everything in here is interesting."

"Tell me."

"Sophie was an initiate of Haitian Vodou. The room is a homage to Erzulie, the Vodou spirit of love and beauty. The powders, icons, tools, and photo placement say she was performing rituals in here. Sophie knew what she was doing."

I nodded as he gestured around the room. The flag on the wall behind him caught my attention: the palm frond symbol was the same one I saw inside Sophie's spell book. The symbol was embroidered on satin in bright-green sequins and surrounded by a black-sequined fleur-de-lis pattern. "Ayizan" was sewn in sequins across the top.

"What is that?" I said, pointing.

Nick looked up. "A drapo—a ceremonial flag of Haitian Vodou. They're rare, never sold, passed from generation to generation. Priceless, in fact."

"What does *Ayizan* mean?"

"Ayizan is the mother of all Vodou initiates. The young apprentice priestess employs her drapo to talk to spirits and start rituals. It's appropriate that it's over her altar. See that yam?" He pointed to the top of the chest. "It's an offering to the spirit Ayizan. She has to be invoked before Erzulie can be invoked."

"What about the heart over the bed?" I said.

"It's the symbol, or the veve, of the love goddess Erzulie. One of Sophie's tasks as an initiate would be to draw it perfectly and I'd say she did an excellent job. The rest of the room is also decorated in Erzulie's honor. Gold was one of Erzulie's favorite colors, and the statue of the Virgin suits the motif."

"You talk about Erzulie like she's real."

"I think Sophie believed she was." Nick started snapping pictures again.

Interesting, but could any of this lead us to her killer? I scanned the room. "Is there a computer in here?"

"No. Maybe the police took it."

On the altar beneath the drapo, I saw Sam Collins's picture behind a red candle. A black candle, burnt halfway, was in front of a blurred photo of Robin. The photo was different from the one left on Robin's front door.

"I'm curious," I said. "If the police took Sophie's computer, why didn't they take anything else, like those photos of Sam and Robin?"

"This isn't a crime scene. Anything the police consider related to her murder would have been removed yesterday. They left the altar set up for me to see."

In the center of the altar, a framed picture of a woman in late nineteenth-century dress was encircled by white votives and a dish of water. Labeled glass jars were lined behind the photos: "Lavender," "Allspice," "Sage," "Black Art," "Catnip," "Brazil Wood," "Betony Root," "Coriander," "Myrrh." Holy cards with pictures of saints, incense sticks, and trinkets littered the bureau top.

"All this clutter is oppressive," I said. "The longer I stand here, the more suffocating it feels."

Nick nodded. "The spirit of Erzulie has a dark and covetous side. Sophie's dedication to her may have provoked the jealousy toward Robin. The burned candle in front of Robin's picture could easily be a black-magic spell, like the symbols on the photo left on Robin's door. The red candle in front of Sam Collins's picture is for love or lust spells. The photo of the old woman and the setup around it is another homage. Interesting. She's not a familiar face in Vodou lore. At least not to me."

"Do you think Sophie was in a voodoo cult?"

He shook his head. "Cult? No. Nothing in here deviates from standard Haitian Vodou practice. It's dark but nothing twisted."

Candles, photos, powders—something was missing. I looked around one more time, then stopped at Robin's photo. "The tarot deck. Did you find it?"

Nick slid his camera into his pocket. "No. No tarot deck."

"Carla knew about the tarot cards yesterday. Maybe the police took it?"

"Dave and Carla wanted me to analyze Sophie's occult paraphernalia. One of them would have told me about a tarot deck. Maybe Sophie kept it in her car."

"I'll ask him anyway," I said. "I brought something much more interesting to show you."

His eyes shone with interest. "What?"

"I think one of your hoodoo spirits tried to spook me last night," I said.

"You? A spirit? I'm surprised, Liz. And I'm sorry I missed your call," he said. "Hoodoo spirits are one of my specialties."

"Exactly the reason I phoned you. I got a cryptic message from a spell book."

Nick paused. "What spell book?"

"You said Vodou was an oral tradition, correct? Nothing written down?"

"Correct," Nick said.

"And you believe Sophie was a Haitian Vodou initiate?"

"Obviously," he said spreading his arms around the room. "Why?"

I smiled. "Because I think I have Sophie's Vodou initiate textbook."

"There is no such thing."

"I think you should see it before you make that judgment. Sophie left an envelope on Robin's desk the afternoon of the concert. I opened it last night and found a notebook inside, filled with handwritten rituals and spells, dating back to the nineteenth century. A sketch of that drapo," I said, pointing to the hanging above the dresser, "is on the title page. The whole book is right up your ancient-manuscript-loving alley."

"And the cryptic message?"

"After the power failed, the book slipped off my bed. By itself. I can't believe I'm going to say this, and maybe I was still a little drunk, but the spell it fell open to read like a warning. It was an incantation to imprison the mind of an enemy."

"You weren't even tipsy when I brought you home. Where is it? Dave should see it, too." Nick's gaze drifted behind me.

I followed his eyes. Crap. Dave and Carla stood in the doorway.

Chapter Nineteen

Carla walked into Sophie's bedroom. "Dr. Cooper, you were told to leave. I could cite you for interfering with an investigation."

"Wait." Dave shouldered past Carla. "Show me what? What do you have, Liz?"

I bit the inside of my lip and looked at him, then at Nick, while they waited for my answer.

"I brought the three tarot cards Sophie used to harass Robin. You and Carla didn't give me the chance to show you so I came back," I said.

Nick wrinkled his forehead, but kept silent.

"Why didn't you give them to me at the station yesterday?" Carla said.

"I didn't have them with me," I said, rummaging through my tote. The cards were tucked into a side pocket. I pulled them out. "I noticed that the rest of the deck wasn't here in the room . . ."

Carla took the three tarot cards and slid them into a plastic envelope. "And you just had to nose around?"

Nick put his arm around my shoulder. "Liz came at my request. I'm curious about the rest of the deck, too. Is it already in evidence?"

Carla flipped out a notebook and paged through some notes. "No."

"What about the deck?" Dave's eyes were fixed on Nick's arm, still around me.

"What if Sophie gave the tarot cards to someone else harass to Robin?" Nick said. "What if that person heard Robin and Sophie argue at the party and was afraid Sophie would expose him or her? Someone who had something to lose?"

"Interesting," Carla said. "I'll have these checked for prints. Who handled them? That you know of."

"Madame Iyå created the deck. Robin, my mother, Nick, and I touched them at one time or another," I said. "And whoever left them on Robin's door."

"Anything else you brought to share?" Carla said.

"No, that's it," I said. "Just wanted to do my part."

Carla scowled.

"I need to get back to the station," Dave said. "Let's close this place up and get out of here."

I left the apartment with Nick; Carla and Dave followed. The elderly man who answered the door was waiting in the corridor.

"Thank you for letting us in, Mr. Marx," Carla said. "Tell Miss Miller we appreciate her cooperation."

"I will. Happy to help, ma'am." Mr. Marx locked the apartment and tipped his fingers to his forehead in a salute.

Carla and Dave took out their cell phones. Both began making calls in the hallway. Nick held the front door open and then followed me outside.

"You kept the spell book from Carla and Dave," Nick said, looking back over his shoulder. "Why?"

"I want some time to read through it before they do."

"Don't get in their way."

"I'll just stay *out* of their way," I said.

"Why are you getting so involved?"

I stopped on the bottom step. "Robin and I have been best friends since grade school. She didn't hesitate to help me if I had a crisis. She dropped everything for me. Why wouldn't I get involved now that she needs my help? Wouldn't you help Dave if he needed you?"

"Yes. I would. I do," Nick said.

I locked my arm into the crook of Nick's elbow, and we walked across the street in silence. We stopped at my car.

"I want to wait for Carla and Dave to leave," I said.

Nick leaned against the trunk of my car. "Okay. Tell me what you thought of Sophie's room. Typical female surroundings?"

I flipped my hand. "Oh. Sure. Typical. Just like my room minus the poltergeist that slides spell books off the bed and leaves them open on the floor."

"I'd like to see that." He smiled.

"I think the spell book is the key, Nick. If Sophie's clients are in the book, I can check their names against the guest list from the party." I looked back toward the apartment building. "Any matches could be good leads for the police and Robin's attorney."

The front door opened. Carla and Dave walked down the steps and crossed the street to my car.

"When will I see a report, Nick?" Dave said.

"I'll go over everything this afternoon and call you later today."

Carla said, "I'm the lead detective on this case. I'd appreciate it if you would call me with your report and copy Dave."

Nick agreed. Dave and Carla went to their cars, then drove off. As Dave passed by, I waved. He looked at Nick and me, side by side on the street, and frowned. Tough. When they were out of sight I opened the trunk and brought out the spell book.

Nick put on his glasses and flipped through the pages. He raised an eyebrow. "This is intriguing. You're right—it's nineteenth-century Vodou and apparently logged with great detail. Let's take it to my house and go through it."

"You take it. I want to drive over to Collins Talent first and get a copy of the guest list. Can I come by later? After the séance? I could have more information by then."

"Okay." Nick leaned back and studied me. "You have my attention. Again. What séance?"

"Madame Iyå is holding a séance here tonight to contact Sophie's spirit." I grinned.

Nick laughed out loud. "You? Miss I-Don't-Believe? Liz, what are you doing? Didn't Osaze convince you that Madame Iyå is a fake? Why are you wasting your time and, I guarantee you, your money on her sideshow?"

"I want to see Madame Iyå put on her show, and it gives

me a chance to talk to Sophie's friends. Sophie told Madame Iyå and Jimmy to leave her alone. Then, after she was murdered, they offer to do a séance like nothing happened? It's strange. I think they're after the spell book. Madame Iyå already lied to me, told me she had it. In fact, she and Jimmy might have been after the spell book the night of the concert. Maybe they followed Sophie out into the parking lot for it. I want to see what Madame Iyå does tonight."

"When did Madame Iyå lie to you about the spell book?" Nick said.

"I saw her yesterday."

"Looking for trouble?"

"No, I'm looking to clear Robin."

"I'll go with you to the séance."

"I have to go alone. Sophie's friends don't know you. They barely know me, but I have to take the chance that they'll accept me."

Nick slid his hands into his pant pockets. "Madame Iyå is a scam artist. She probably set up the séance to pick up some cash at the door."

"You might be right." I looked at the ground, then up at him with a grin. "But I'm going anyway."

Nick touched his forehead to mine and smiled into my eyes. "Watch yourself tonight. Madame Iyå may be a fraud and you don't know what the rest of the people there could be into."

"I'll be careful." I closed the trunk and dug in my tote for my keys.

Nick crossed the street to his car. As I watched him drive off, Dave's warning about Nick niggled at the back of my mind. But I didn't have time to dig into Nick's social life and track down a murderer all in the same day.

Mr. Marx came down the front steps of the apartment building in a green sweater and coordinated tweed hat with wisps of white hair poking out from the sides. When he wobbled on the middle step, I went over and gave him my hand.

"Thank you, young lady." He smiled, tipping a finger to his hat. "Did you find your clues inside?"

"No," I said, smiling back. "I was observing today."

"But not by invitation, eh? You lied to me, Dr. Cooper. They were talking about you in the hall," he said. "That lady detective was mad as hell at you. The other detective tried to calm her down. He likes you."

I laughed. "He's my brother—he has to like me. And I didn't lie to you. The other man inside really was expecting me. Please, call me Liz."

"Henry Marx," he said. "I own the building."

"So my big brother defended me? I'm glad to hear it," I said.

"That lady detective said that she'd file a complaint against him if he let you get in the way," Henry said. "Are you going to listen to her?"

"Nope. But I'm going to be more careful of who I talk to. Can I count on you to be discreet?"

"I don't know what you're talking about," he said with a twinkle in his eye.

Henry was about four inches shorter than my five foot five. As I looked down at him, I saw three commemorative pins tacked on the band of his hat. One was purple with a deco Indian head drawn beneath a Santa Fe Super Chief logo; the other two pins were deep yellow, surrounding a black Super Chief cross.

He caught me studying them and said, "Do you know the Super Chief?"

"The Super Chief was a train, wasn't it?"

Henry laughed. "It was the most famous train in the world, young lady. Your generation missed out on luxury travel. Do you have a minute? I want to show you something."

It may not have been the cleverest come-on ever, but I had a feeling that Henry Marx didn't miss much. He probably saw everyone who came and went from his building. I didn't want to waste the opportunity, so I took his arm and we ascended the steps together.

Henry unlocked his apartment door and led me into the light-blue living room. A gold-tapestry sofa and matching chairs nestled near the front window around a mahogany sofa table. The scent of sweet cherry tobacco hung in the air. On the far wall was a huge mahogany china cabinet filled with matching dishes.

"Come sit down. Let me show you something."

We sat on the couch. Henry opened a scrapbook with a collection of yellowed newspaper articles and photos.

"See? Here's Humphrey Bogart and Lauren Bacall getting off the Super Chief in Pasadena." Henry tapped my knee. "And here's Jimmy Cagney. My family and I rode with him on his way out here to make *The Time of Your Life*. Cagney gave me his white china mug from the dining car as a souvenir. It has an art deco lizard painted on it. I've been collecting the rest of that Mimbreno china set for sixty years. I don't think the gecko on his mug was lucky, though. His movie flopped."

"Oops," I said, wincing. "Are you superstitious?"

"Liz, at my age I believe everything and nothing. Sophie understood. We talked about spirits quite often after my wife, Maria, died last year." He looked up at me over his glasses. The childish delight over the Super Chief faded from his face. "Sophie knew things."

"Did she do spells for you?"

"Ah." Henry locked his hazel eyes on mine and held them there. "I'm old, but I'm not stupid. I can't talk about that."

"It sounds like you and Sophie were good friends. I'm so sorry for your loss."

He shook his head. "Sophie was a feisty one. She could hold her own if someone crossed her. But she was a great kid, too, like Linda. My best tenants. I don't know why they wasted their time with that Nola girl, though, always gossiping and arguing in the hall." Henry closed his scrapbook and slid it back on the table. "She's nothing like Sophie was. Sophie wouldn't let her forget it, either."

"But they were cousins," I said.

He got up and went to the window.

"What, Henry? Is there something wrong?"

"I won't start trouble." He turned. "That's why I didn't say much to the police."

"I'm not the police," I said. "Do you know something?"

"I heard things. Sophie and Nola fought a lot. Maybe that's the way young girls talk to each other these days," he said, walking into the kitchen. "One day they're shouting and then the next day they're best friends again. Now Nola has it in her mind to move in with Linda and take Sophie's place."

I followed him and slid into a chair at the Formica table. "This is your building. You can prevent Nola from moving in if you want. You have control over that, Henry."

"Linda can't afford the apartment on her own. I don't

want to lose her as a tenant. She's a good girl. She pays her rent on time. If it makes Linda happy to have Nola here, then I won't stop her. But I don't trust Nola," he said.

"Why not?" I said.

Henry filled a teakettle in the sink and put it on the stove. "When Sophie came to town, she stayed with Nola's parents. It was Nola who put Sophie and Linda together as roommates. Sophie told me Nola wanted her away from her uncle's house. Then, when she moved here, Nola got jealous that Linda and Sophie became close friends."

"But if it was Nola's idea for them to live together . . ."

"Go figure. Nola wanted what Sophie had, and Sophie had everything. Sophie got all the attention. That's where the trouble was." Henry reached for mugs from the kitchen cabinet. "Tea?"

"No, thanks. What trouble?"

"First it was Sophie and Linda being friends. Then Sophie's friendship with Jimmy, in the apartment upstairs."

"Jimmy Johnson? Madame Iyå's son?" I said.

"Yes. You know him?"

"Sort of," I said. The pieces were coming together. Jimmy must have introduced Sophie to Madame Iyå. "Tell me more, Henry."

"Next thing, Nola started complaining about that new boyfriend of Sophie's. The rich one who never came over here."

Jealousy was a precursor to domestic and sibling abuse. Maybe Nola was bitter about Sophie's alleged engagement to Sam. I remembered her snide comment at the party about Sophie serving coffee on her knees. I wondered how jealous Nola really was.

Henry poured his tea, and I followed him back into the living room.

"Did Nola ever threaten Sophie?" I said.

"They think I don't hear." He set the cup near his pipe on the table and started to sit down.

The doorbell rang.

Chapter Twenty

Henry went to his front window and pulled back the curtain. Over his shoulder, I saw the Channel 9 News van parked outside the apartment building. A man in a baseball cap and jeans waited at the foot of the steps with a video camera perched on his shoulder. A woman in a business suit backed away from the front door, looking toward Henry's window.

"Ach. I shooed the other two reporters away yesterday," Henry said. "They're all sniffing around, asking if I saw some singer here with Sophie."

My stomach clenched. "I can't get caught on camera here, Henry."

"Go down the corridor and out the back door." Henry dropped the curtain. "I'll distract them. The alley in back will lead you to the street. Don't worry. You won't be seen."

"You're my hero, Henry. Thanks." I kissed his cheek.

He left the apartment and cracked open the door to the street. As I dashed down the corridor, I heard him say: "You can't film here. This is private property."

I exited through the back door and walked down the alley. When I came around the corner onto the street in front of the apartment, I saw the news van drive away. Henry watched from his window. He tipped a finger to his forehead in salute and smiled at me.

In my car, I put on my headset and dialed Collins Talent. I needed that guest list.

"Collins Talent, this is Lulu."

"Hi, Lulu, it's Liz Cooper."

She paused.

"Liz. Robin's friend. I just saw you at Hissy Fit . . ."

"Oh, hey, Liz. Sorry. Brain freeze. The phones are going insane and ninety percent of the calls are from the press. Robin's not here. Did you hear the news?"

"I know, Lulu," I said. "I need a copy of the—"

"Hold on, another call."

Afternoon traffic across town would be a nightmare. I started my car and headed toward Beverly Hills.

Lulu came back on the line. "Sorry. The damn calls won't stop. Between Sophie and Buzzy, you'd think I didn't have any other work to do around here. Freakin' crazy about Buzzy, isn't it? He was just here yesterday afternoon."

"What are you talking about?"

"I thought you said you knew. Wasn't it on the news? Buzzy got hit by a truck on PCH last night."

"Buzzy got hit? Do you mean his car?"

"No—that's the freakiest part. He was walking. I mean, who walks across the Pacific Coast Highway? He was meeting Sam and Zack Tate at Gladstone's. Did you meet Zack? Really cute. He's a junior agent here."

"Lulu—what happened to Buzzy?"

"Zack told me the whole story this morning. Then Sam calls and tells me to give the press a no-comment and only take messages. I knew that. Like I have time to sit on the phone all day and talk anyway."

"Is Buzzy okay?"

"He's *dead*," she said. "Zack and Sam were outside the restaurant watching Buzzy cross the street to meet them. Buzzy steps off the curb, something drops out of his pocket, he bends down to pick it up, and *bam*. A truck came tearing around the corner and hit him. Zack said Buzzy flew up in the air and got hit again by another car. Nasty. Can you believe it? After the ambulance came, Zack went over to the curb. Buzzy's wallet was lying there. Ugh. Freaky."

I put a hand to my chest and took a breath. I pictured Buzzy at the lunch counter yesterday, laughing and gossiping about Sophie. And now he was dead. "That's horrible."

"So Zack told me not to tell anyone anything about anything until Sam comes back to the office. And with all the bullshit going on around here, who knows when that will be? You wouldn't believe how many reporters I had to take messages from today. Two of them invited me out for a drink. I almost said yes because I need publicity for my showcase tomorrow, but . . ."

"I'm so sorry for Buzzy and his family."

"Yeah. I'm a wreck, too. Buzzy was going to help me with publicity. It sucks."

"I feel bad for Sam. First Sophie, then Buzzy. He and Buzzy were close, weren't they?"

"Yeah. We all liked Buzzy. There was this one time—"

"Lulu, I know you're busy, but I need your help. You're the first person I thought of."

"Of course I'll help you. I turned you on to Hissy Fit, didn't I? You loved it, didn't I? What can I do?"

"I need a copy of the guest list from the party Tuesday night."

"Sure. Easy. For Robin's lawyer? Want me to fax it to you? Messenger it over? I can bring it to your house."

"I'll come pick it up. I knew you'd help, thanks," I said.

"No problem. I'll leave it at the desk with the guard downstairs. Oops. Another call. It's Sam. Gotta go."

As I drove across La Cienega Boulevard, the two lanes narrowed to one to make room for a truck and crew trimming the palm trees. With traffic bottlenecked and no alternate route to take, I decided to return my mother's call.

She picked up on the first ring. "Elizabeth, where have you been? I've been waiting all day for you to call."

"I've been busy, Mom. Robin's still in jail. I'm trying to help her if I can."

"Oh dear. Should I call your brother, Dave?"

"No—please don't. He knows."

"Okay. By the way, did you get my incense from that little shop?"

"No. Madame Iyå didn't carry your brand." I could tell by the tone of her voice that something other than incense was on her mind. "What else is going on, Mom?"

She let out a long sigh. "Well, I know you're busy but I'm worried about Jarret. You know he lost the game last night and flew back to town. He called me this morning."

Of course he did. Whenever Jarret couldn't get what he

wanted from me, he used my mother. He toyed with her loyalty, knowing she liked to brag about her son-in-law the sports celebrity. She excused his indiscretions and addictions as an occupational hazard. Mom treated our divorce as a minor misunderstanding.

"I forgot he was pitching." I switched lanes to turn left onto Santa Monica Boulevard into Beverly Hills.

"Oh, Elizabeth. His loss took the Dodgers out of the play-offs. I can't believe you didn't know that. You should call him. He's devastated. You know how upset he gets." The whine in her voice frayed my nerves.

"That's not my problem anymore—or yours."

"But he's alone. He was so down when he called."

"Oh, poor thing." My sarcasm came with ease. "Reminds me of how down and devastated I was when he cheated on me."

"I'm sorry, dear. I know. But people change. He's a nice boy. He needs a friend."

"Jarret is an adult. He'll learn how to deal with life on his own. I did."

"You should talk to him, Liz," she said. "Now that his season is over, maybe the two of you could spend time together again, as friends. It's not like you're seeing anyone else."

The last line was tossed like a worm at the end of a fishing line. I wasn't going to bite. "I have to go."

"You work too hard," she said. "You're going to get lines on your face. I don't know why you don't use your divorce settlement to enjoy yourself."

"Mom, I have to go. Give Daddy a kiss for me," I said. "I love you."

"I love you, too, honey. Call Jarret."

I parked in the loading zone in front of the Collins Talent office building, walked up the steps, and entered through the glass doors. I gave the guard at the desk my name. He handed me the envelope from Lulu, and I thanked him. Inside was the four-page guest list to the Steve Weller after-party. When I got back in my car, I scanned over the names. Missing were Sam, Lulu, Robin, and, I assumed, the rest of the Collins Talent staff who worked the party. But I had the names of invited guests.

It took almost an hour to drive back over the hill to Studio City and my townhouse. If I had a dollar for every minute I wasted in traffic, I could buy a house at the beach.

Once home, I went through my mail, plugged my phone into the charger in the kitchen, then checked for phone messages. No calls. I called Ralph Barnes for an update. No news on the DNA test. I went into the bedroom and stretched out on the bed to rest. Hissy's workout had caught up with me. Every muscle ached.

I jerked awake at six o'clock. A hot shower revitalized my burning muscles. I dotted rose oil on my neck, put on a long-sleeved silk coral blouse, slid into jeans, and stepped into beige pumps. I tucked the guest list into my purse to show Nick after the séance, threw on my black coat, and drove over the hill again to Sophie's apartment.

Streetlamps lit the sidewalk and the steps to the building. The lights were on in Henry's apartment, but he wasn't at the window. I rang the doorbell to apartment 3 and announced myself on the intercom. Linda buzzed me in.

When I got to the end of the corridor, Linda opened her

WHO DO, VOODOO?

apartment door, barefoot, in an embroidered white Indian
shirt over white silk pants. "Come on in. I'm glad you made
it. Can I get you a glass of wine?"

"Yes, thanks," I said, following her into the living room.
The low hum of a flute played beneath the buzz of conversation. The furniture was pushed against the wall, leaving a
large open area in the middle of the floor. A donation basket,
layered with twenty-dollar bills, sat on a table in front of the
kitchen counter. I took a twenty from my wallet and dropped
it on top of the others.

Nola, Madame Iyå, and Jimmy chatted outside the
kitchen. A plump redhead in a ruffled red camisole teetered
on black platform sandals on the other side of the living
room. She was talking to—oh my God—Henry Marx. A
bolt of nerves shot through me. Henry was the only one who
knew about my connection to the police. I tried to catch his
eye. He saw me and lit up in a smile. I pressed my lips
together and shook my head in a plea for silence. He turned
away. I loved that man.

Linda handed me a glass of red wine. "Come on and meet
everyone." She led me across the room. She introduced the
redhead, Tawny Dalton, as Sophie's friend and coworker at
the Chic Boutique in Beverly Hills.

"I can't believe this. Last week Sophie and I tried on
bridal dresses at Saks on our lunch hour." Tawny twirled the
wine glass in her hand. "I was going to be one of her brides-
maids. Sophie wanted us to wear lavender dresses. I miss
her so much. I don't know what I'm going to do without her."

I set my hand on her shoulder. "Just being here and talking about Sophie among her friends is healing."

"Do you think we'll be able to talk to Sophie tonight?" Tawny said.

"I don't know what to expect," I said. "I'm keeping my mind open."

"I expect she'll float in and tell us to drink champagne in her memory," Henry said with a smile. His green woolen sweater smelled of musk cologne. "She'll love that her pretty friends are here tonight. Did you work with Sophie, too?"

"We had mutual friends," I said, wanting to kiss him. "I'm Liz Cooper."

He covered my hand and squeezed.

Tawny turned to me, her eyes searching. "I don't remember Sophie mentioning you. What do you do?"

"I'm a psychologist. I have a practice in Studio City."

"Was Sophie your client?"

"Hardly." Nola joined us, towering over Henry in three-inch spike-heeled, black-leather boots. The silver bracelets on her arms jangled as she pointed her wine glass at me. "She's best friends with Sophie's killer."

"Who?" Tawny said, wide-eyed.

"Sam's secretary." Nola sneered, then walked away.

Tawny and Henry looked at me. I felt I owed Henry at least part of the truth.

"Nola's wrong. She wants answers. So do I. But nothing's been proven. No one's been arrested yet," I said. "I met Sophie when I visited my friend Robin, who works for Sam, at Collins Talent. Sophie was there with Sam. I came tonight, hoping to gain insight from Sophie about what happened the night she died. What about you? Why did you come?"

"I came because I miss her," Henry said. "Sophie moved

into this building while my wife was still alive. After Maria died, Sophie came and sat with me, kept me company." He looked around, then leaned in to Tawny and me. "She did a ritual to help Maria pass into the spirit world. Sophie knew things."

"What do you mean? What kind of things?" I said.

Henry stared at his feet. He wiped his chin. He looked up at me. "Sophie knew how to contact the dead."

Not a point I would argue at a séance. "Did she tell you who taught her?"

"Her grandmother, down in New Orleans," Henry said. "The one who raised Sophie."

"Is her grandmother still in New Orleans?"

Henry shook his head. "Such a shame. They were evacuated to Houston when Katrina hit. The grandmother died in a hospital there. Sophie came out here with nothing."

"She found a good friend," I said. "I can see that you cared about her."

"Yes, I did. I came tonight to show I wouldn't forget her."

"None of us will forget." Tawny raised her glass. "Here's to Sophie."

Henry clinked his glass to Tawny's. "To Sophie."

"If you two will excuse me, I want to say hello to Madame Iyå." I walked toward the dining room table, where Madame Iyå, decked out in a purple caftan embroidered with stars, was emptying a large shopping bag.

I tapped her arm and she turned to me, a box of cornmeal in her hand.

"Madame Iyå," I said. "Do you need any help?"

"No, dear. I'm almost ready." Madame Iyå glanced at the donation basket at the side of the table. "But you can show your generosity to the spirits. We have to encourage them to bring Sophie to us tonight."

"Oh, I already did."

Madame Iyå stared at the basket. I slipped a hand into my coat pocket, pulled out a couple of bills, and added them to the top of the pile.

She smiled, watching the bills settle. "The spirits will be very pleased. Now if you'll excuse me, I have to finish unpacking and set out the candles. You can shut off the music so we can begin."

As I turned off the CD player, I saw Jimmy slip out of Sophie's room. He sauntered down the hall toward me.

"I'm Jimmy Johnson. I don't think I know you." His eyes drifted to my chest.

"Liz Cooper." I held out my hand.

Instead of responding with a handshake, Jimmy took my hand and kissed it. "Enchanted. I can't resist beautiful women."

I fought the impulse to wipe my hand on the back of my jeans. "You and Sophie were friends?"

"*Very* good friends." He smoothed back his hair and grinned. "Sophie was hot."

Nola came over and locked her arm into Jimmy's. "What are you up to, shrink? Flirting with my pal now?"

Jimmy looked me over and said, "Are you a shrink?"

I nodded. "Psychologist."

Nola downed the rest of her wine. "Do your clients know you slum with the Hollywood crowd at night?"

"Ease up." Jimmy unhooked his arm from hers.

"No, seriously, I still don't get why she's here." She pointed at me with her empty glass.

Linda, listening a few feet away, moved between us. "Your negative energy isn't welcome here, Nola. If you don't lighten up, you can leave."

"Oh, come on," Nola said. "Get serious. We all know who killed Sophie."

And I was counting on learning the truth.

Chapter Twenty-one

"Everyone, please. There's too much chaotic energy in the room. We need peace to create a spiritual environment." Madame Iyå came out of the kitchen and set a bowl of water in the center of the living room. Jimmy helped her ease down cross-legged onto the floor behind it, her long earrings jangling in the effort. He set two baskets to her side.

"I'm ready to begin," she said. "Turn off your cell phones. I want everyone to take a piece of paper and write out a question for Sophie. When you're finished, fold it, put it into the bowl, and join me in a circle on the floor. The water will invite Sophie's spirit and protect the room from unwelcome forces."

I searched through my purse, then swore under my breath for leaving my phone charging on my kitchen counter.

Clever to juice it up before I left, not clever enough to remember to bring it with me.

Jimmy took paper from the table and gave each of us a piece.

"What are you going to ask, Liz?" Tawny said.

I lowered my voice. "I think I'll ask Sophie to name her attacker. What about you?"

"Sophie's up there now." Tawny looked up. "She knows if my new boyfriend is a keeper. I used her love spell to find him. So, that's my question: 'Is Marvin the one?' I wonder if we can ask more than one?"

"Why not? Ask away." I wrote out my question, folded the paper, and dropped it into the water, deciding to corner Tawny after the séance about her spell. Then I sat on the floor with the others, across from Madame Iyå, and waited for the show to begin.

"Before we go on, everyone take off your jewelry." Madame Iyå slipped off her earrings and continued, "Do any of the women here have their period right now?"

What a bizarre question. Henry blew his nose. Nola and Linda shook their heads no. Tawny giggled.

Madame Iyå shot her a look. "Don't laugh about this. The dead have no joy. They'll think you're mocking them. Menstrual blood draws demons. Do you have your period?"

"No." Tawny dropped her head.

Madame Iyå looked at Jimmy. "Create the circle of protection."

He picked up the cornmeal, pulled a switchblade from his pocket, and punctured the top of the box. I shifted, uneasy at the casual deftness with which he handled the blade. Tawny gaped, but neither Nola nor Linda appeared surprised that Jimmy pocketed a weapon.

"No. I said no metal. Put that thing away, Jimmy. It will repel the spirits," Madame Iyå said with disgust.

He grunted as he put the knife away, and then sprinkled a line of grain around us.

"Very well, then." Madame Iyå picked up a white candle from the basket beside her. "I'm passing candles around the circle for each of you to hold, then pass on. We're charging them with our energy to unify our purpose as a group."

She handed the first candle to Nola, on her right. Nola passed it to Linda, and the candle made its way around the circle from Linda to me to Henry to Tawny and at last to Jimmy. He lit it and set it in front of Nola. Seven candles went around. When the final one was lit, we each had a candle burning in front of us. Jimmy got up and turned off the lights. The faces around me were illuminated with a golden glow.

Madame Iyå reached into the other basket and took out seven white roses. "Sophie's favorite flower."

We each set a rose in front of us with the bud facing the bowl in the center.

"Until we release the spirits at the end of the séance, we have to keep the circle unbroken. Link little fingers with the person on each side of you. Don't touch knees or anything else besides your fingers."

I felt Linda touch my left pinkie. I moved my right finger to seek Henry's. Linked, we rested our hands on the floor. I shifted to get comfortable and looked around. Tawny, Linda, Nola, and Henry sat erect, watching Madame Iyå.

WHO DO, VOODOO?

Madame Iyå positioned four candles around the bowl of water, forming a cross. "The spirits seek the light." She lowered her voice. "Focus on the candles and the water, then close your eyes. Sophie will come to us through our senses. In scent, in feel, in sound, through the vision of your third eye."

I focused on my breathing, my senses heightened in the darkness. The scent of the roses wafted in through the air. No one spoke. I felt the touch of Henry's and Linda's fingers on mine. A chill of anticipation washed through me.

Madame Iyå began to hum. Linda joined in, and then Tawny, Nola and the rest of us followed. I inhaled, then exhaled a tone that vibrated from the back of my throat to the top of my head. The room came alive with sound.

As the low, steady chant continued, I cracked open my eyes a slit. Okay. No one was levitating.

Madame Iyå rocked back and forth, shaking a small brass rattle. "I call to the spirits to welcome us and bless our circle. We humbly ask you to send the spirit of our beloved Sophie here to join us. We open our minds and our hearts to be with her here tonight. Sophie." Madame Iyå chanted: "So-phie. So-phie. So-phie."

A clock ticked in the background. A car passed outside. Air hummed out of the heat register.

"Come to us, Sophie darling," Madame Iyå said.

Linda curled her pinky tighter around mine. I squeezed back.

Madame Iyå hummed, then spoke. "Sophie, your friends are here. We miss you. We love you."

"I don't feel anything," Tawny said.

Neither did I. I was waiting for a sheet on a wire to float over my head.

"Shhh. Focus on your breathing. Spirits will follow the resonance of our breath." A full minute passed, then Madame Iyå spoke again. "Sophie is here. I feel her. She wants to communicate with each of you in her own way. Some with words, some with feelings. Open yourself up. She will contact you."

I stared into the candlelight reflection in the bowl of water, aware of the subtle movements from the people in the circle. I decided to mimic their body language to see if I could read them. Linda's body was open and peaceful; her face relaxed. Tawny fidgeted. She rolled her shoulders. Her eyelids were pinched shut, her face twitching. I copied the movement and felt her nervousness. Henry nodded with his eyes squeezed tight. His shoulders were slack, showing no tension. Nola sat erect, biting her lower lip. I stiffened, bit my own lip, and picked up on her anxiety. Jimmy's shoulders were hunched. His eyes darted around the room. I mimicked him and felt guarded, cautious. Then I relaxed myself, letting my body ease.

Madame Iyå inhaled, then released her breath. "Sophie thanks us for the roses, the flower of love, and she feels the love in the room tonight. She's at peace."

A candle popped. Shadows flickered on the walls outside of the circle. Henry and Tawny still had their eyes closed. Nola and Jimmy looked at each other and smiled. Linda didn't move. Her eyes fixed on the candlelight in the center.

"Tawny," Madame Iyå said. "Sophie cherished your friendship. She wants you to take her violet sweater and wear it when you miss her."

"Oh, I will. I know just which one. It was her favorite. Thank you." Tawny looked up, as if to glimpse Sophie's ghost above her.

I recalled the violet sweater on the drawer pull in Sophie's room. Was that why Jimmy went in there? Scouting for tools for Madame Iyå?

"Henry." Madame Iyå's words were slow and direct. "Sophie has a message from your dear wife. She loves you and wants you to take care of yourself."

His wife's name was Maria. Sophie would know that. Madame Iyå had to do better than a sweeping generalization to convince me. And using Henry to feign familiarity made me bristle.

Henry opened his eyes.

"There's a pink candle in Sophie's bedroom for you." Madame Iyå said to him. "Burn it at night, and you will dream of your wife."

He nodded and sighed. His finger trembled a bit as it held mine.

Although my experience with séances was limited to this one, I didn't recall hearing that participants left with party favors. How much time had Jimmy spent in Sophie's bedroom? Enough to search for the spell book, too?

The living room got colder. A draft swept across the floor and flickered the flames of the candles. The scent of rose was strong. I thought I saw a shadow move behind Jimmy and Tawny. I brushed away the sensation that someone else was in the room with us. Silly. And yet, I tensed up. Something shifted.

"Nola. Sophie wants you to publish her spell book." Madame Iyå hesitated. "No, Sophie. I couldn't. Yes, then, as you wish." Her face wrinkled. Madame Iyå shook her head and let out a deep sigh. "She wants me to help you complete it. She said it would benefit the family."

Aha. The money pitch. Nick was right. This evening was about money. More than a basket full of twenties. Madame Iyå wanted to get her fat paws on Sophie's spell book.

Linda's body went rigid. She clenched her hand over mine and began to rock. She spoke in a deep and insistent voice—a voice I didn't recognize. "No. I don't want that. My secrets have to be protected. There will be danger. No."

"What are you talking about, Linda?" Nola said.

Linda stared across the room. "Linda's not here, my treasure."

"Who are you?" Nola's words came unsteady, searching. "Sophie?"

"Not Sophie. I'm Callia."

The back of my neck tingled. Who was Callia?

Linda gazed around the circle. She stopped when she got to me. Her face had changed: the softness drained from her features. She looked tired, older. Her eyes were vacant.

A small terror edged my rational mind aside. I had a fleeting sensation that someone else's eyes were staring at me from Linda's face. Was Linda acting? In a trance? I willed myself to stay calm.

"You have to keep my secrets safe and with my family. Your question is answered inside." She held her eyes on mine. "Promise me."

I nodded warily, not knowing what she meant. "I promise."

A door down the hall slammed shut with a force so hard it rattled the windows. Tawny screamed. I jumped.

Jimmy spun around and looked behind him. "Jesus."

"Holy shit," Nola said.

Madame Iyå raised her arms in the air. "Be quiet. Look at me, everyone. Look at me and stop talking. We have an uninvited presence. We're safe if we stay inside the circle."

She looked at Jimmy. He shrugged, wide-eyed.

Then Madame Iyå said, "Linda. Listen to me. Exhale. Let the energy float on your breath and send it back into the night. Follow my breath. Everyone, help her."

Madame Iyå began to inhale and exhale deeply. We followed her until Linda joined in.

"We have to close the circle now," Madame Iyå said. "We've kept Sophie's spirit out of the light for too long. Sophie, we honor you and thank you for your visit. You may go with the other spirits in peace. Everyone repeat after me. Go in peace. Blessed be."

We recited in unison: "Go in peace. Blessed be."

Linda sat rigid. Her eyes were closed. Tears rolled down her cheeks. I slipped my finger out of her grip and rubbed her arm to bring her into the moment. "Linda, it's Liz. Can you hear me?"

Her eyelids flickered open. She touched her face. "What happened?"

"Linda." I kept my eyes steady on hers to orient her. "Look at me. Do you know where you are?"

"No." Linda braced herself to stand up, then buckled back to the floor.

"Henry, please get her some water. Tawny, help me get her onto the sofa."

"Can we get up?" Tawny looked to Madame Iyå.

"Of course we can." Henry got to his feet and stepped over the bowl on his way to the kitchen. "It's over."

Chapter Twenty-two

Jimmy flipped on the lights. The ghostly, candlelit mood of the séance was erased by the fixture overhead, which bounced a harsh glare onto the walls. Tawny and I eased Linda onto the sofa, while Henry brought a glass of water. Linda was dazed, her face as pasty as the white wall behind her.

Nola sat down and gripped Linda's arm. "How do you know about Callia? Did Sophie tell you?"

"Let's let her rest a minute. She's shaking," I said, noting that Nola didn't ask *who* Callia was. Linda said the answer to my question was in her secrets—what secrets? The spell book? She must have overheard me say I wanted Sophie's spirit to name her killer. Was Linda's message connecting Madame Iyå to the murder and the spell book?

In the center of the room, Madame Iyå pushed herself up from the floor, straightening her caftan. Jimmy brought a broom and dustpan from the kitchen and began to sweep the circle of cornmeal off the floor. I brushed random grains from the back of my jeans and started toward Madame Iyå to get her opinion of how the séance unfolded.

"How is Linda?" Madame Iyå looked back to the sofa.

Henry and Nola sat on each side of Linda, stroking her arms.

"Disoriented," I said. "She may have been in a suggestive trance. Who is Callia?"

"I don't know." Madame Iyå shrugged. "Some other spirit who followed Sophie into the circle. Its presence is still in this apartment and needs to be expelled."

"Like, you mean, exorcised?" Tawny came up to us, wide-eyed. She looked across the room to Linda, then back to Madame Iyå. "I'm getting out of here." Tawny reached for her coat. "I'll get the sweater another time. This place is too freaky."

"Wait." Madame Iyå grabbed Tawny by the sleeve. "An uninvited spirit is here and may attach to your soul if you try to leave. The only way to prevent it is to put money in the basket as you walk out the door. The spirit will have to take the money to its spirit master before it can possess you."

Tawny's mouth dropped open. I smirked. Madame Iyå knew how to stay on point. No matter what happened, the woman kept her eye on the dollar. Tawny threw a bill into the basket, opened the front door, and left without a look back. Madame Iyå snatched the wad of cash from the basket and tucked it into her side pocket.

I leaned against the table. "Everything go according to plan?"

She studied me for a beat. "Each séance is different, depending on the energy in the room. There was a lot of restless anticipation tonight. Linda's energy was open to accepting the spirits. Callia's spirit used her to connect to you. I can help you decipher the meaning."

"What do you think Linda was talking about?" I said.

"Callia." Madame Iyå gave Jimmy an empty bag and told him to pack up. Then she turned to me. "Linda was speaking as Callia. I saw how you reacted. Whoever Callia is, she came to you for help. Let me guide you, while Callia's spirit is close."

"Actually, it sounded to me like she was talking about you and the spell book."

"The spell book?" Madame Iyå said. "Sophie's spirit gave instructions. She wants me to work with Nola and I will. Whatever Linda was channeling had to do with you, not me."

Jimmy set two bags on the table and helped Madame Iyå put on her coat.

"So you're going to publish Sophie's spell book?" I said.

Jimmy stopped. Nola crossed the room to us.

Madame Iyå pulled her purse onto her shoulder and picked up one of the bags. "Of course I am. That's what Sophie wanted. And that's what we agreed on."

I smiled. "Really. I know Professor Garfield would love to see the spell book. How about if we stop by tomorrow, and you can show it to him?"

She hesitated. "It's not ready yet."

"Oh, but Nick might be able to help you and Nola now that Sophie is gone. What time are you opening the store?"

"What do you know about Sophie's spell book?" Jimmy took a step toward me.

"I only know what Madame Iyå already told me," I said. "But I'm a little confused. I was under the impression that

Sophie kept the spell book to herself before she died. But she gave it to you?"

Nola joined the edge of our group and faced Madame Iyå. "Did Sophie give you her spell book?"

"Well, I . . ." Madame Iyå looked away.

"I don't think so. In fact, I think Madame Iyå was counting on getting the spell book from you, Nola," I said. "Do you have it?"

"If I did, I wouldn't tell anyone." Nola turned to Madame Iyå. "No matter what you channeled Sophie to say."

Madame Iyå narrowed her eyes. "That book belongs to me now. Sophie and I had a deal."

"You did?" I faced Madame Iyå. "I think Sophie made other plans before she died."

"We were partners. I have a right to it." Madame Iyå's earrings jangled as she tossed her head.

"That's not what I heard Sophie tell you at the party," I said.

"I don't know what you're talking about. Sophie and I agreed to publish that spell book together. We had a deal." Madame Iyå pointed her finger at Nola. "And she wants you to help me finish it. Don't listen to this stranger. That spell book can help your family."

"Are you insane? Sophie had no right even showing it to you." Nola pushed Madame Iyå's finger away, then turned to me. "How do you know so much about the spell book?"

"I don't," I said. "But I have a feeling Madame Iyå set up the séance so she could get into this apartment and search for it."

"That's a lie," Madame Iyå said.

"Is it?" I said. "Jimmy came out of Sophie's room before

the séance tonight. I suspect he was scouting for a few things to hand out for effect—like the violet sweater—while he hunted for the spell book. And when he didn't find the book, you assumed Nola had it. Was Jimmy instructed to leave a window open so the wind could come through and slam the door shut—all to add to your little production? Nicely done, Madame Iyå. It's a shame Linda interrupted so you couldn't get what you came for."

Madame Iyå put her face close to mine. Her face was crimson, eyes squinting. "You'll be sorry you said that. I am not a fraud. There's karma in the spirit world, honey. Unknown forces were here tonight—dark spirits. And dark spirits like to turn on lying doubters like you." She left, with Jimmy following.

Chapter Twenty-three

I closed the apartment door and leaned against it. My nerves were doing a fast jig throughout my body. Inside of two days I was threatened by a spell book during a blackout, promised to help a door-slamming spirit, and was cursed by a fake seer. I needed a moment to catch my breath and clear my mind.

Nola stood in front of me with her arms crossed. "What do you know about the spell book, shrink?"

"I know that Madame Iyå and Sophie talked about publishing the spell book together," I said. "Tuesday night at the party I overheard Sophie tell Madame Iyå that the deal was off."

"That's it?"

"I know Sophie was selling spells from the book." I looked around Nola for Linda. She and Henry were on the sofa, talking.

Nola pulled my arm. "How do you know Sophie was selling spells?"

"I knew one of her customers," I said.

"Oh no." Nola dropped my arm and pushed the hair away from her face. "That person was an idiot to tell you. They have no clue how dangerous it is to talk about those spells."

My heart froze. Buzzy was dead. "What do you mean?"

"The spells are cursed," Nola said in a whisper.

"How?" I flashed on the spell book open on my bedroom floor. *How to Imprison the Mind and Spirit of an Enemy.*

"Drop it."

"No, we can't drop it," I said. "Information in the spell book might connect to Sophie's murder."

"Not now. I can't talk in front of them." Nola looked across at Henry and Linda. "I want to make sure that Linda is okay. I don't think she should be here alone tonight."

"Because of what she said as Callia?" And then I got it. I took Nola's wrist in my hand. "Callia is connected to the spell book and the curse."

"Callia was the matriarch of my family."

"Does Linda know that?"

"Only if Sophie told her. I used to think Sophie kept the secret—now I'm not so sure," Nola said.

Henry got up and lent Linda his hand. They came toward us.

"I'm going to my boyfriend's," Linda said. "Henry and I were just talking about how strange it feels in here. He offered to have the apartment painted for us this weekend. I'll stay at Gerard's until it's finished."

"I'll schedule the painters for Saturday morning." Henry

touched Linda's shoulder and smiled. Small beads of sweat lined his creased brow.

"I'll call Gerard right now. Don't worry, Henry, I'll be okay. You're so sweet." Linda kissed his cheek and went down the hall, into her bedroom.

"I'm going through Sophie's things tonight, then," Nola said. "If that spell book is still here . . ."

Henry flung a dismissive wave toward Sophie's room. "Not tonight. Don't upset Linda anymore. She doesn't remember what happened to her tonight, and I didn't tell her."

"I'll get the pink candle that Sophie wanted you to have," Nola said.

He held up a hand. "I don't want it." He pointed a finger to his heart. "Maria is in here. With Sophie. I have my memories. I don't need nothin' else."

Linda came back and gave Henry a phone number. "I'll be at this number if you need to reach me. But I'll come back tomorrow and help Nola pack Sophie's room."

He pocketed the paper and went to front door. "Don't hang around here too long—any of you," he said, looking at me. He saluted Linda and Nola. "Monday this apartment will feel like a brand-new place."

Henry left. Linda went to her room to pack.

Nola started down the hall toward Sophie's room. "I'm going to look for that spell book."

"I'm going with you," I said, grabbing a bottle of wine and two glasses from the counter. "I'm not leaving until you tell me the whole story."

"You are one nosy chick, shrink," Nola said.

Sophie's bedroom door was stuck. Nola jiggled the knob

and pushed the door with her shoulder until it popped open. I followed her in. She turned on the light on the dresser. The window was closed.

I stopped short. If Jimmy didn't open the window, what made the door slam during the séance? A draft from the hall would have swung the door open, not shut.

"Are you going to help me or what?" Nola said.

I set the glasses on the dresser and poured us each some wine. Nola downed half of hers in one gulp, then opened a dresser drawer and began to rummage through it.

"Can we agree to help each other for tonight? I'll help you search while you tell me the story." I slid my arm under the mattress, pretending to search for what I knew wasn't there.

Nola searched the rest of the dresser drawers, then went to the closet, finishing her wine on the way. "I hope we're the only two souls in here listening. Sure, I'll tell you. It's a family legend. I've heard it from my old man so many times that I can recite it from memory."

I took the violet sweater off the drawer pull and set it aside.

Nola pushed the clothing in the closet apart and talked as she went through the shoe boxes on the floor. "Callia was my great-great-great-grandmother, born in Haiti in the 1840s. Her father was a French plantation owner. Her mother was an African slave who practiced Vodou in secret while the missionaries tried to convert the slaves on the island to Catholicism.

"Callia was half French so she was schooled at the white French academy. She hated it. She adored her mother and wanted to learn the Vodoun culture, but the missionaries kept Callia isolated on her father's orders."

I got on my knees and looked under the bed. Dust.

"When Callia got older, she snuck out to the mountains at night to watch the Vodoun tribal rituals practiced by her mother—totally something that I would do," Nola said. "And when she came back to the plantation, Callia would secretly write out the spells into a leather-bound book so she wouldn't forget them. The missionaries caught on and knew they couldn't harness Callia's wild spirit—I love that about her. They told her father, and he got so pissed that he forced Callia into an arranged marriage with a French merchant from Louisiana. She was only fifteen when her husband dragged her to the United States with him, the old lech."

"To New Orleans?" I said.

"Yeah," Nola said, opening the drawer in the nightstand. "Callia smuggled her spell book with her, tucked in the folds of silk lingerie and linens the merchant bought for her boudoir. She bore him two daughters. He traveled a lot, and while he was away, Callia practiced the rituals and spells from her spell book. Her husband caught her, but she refused to give up Vodou even when he threatened to take away the children and have her committed for practicing black magic. The more he threatened, the more protective she became of the spell book and the spells in it. Eventually, her husband ran off with some white showgirl and abandoned Callia and their two daughters alone in a house in the French Quarter. Callia needed money. She began to sell spells to people she trusted. The spells worked, and more people came to her, but Callia was convinced she'd be arrested and separated from her children if she was caught. That's when Callia created the curse. She didn't understand New Orleans was filled with voodoo practitioners at the time. She only remembered the missionaries separating her from her mother in Haiti."

"I can't imagine what it's like to worry about having your children taken away," I said, glancing at the black-and-white photo surrounded by white votives on Sophie's altar.

The woman appeared to be in her thirties, dressed in nineteenth-century garb. She was looking to the side, away from the camera, with her chin slightly tilted down. The whites of her eyes made the irises appear to be black. Her rich, dark-toned complexion seemed flawless. A small mouth, delicate eyebrows, and high cheekbones framed a broad nose. Black hair was pulled off her face; wisps graced the sides of her slim neck.

I pointed to the photo. "Is that Callia?"

"Yes." Nola sat on the corner of the bed, staring at the image of her ancestor. "Callia became more and more obsessive. To protect herself, she made every buyer sign and date the page of the spell they bought. She forced them into a covenant saying they couldn't reveal the spell or where it came from, or they would trigger the curse. The legend goes that anyone who signed Callia's spell book and then talked about the power of her voodoo died a violent death."

I thought of Buzzy. "And did that really happen? Or was it only a myth?"

"It happened once, for sure. When I was a kid, I visited my grandma Florence in New Orleans. She sat Sophie and me down and showed us a newspaper clipping from the New Orleans *Picayune* dated in the eighteen-somethings," Nola said. "The article was about two sisters from New Orleans who went to a voodoo queen to buy love spells. One sister— what the hell was her name? Alice maybe? I forget. Anyway, she bought a spell to keep her husband faithful, and the other sister bought a spell to destroy her lover's marriage. The voodoo queen made the married sister a potion to spread across her conjugal bed. What a weird word—*conjugal*. Who talks like that? Anyway, she sold the other sister a talisman to wear only when she was with her married lover. The sisters ignored the warning about the curse and showed the potion and the talisman to each other. But what the married sister didn't know was that both spells were intended to keep the same man. Her husband was cheating on her with her own sister."

"You're kidding," I said.

"I'm not. It said so in the paper." Nola picked up Callia's photo. "The wife went through her husband's coat one day and found her sister's talisman in the pocket. She confronted him, told him about the voodoo queen in the Quarter and that she knew the talisman belonged to her sister. He blamed her sister for seducing him. The wife left the house, found her sister, and shot her. Then she shot herself."

I blinked and took a swig of wine. "So both spells worked. The husband would never be unfaithful to that wife again, and the other sister caused the end of her lover's marriage."

Nola smiled. "Weird, huh?"

Not that weird. It wasn't far off from family problems I encountered in my practice. Minus the voodoo, duplicity, and murder.

"The cheating sister was a reckless liar, a real bitch. The

husband told the police everything, but Callia's name never hit the papers. He didn't know who she was." Nola put the photo back onto the altar and studied it. "Grandma Florence showed us the sisters' names in the spell book with the date that matched the clipping. Here's the point: it didn't matter if a spell was for love, money, or revenge. The curse on Callia's spell book protected her from being exposed."

I shuddered a little and pictured Nick poring through the spell book at his house. "Why was the spell book passed on to Sophie instead of you or your father?"

"Callia believed women were very, very powerful. The spell book went through the family from daughter to daughter," Nola said. "My grandmother had two kids: Sophie's mother and my father. When Sophie's mother died, Grandma Florence raised Sophie in the same house in New Orleans that Callia had lived in. Sophie was the daughter of the daughter. I'm the daughter of the son. So, when Grandma Florence passed away, the spell book went to Sophie."

"Did Sophie show you the spell book when she came to town?"

"Hell no." Nola finished her second glass of wine, sat on the bed, and leaned against a pillow. "She was *the one*, Miss-Aren't-I-Special. We just didn't talk about it. I know voodoo, but Sophie was deep into it by the time she moved here. I knew she wasn't supposed to cast spells from the spell book until she was initiated as a Vodou queen. Another big freakin' deal that was all about Sophie. I didn't know that Sophie was showing around the spell book until Jimmy mentioned it to me."

"Sophie and Jimmy were good friends?"

"She dated him for a while when she moved into this building. I suppose that's when Sophie got swept into

Madame Iyå's bullshit. But when Sophie met Sam, every-thing changed. She dumped Jimmy and became obsessed with Sam. She even practiced love spells on him."

"Didn't you warn her not to talk about Callia's spells?"

"Sophie?" Nola stood up in a wobble, then sat back down. "Are you kidding? She survived Katrina. She thought she was invincible. And she was in love. She didn't pay attention to anyone or anything. God only knows who else Sophie sold spells to or if she warned them about the curse."

I emptied the bottle into her glass. "I wonder if she wrote the names of her customers in the spell book the way Callia did. I can't say that Sophie was killed by a curse, but it is possible that someone who bought a spell from her was troubled enough to either want retaliation if the results were bad or was paranoid that Sophie knew too much about them. And since most murders are committed by people the victim knows, the spell book might provide us with a suspect list."

"Yeah, good thinking," Nola said. "But you notice that the spell book isn't in this room. Until we find it, no one's going to discover anything."

"I'll keep looking." I picked up the violet sweater and held it up. "Tawny will want this. She worked with Sophie and might have other information we don't know about. Do you have her number?"

"Linda does."

"By the way, did Sophie have a tarot deck?"

"Tarot?" Nola scrunched her nose, shaking her head. "No. Tarot has nothing to do with Vodoun or New Orleans voodoo. Why do you ask?"

"Just curious." Very curious.

We closed Sophie's room and found Linda in the living room. Her suitcase was resting at the front door. I gathered my coat and purse, and then asked Linda for Tawny's number.

"Are you going to be okay?" I said.

"It'll be good to be away from here tonight," Linda said. "Thanks for taking the sweater to Tawny. I'm sure she'll appreciate it."

Nola walked me to the door and gave me her number, too. "If you stumble upon the spell book, call me."

"I will."

"And if Tawny tells you anything . . ." Nola said.

"I'll call you."

"Thanks for coming," Linda said. "Tonight was more than I expected, but I felt Sophie was here in spirit. I hope she found peace."

I touched her arm. "Try to stay centered. You had a rough week. Be safe. I'll be in touch. Maybe I'll see you at Hissy Fit again soon."

"I'd like that." Linda smiled.

Henry's lights were out when I left the building and crossed the street to my car. I drove home and parked in front. I needed to dash inside for my cell phone. I walked up the steps, fishing for the key to the front door in the bottom of my purse. When I reached the landing, I still couldn't find it. Damn. I tucked my wallet under my armpit, shoved my checkbook between my teeth. Things were getting looser in the bottom of my bag. I tipped it halfway to separate the soft from the heavy. When I finally got a finger around the heart-shaped key ring, I heard a soft thud at my feet.

I looked down. The pouch of Madame Iyås lust gris-gris

was spilled over my welcome mat. Oh, great. I shook my head, remembering her ridiculous instructions for it. There wasn't a chance I'd be leaving this across my threshold to entice Nick's lust. I would sweep it up in the morning. I went inside and called Nick to tell him I was on my way. I stopped at the mirror for a lipstick check. And to fluff my hair.

Chapter Twenty-four

Trees framed the amber light that swept from Nick's porch and across the lawn. When I pulled up, he was waiting at his front door and gestured for me to park in the driveway.

As I walked up the two steps onto the wooden porch, he leaned against the doorframe in jeans and a faded black T-shirt that hung from his wide shoulders. He smiled and touched the back of my neck. The dull ache that had built up in the past four hours relaxed. I looked at him, returning his smile.

"Well? Meet any ghosts tonight?" Nick said.

"One or two." I grinned.

He led me into the living room. The blaze in the fireplace glowed golden against the mustard-colored walls. I took off my coat and held my hands in front of the fire to warm them. I noticed the ivory-toothed, turquoise mask on the mantle.

Nick came up beside me. "The mask is a replica of a

Mixtec-Aztec relic from the sixteenth century. The original is in the British Museum. This was a gift from a friend I met in South America last summer."

"It's extraordinary." I looked down at the black, rust, and beige Aztec rug covering the dark wood floor. "Did you get this rug in South America, too?"

"Different trip, but yes. I bought it from a rug dealer when I was researching Mesoamerican human sacrifice rituals of the Incan Empire."

Oh, yeah, I shop that way, too.

Across from the mask on the mantel, the Bible, the Koran, and the Gnostic Gospels were stacked between brass bookends. I moved away from the fire and set my purse on a chair in front of the bookcase. Plato, Poe, Augustine, and Yeats were on one shelf; *The Ultimate Football Almanac* and the *Sports Illustrated History of Baseball* were tucked in among sports biographies and reference books on another.

Nick leaned against his desk in front of the window, watching me. Behind him, a black laptop was open to Google search. Next to the computer, a legal pad scribbled with notes sat beside the open spell book.

Music played in the background. My head fell into rhythm with the slow shuffling beat. "Muddy Waters?"

"Yep. Chicago blues remind me of home." Nick reached for my hand and slowly twirled me around. "Want to dance?"

"Later. I have a lot to tell you."

We settled onto the paprika twill sofa, his arm across the cushion behind me, his body warm next to mine. He smelled woodsy, like pine mixed with lavender, and I noticed his hair was damp. I tucked my legs beneath me and sunk into the soft cushion.

"I want to hear it all," he said. "Was the séance what you expected?"

"I think it was more than Madame Iyå expected." I gave him the details, ending with Linda's trance and the slamming door.

Nick nodded. "The girl and the slamming door could have been part of the act."

"I don't think Linda was acting. And Madame Iyå looked as shocked as the rest of us when she ended the séance."

"What makes you think Linda wasn't part of the show?"

"When she turned to me, I felt like I was looking at a different person—the way she held her body, how her mouth was set. And her eyes appeared to be dark brown or black—Linda's eyes are blue."

"Contacts?"

"She didn't have time to remove them."

"Was she exhausted afterward? Did she remember anything?"

"No memory. She was disoriented and could barely stand. Her face was colorless."

Nick nodded, a finger to his lips, his eyes narrowed. "I witnessed possession once, in Haiti. It was intensely draining on the subject, a soldier in the mountains. He collapsed and had no recollection of what happened to him. In general, a spirit is known to take over a practitioner or finds an unguarded participant in a ritualistic circle. Someone like Madame Iyå is too sidetracked by her own scam to be open to a possession. I don't know about the others, but you're a doubter. There's not a respectable spirit around that would select you for possession at a séance."

"Oh, thanks. An added bonus to my complete and utter sanity."

"From your description, I would have guessed Tawny was most vulnerable to possession. But if the spirit chose Linda, then she was the most impressionable target in the room. Interesting. But possessed or not, someone wanted you to get the message about the spell book. What happened after the séance ended?"

I told him about my face-off with Madame Iyå.

"Why did you confront her?" Nick said.

"I lost my patience when she scared Tawny into making another donation."

"That's how Madame Iyå earns her living." Nick got up to poke the fire. "Okay, so you accused her of being a fraud. What if she has more information about Sophie? Or you find evidence in the spell book that marks her as Sophie's killer?"

"If I need to talk to her again, I'll buy something. I already know that works." The music stopped. My stomach growled, breaking the silence. I folded my arms and leaned back into the cushion.

"When was the last time you ate?"

I wrinkled my forehead and tried to remember. "I don't know."

"I can fix that. Come with me." He took my hand and led me into the kitchen.

I sat on a red-leather padded chrome stool at the eating bar. "What did you learn from the spell book?"

"Let me heat this up, then I'll show you."

He took a covered glass bowl from the refrigerator and scooped pasta with red sauce into a pan on the stove. He slid garlic bread into the toaster oven and poured out two glasses of red wine while I told him Nola's story about Callia. The spicy scent of tomato, garlic, anchovies, and olives filled the room. He spooned the hot pasta onto a plate, grated fresh Parmesan cheese on top, and set the plate in front of me.

I bit into a forkful of rigatoni and closed my eyes. "This is delicious. Who taught you to cook?"

"My dad's buddy had an Italian restaurant in Chicago. They'd leave me with the guy's old grandmother in the kitchen. She taught me." He sat on the stool next to mine. "You eat—my turn to fill you in."

"Please." I took a sip of wine and picked up my fork again.

"Callia's spell book contains a collection of Haitian Vodou rituals and their effects—some of the rituals I haven't seen for years, some I've never seen—along with the prices she charged. And I found the curse."

"How did you know to look for one?"

"I always look for curses before they pop up on their own. I hate otherworldly surprises, don't you?"

"Yes, I do." I popped the last bite of garlic bread into my mouth and finished my wine.

Nick left the kitchen and put the music back on, returning with the spell book. He traced his finger around the leather cover's gold-leaf border. "There are three lines here. The script is so small that it's only legible under a magnifying glass. The centerline is an incantation in French to protect the contents. A curse of death for revealing the contents repeats around the cover from front to back."

"Is Buzzy Lacowsky's name inside? Yesterday he told

me about a spell he bought from Sophie. Last night he died in an accident."

Nick rubbed his chin and set the spell book on the counter. "The curse in action."

"Or coincidence. But if I were to believe that Callia's curse brought death to anyone who betrayed the promise of silence, I wonder, does it have a lesser punishment for a nosy, just-looking violation? Do you think the curse made the lights go out last night when I tried to read the spell book?"

He smiled. "I doubt if offended spirits would shut down the power in Studio City to annoy you. What do you think?"

"I'll hold on to common sense for the time being and agree it didn't." I glanced at the spell book. "I'm sorry, I interrupted—did you see Buzzy's name?"

"I can't remember all the names I saw. Entries in this century only had initials." He opened the book. "The earliest date was 1866. I recognized some of the names on the older entries. American voodoo was thriving in New Orleans. Marie Laveau and the voodoo king Don Pedro were well-known practitioners, notorious for their promises of love, fame, and wealth. Their signatures are inside, along with those of a few Louisiana politicians. I imagine they were all happy to agree to anonymity for themselves and Callia. Spells were sold until 1930, dates and prices entered by the same hand—Callia's, I presume—then stopped. In October of 2005 entries began again, this time in two different hands."

I looked at him. "One may be Sophie's?"

"Could be." Nick flipped to a "Fidelity Spell" and pointed. "Here is an entry in Callia's hand, dated 1885."

The spell was written in cursive letters, elegant and fluid, but careful and clear. Spell dates and prices were in the same hand but appeared more rushed, less reverent. The first name on the list was Alice Gillette. She purchased the "Fidelity Spell" for ten dollars.

I pointed to the entry. "Nola claimed one of the doomed sisters was called Alice."

"Nola told you there was a newspaper clipping. Let's see if I can find the archived article."

I stopped him, then slid off my stool and planted a kiss on his cheek. "Thanks for dinner, Nick. It was yummy."

He blushed.

I followed him to his computer in the living room, pulled a chair close to his, and sat down. With my elbow propped on the desk and my chin resting in my hand, I watched Nick search for the article. He looked like a college student in his thick brown eyeglass frames and faded T-shirt. I was close enough to see the freckles on his aquiline nose. A shadow of a beard was beginning to show. Why didn't I notice how sexy he was twenty years ago?

He must have felt my stare because he glanced at me as he typed. I grinned. He kept typing. Four screens later, he pointed to a *Picayune* article on the Gillette sisters from July 1885.

I skimmed the article over his shoulder. "That's it."

He closed the laptop screen. "So—we know that the curse played out with the sisters. Now let's see if we can find Buzzy Lacowsky's initials in here."

"And anyone else Sophie sold spells to."

Nick turned the pages of the spell book while I read alongside him. He pointed out specific spells—"Break a Bad Marriage," "Good Luck," "Revenge."

A shift in handwriting on a "Safety Spell" dated August twenty-seven, 2005, caught my eye. "Here's something entered after Hurricane Katrina, before Sophie moved to Hollywood."

Initials and amounts listed beneath the spell ranged from twenty to one hundred dollars. "Sophie and her grandmother were evacuated to Houston. Do you think they sold "Safety Spells" to other evacuees?"

"Let's see if more recent entries are all in one hand, after the grandmother died. That would confirm this is Sophie's writing." Nick flipped pages while Howlin' Wolf's "Evil" played through the speakers on the mantle.

Five pages later, I stopped him. The heading read "How to Imprison the Mind and Spirit of an Enemy." "That's the spell that fell open in my bedroom last night."

"I recognize it," he said. "A voodoo king named Noble Roup claimed he created the spell. Noble would take his followers to Lake Ponchartrain to conjure voodoo. He closed his meetings with an all-night orgy. One night the state police busted them and found the governor's wife naked and in a compromising, well, position with her butler and a bartender from Metairie."

I grinned. "Are orgies part of your philosophy lectures?"

He wiped his forehead before he answered. "No, Liz. I don't do orgy lectures. Well, maybe a mention." Nick gave me a wicked smile, and I caught my breath. "Back in the nineteenth and twentieth centuries, the voodoo kings and queens needed an added attraction. The orgy business was a bonus for their customers and brought more money to the till. Orgies are not a requisite part of voodoo practice and not my style."

My cheeks burning, I returned to the mind-control spell. It required voodoo dolls, black candles, blood, and oils, including patchouli. At the bottom of the page was an invocation. I read it in singsong. "'Turn his mind weak and fitful, his soul possessed will be. Choke his spirit with his mind and bring it—'"

"Don't." Nick laid his hand over the invocation.

"What?"

He started to croon "That Old Black Magic," and I stopped him.

"Good thing you have academics to fall back on in case that singing career doesn't pan out. You're trying to distract me. Suppose I'll put the curse in motion?"

"You'd have to purchase a spell and sign the book to trigger the curse." Nick closed the cover and peered over his glasses. "And as for the 'How to Imprison the Mind and Spirit of an Enemy,' not believing won't protect you from invoking the spell. Repetition is an important tool in the occult. Don't read out loud, unless you *want* to play with the spirits. But they might want to play back."

I shrugged. "Okay. Sorry."

"I don't want anything to happen to you."

"Thanks. You can be my bodyguard against the supernatural."

We were halfway through the spell book and found no entries later than 2005. I began to worry that Sophie didn't log in her new clients at all.

Nick turned to the next page: "To Find a Lover." "Here's an entry dated last month and initialed T. D."

I leaned in, and a surge of adrenaline made my hands

tingle. "T. D. could be Sophie's friend Tawny Dalton. She told me tonight that she bought a spell."

I tore a blank sheet from the back of Nick's notepad and started a list, with "T. D.—Tawny" on top.

A few pages later, Nick said, "Look. 'B. L.' is the last entry under the 'Attract Money Spell.' It's dated the week before last."

"That's definitely Buzzy. He told me he bought a 'Money Spell' from Sophie." I gripped Nick's shoulder. "Last night he bent to pick up his wallet and was hit by a truck. What a strange coincidence."

Nick sat back and folded his arms, staring through the window in front of his desk. "You said coincidence earlier. I don't believe the wallet or his death was a coincidence. Now we know this is Sophie's writing."

I wrote "B. L.—Buzzy" under "T. D.—Tawny" on my list.

"Here's another one: 'R. B.' under the 'Family Protection Spell,' " Nick said.

"R. B.?" I leaned in to look. When I saw the signature, my stomach did a flip. The *R* had a heart at the end of the loop—the same heart and loop Robin had been using since the eighth grade. The spell included an incantation and the instruction to create a talisman—a childlike stick figure with stars circling the head—for each member of the family to wear.

"That's Robin's handwriting. She gave Orchid a talisman like that on a chain for her birthday. She claimed it was a good-luck charm she found at a psychic fair."

"She lied to you," Nick said. "Robin knew Sophie was into voodoo."

I stared at the page, stunned.

"Why would Robin have us chasing around town looking for tarot decks if she knew all along it might be Sophie?" Nick said.

"It was my idea to search for the tarot deck, not Robin's. Why would Robin assume Sophie left the cards? Nola said Sophie wasn't into tarot. Plus, Robin is extremely superstitious. If Sophie warned her about the curse, Robin wouldn't talk to us about Sophie. She'd be too afraid." I shifted in my chair, uncomfortable with my uncertainty. Was it that easy for Robin to lie to me?

"Afraid enough to kill Sophie?"

"For what? Leaving tarot cards? You sound like the police."

"What if Sophie and Robin had a falling-out? What if Robin threatened to tell Sam that Sophie was peddling voodoo as a sideline? If Sophie thought it would ruin her relationship, she may have decided to spook Robin, distract her. Then Robin found out . . ."

"That doesn't make sense, Nick. Sophie had the curse for insurance. How could Robin tell Sam about Sophie without talking about the spell book and exposing herself to the damn curse?"

Nick got up and threw a log on the fire. "What if the night of the party Robin let something slip about the spell she bought and believed she triggered the curse? If Robin was that superstitious, she would be afraid of the consequences. We didn't hear the whole argument between Robin and Sophie. Sophie threw out another curse at Robin before she left the party. What if Robin decided the only way to protect her family was to kill Sophie?"

My mind was reeling. Everything Nick said was possible. "No. You're way off track. Robin's not a killer."

"You're so certain."

"Yes, I am. I want to find the rest of the names."

Nick sat back down at the desk. When we finished paging through the book, I had five sets of initials:

H. M.

L. M.

T. D.—Tawny Dalton

R. B.—Robin

B. L.—Buzzy

I took the Steve Weller after-party guest list from my purse and unfolded it on the desk to find names matching the initials I had. Out of four pages of guests, there were two matches: Linda Miller and Buzzy Lacowsky.

I noticed something else on the guest list. "Everyone invited had a plus-one."

"What does that mean?"

"It means that half the people we saw at the party were spouses or tagalongs. The Collins staff isn't listed, either."

"What do you want to do?"

"Follow the leads we have. If L. M. is Linda Miller, H. M might be a relative or . . ." I sat up straight. "Henry Marx."

"The landlord? The old man wasn't at the concert, and even if he was, he doesn't look strong enough to carry out the attack on Sophie. If Linda is the killer, why would she tell you the answer to your question is in the spell book?" Nick leaned back and folded his arms.

"Linda was in a trance. It's easy to find out if H. M. is

Henry. I'm only guessing the other initials are Tawny and Linda. I have to talk to them."

"Talk without exposing them to the curse," Nick said.

"I'm not worried about the curse. I'm worried about Robin."

"What are you going to do? Coax them out of their superstition?"

"Give me some credit for respecting their beliefs, Nick. I'll find a way." I started to pace. "I'll see Robin in the morning. Then I'll meet with Tawny and go from there."

Nick closed the spell book. "Meanwhile, I want to show this to Osaze tomorrow. He might know how to reverse the curse."

I walked over to him. "I'm going with you."

"I don't know when he'll be home."

"I'm going with you, Nick."

He got up to face me, brushing a hair back from my forehead. "You're impossible to say no to."

"I'll use that to my advantage. I have to go home."

Nick picked up my coat and held it for me. "I like having you here." He turned me around and tilted my chin up. "And Liz? When you're ready to dance, let me know."

"I will."

He handed me the list of names. "Don't forget this."

"Thanks. I'll see you tomorrow. What time?"

"Right after my last class ends, about one. I want to give Osaze enough time to go through the spell book before I drop it off at the police station."

I snapped my head around. "What?"

"We have to turn the spell book over to Dave and Carla."

I took the book off the desk and held it to my chest. "You

can't do that. We'll show the spell book to Osaze, but after I'm done with it, it goes back to Nola. It belongs to her family."

"The spell book could be evidence, Liz." He pried it out of my hands and laid it back on the desk. "You think it holds answers to Sophie's murder—so will Carla and Dave. And I won't risk hindering the investigation by keeping it from them."

"Please don't do this, Nick."

"The initialed entries could provide motive. The police will want to talk to these people, too." Nick's voice was even; his eyes held mine. "It's the ethical thing to do."

"Carla will see Robin's initials and stop there. Damn it. Won't you please give me time to find the people on the list? There might be something inside the spell book we missed. I thought you couldn't say no to me."

We stood in the center of the living room. The only sound was the crackle of burning wood.

Nick walked to the front door. "I'll give you until the end of the day. Then Dave or Carla gets the spell book."

"That's not enough time." I didn't move.

"I'll meet you at your house at one."

"Fine." I picked up my purse.

"Fine." Nick opened the front door and followed me to my car. He leaned inside the driver's side. "Be careful on the way home."

"I'll see you tomorrow." I closed the door. As I backed out, I waved at him and smiled so he wouldn't change his mind and bolt over to the police station in the morning with the spell book and his Boy Scout conscience. He went inside and closed the door. I slammed my fist on the steering wheel and drove away. Damn him.

Ten minutes later, I pulled into my garage. Once out of the car, I heard the phone ringing in the house. It had to be Nick, calling to apologize. Of course he wouldn't turn the book in as evidence tomorrow, he'd say. We'd take as much time as needed to clear Robin.

I locked the kitchen door behind me and picked up the phone. "Hello?"

"Are you naked?"

I stopped. The line that used to make me giggle sent a ripple of repulsion through me. "What do you want, Jarret?"

"I've been waiting for you to get home, Lizzie Bear." He slurred his words. "I'm back in town and I was missing you. I'm out front. Let me in. Let's have a drink and talk."

"Go home, Jarret." I hung up.

The phone rang again. I stared at the receiver until it stopped. Great. My ex was drunk-dialing me, and Nick was on track to keep Robin locked in jail.

I secured the bolt on the front door, then went upstairs. A car engine started on the street outside. I peered between the shutter slats of my bedroom window and watched tail-lights disappear down the block.

After I brushed my teeth, I burrowed under the covers, took a deep breath, and tried to fall asleep. My mind, however, was cranking out a to-do list: Ask Robin why the hell she lied to me. Get the spell book away from Nick. Figure out how to vet possible murderers while dodging a curse. Remain rational about curses. Wash and condition my hair.

Chapter Twenty-five

Incessant cawing outside my bedroom window woke me. The morning sun through the open shutters glared like a high-powered flashlight beam in my eyes. I covered my head with my pillow until I could get my wits about me. A murder of crows. Murder . . . Robin . . . Voodoo . . . Nick. I threw the pillow on the floor, got up, and went to shower. The hot water did nothing to erase the dull thud of last night's four-glasses-of-wine hangover so I rinsed myself with a blast of cold water. Shocking, but effective to jolt me into action.

After I dressed and started a pot of coffee, I went to the den and did a computer search for the Van Nuys jail. Visiting hours began at ten. If I moved fast, I could be the first in line. A cup of Kona blend and a toasted English muffin later, I grabbed my purse and coat and picked up Sophie's sweater.

I backed the car out of the garage, opened the driver's

window, and drove down the hill. The sky was clear; the air was crisp. Sunlight sparkled on the traces of autumn color in the neighborhood foliage. "Halloween Sale" signs beckoned from retail shops on Laurel Canyon Boulevard. Girls in shorts and wool scarves jogged along Burbank Boulevard.

The streets around the Van Nuys Government Center teemed with cars and pedestrians. I cruised around the long blocks, found a parking space, and fed twelve quarters into the meter. The jail was somewhere inside the maze of federal, state, county, and city buildings; police and fire departments; superior courthouses; and a public library. If I got lost, at least my car wouldn't be ticketed or towed.

A suited man with a briefcase directed me to the Van Nuys Community Police Station, on the east side of the complex. Bondsmen in black "Kennymo Bail Bonds" T-shirts touted their services at the stairway beneath the entrance. I bypassed the hawkers and climbed the steps to the double glass doors. Inside, three policemen signed in visitors at the counter. I gave my name and sat on a bench near the window.

Thirty minutes later, I was led into a tiny visiting room that smelled like an odd mixture of cleaning fluid and dust. Robin sat behind a Plexiglas barrier. She wore a blue jumpsuit, her hair pulled back into a ponytail. She picked up the phone receiver on her side, put her hand against the window, and smiled weakly.

My heart tugged when I saw how pale and drawn she was. I sat down, put my hand on the glass to hers, and picked up the receiver. "How are you?"

Her face crumpled, and words came out in sobs. "I'm being arraigned on Monday. The DNA test came back a match to Sophie's blood."

"Oh my God, Robin," I said, her words prickling through me like an electric shock.

"The police want me to confess. Said it would be easier on me. They told me they have a witness."

"A witness?" I leaned in toward the divider. "Witness to what?"

She wiped her eyes. "Someone claimed they saw me leave the lot where Sophie's car was parked. That's a flat-out lie, Liz. Why won't the detectives believe me? Orchid's car was in a different lot. I was nowhere near Sophie's car."

I wanted to take Robin's hand, reassure her with a hug. All I could do was shake my head in disgust. "The witness must be mistaken. Eyewitnesses aren't always reliable, if there really is a witness to begin with. Police don't always tell the truth when they're looking for a confession."

"The detectives keep asking me the same questions, over and over: Why did I kill Sophie? How did I do it? What did I do with the weapon? Your brother and that Detective Pratt made me retrace my steps a million times."

"Did they tell you the witness's name?"

Robin rubbed her forehead. "No. Barnes told me they didn't have to—yet. What am I going to do? I don't know where the blood came from. I can't erase my argument with Sophie. Everyone at the party heard us. How will I prove I'm innocent?"

"Tell me about your purse. You had it with you when you walked Orchid to her car. Then what?"

"I stopped in the ladies' room, then came back into the artist lounge. I put my purse behind the bar until every-one left."

I pictured the small bar. There was only room for the

bartender to stand. "The bartender would have noticed someone going behind the bar. Have Barnes check him out. Who was in the ladies' room?"

"I can't remember. Women came in and out. The bathroom was jammed. After the scene Sophie made, I wasn't in the mood to talk to anyone."

"Did you ever lose sight of your purse?"

She paused. "Only when I reached for the towel to dry my hands. My purse was on the counter, next to the basin. Do you think one of the women could have swiped the blood then?"

"Maybe. Keep trying to recall who was in there. Same thing with the parking lot. Something may come to you," I said.

"I told Barnes to talk to Buzzy. Buzzy walked Sophie to the lot. Maybe he remembers seeing me out there. You could talk to him. Would you? Ask him?"

I squirmed, searching for words to soften the news. "Buzzy was in an accident Wednesday night. He's dead, Robin."

Her jaw dropped. "How?"

"He was hit crossing PCH on foot. I'm so sorry. I talked to him that afternoon. The night of the party he left Sophie at the curb with her friends and went back inside. He didn't walk her all the way to her car." I hesitated. "He also told me about Sophie's spell book and the voodoo spell she sold him."

Robin shook her head, slowly at first, then rapidly, holding up her hand up as if to push the words back at me. "No. No. Don't say any more."

"We have to talk about this, Robin, so I can help you. It's time to stop lying."

"Lying about what?"

"About the deal you made with Sophie. I know you bought a 'Family Protection Spell' from her. You knew all along she left the tarot cards."

She looked away. "I don't know what you're talking about."

I squeezed the receiver. "Yes, you do. I saw the spell book, Robin. It was inside the envelope Sophie left in your office. I found your initials under a 'Family Protection Spell.' The locket you gave Orchid is the talisman for that spell. And I know all about the alleged curse. Nick translated the French from the spell book's cover. You lied because Sophie told you you'd die if you talked about it."

"Are you crazy?" Robin's face went red. "How can you sit there and talk about it so freaking casually? Do you know what you've done? You triggered the curse. Why? I wanted to protect my family—you wouldn't understand that, would you? You probably think I'm guilty." She started to get up. "I'm done. Don't come back."

"Wait." I yelled into the phone, touching the glass to hold her attention. "Nick has a friend who can stop the curse."

She fell back into the chair and hissed into the receiver, "Who?"

"His name is Osaze Moon. He's a voodoo master. Nick and I have an appointment with him this afternoon. Robin, I know you're not guilty. And I didn't trigger the curse. Nick said it's literal. You'd have to tell me you bought it, not the other way around. I know you and Sophie made some kind of deal. But Nick wants to turn the spell book over to the police. I want to avoid that until we find evidence to prove you're innocent."

"If they see . . ."

"Your initials in there? I know. Nick and I plan to talk to Sophie's other clients this afternoon. If you have information about Sophie to get them to open up . . ."

"Even if Nick's friend revokes the curse, I have nothing to tell you. You probably think that's a lie, too."

"What I think isn't at issue, Robin. I'm here to help *you*. I understand why you lied," I said. "But Sophie's murderer could be tied to her spell book. Were there any other conditions on the spell you can talk about?"

"You don't get it. Buzzy was crazy to give you information. Don't you see? He set the curse in motion and died as a result. Damn Sophie. Damn her." Robin slammed her hand on the ledge in front of her.

"Okay. Then tell me about your other conversations with Sophie."

"She didn't mention her personal life, and I didn't care enough to pry. The first few times we talked, she asked about my family. I told her about Orchid and Josh. That's it."

"How did the occult come up?"

Robin didn't answer.

"We're not talking spells," I said. "Who brought up the occult in general?"

"I did. I told her about the tarot reading the night before Josh died. Sophie wasn't into the tarot. That's the reason I didn't think she left the cards on my door. The most I'll say is that Sam's girlfriends try to get chummy by bringing me little gifts, thinking their favors would grant them open access to Sam at work. Sophie's offer was different." Robin shrugged. "I trusted her for a moment, and I wish I hadn't."

I wished she hadn't, either. "If Sophie expected you to

give her free rein of Sam's office after she gave you the spell, did she threaten you when you didn't?"

"No. You saw her. She just tried to sidestep or bully her way in."

"She never talked about the spell or the curse again?"

"Stop pushing, Liz."

Robin's eyes burned into me, but I gave it right back to her. "I'll stop pushing when you're cleared. One name or incident could resolve who killed Sophie and framed you. When you get home, you can smack me in the face with a cream pie if you want to." That drew a snicker from her. "Until then, you have to ignore your superstitions. Search your memory. Buzzy's death was a horrible accident, not the result of a curse."

"You don't believe. I do."

"This is a lousy time to let the supernatural cloud your thinking."

"I'm sorry, Liz." Robin's shoulders sank. "I really didn't think Sophie left the tarot cards. My mind is spinning right now. I'll try to think back on what she and I talked about. If something comes to mind, I'll tell Barnes to call you. No more lies. Forgive me?"

"Sure. But to even things up, maybe you should make two cream pies when you're out of here." We grinned at each other. I glanced at my watch. It was almost eleven. I wanted to see Tawny before meeting Nick. "I have to go. Are you going to be okay?"

She shrugged. "I'm trying my best. I'm happy you came. You're the only one except for Barnes who's been here. Sam won't even take my calls. I wonder if I still have a job."

"Now you're being silly. Sam can't run his business without you there to direct traffic. I bet he feels guilty as hell for missing your calls. I'll come back tomorrow. Tell Barnes to find me if you need anything. I'll make sure you get it." I gave her a thumbs-up, something we did in high school before tests. This was our biggest test yet. She returned the gesture.

On the walk to my car, I went over what Robin said. Despite my comment, I was curious why Sam didn't take her calls. And who was the parking-lot witness the police claimed they located? Had to be someone from the party; the rest of the theater was empty by the time Sophie was escorted out.

I slid in behind my steering wheel and dialed Tawny's number. She answered on the first ring.

"Tawny? It's Liz Cooper. We met at the séance last night. Do you have some time right now? I have Sophie's sweater for you. I'd like to bring it over and talk a little."

"Oh, sure," she said. "I was just cleaning up the place for my date tonight if you don't mind a little mess. I'll make a pot of coffee and we can chat." She gave me the directions to her rented guesthouse in the hills off Outpost Drive.

I raced down the freeway through the Valley toward Hollywood to have as much time as possible with Tawny. I exited on Cahuenga and when I turned right onto Mulholland Drive, my cell phone rang.

"Hi, honey—it's me." My mother's voice was too chipper.

"Hi, Mom," I said, cautious. "How are you?"

"Wonderful. Listen, I'm having some people over tonight . . ."

"I'm sorry, Mom. I can't come. I have plans. If I had

known sooner . . ." It wasn't a complete lie; my aim was to spend the whole day with Nick.

"You're not invited, dear. It's Daddy's and my night to host our card club. But I want to make a couple of quiches and I only have one quiche dish. Can I borrow yours?"

"Sure, except I'm not home right now."

"Oh, I'm sorry. Did I bother you at work?"

"No. I'm running an errand. I just left Robin at the Van Nuys jail."

"How is she? Poor thing. I feel so bad for her. I heard on the news this morning that charges are about to be filed. Thank goodness they didn't give her name. Robin and her poor daughter must be beside themselves with worry. I am."

"I am, too."

"I pulled a tarot card for Robin in my reading this morning—the Seven of Swords. Someone is deceiving her."

No kidding. "I'll be sure to tell her lawyer to be on the lookout."

"Anyway, honey, that beautiful Italian porcelain pie dish Aunt Minnie gave you for your wedding would be so perfect for my table. I was going to send your father or someone over to pick it up. I won't need it until later this afternoon."

How did my mother keep track of my wedding gifts after fifteen years? I used the dish once, for vegetables. "Tell Daddy I'll be home at one to meet a friend, but we're leaving right away."

"Good. I'll send him over. Why so busy? Where are you going now?"

"To see someone in Hollywood. Then Nick and I have an appointment." Oh no. I didn't mean to blurt that out. Here it comes.

"Your brother Dave's friend Nick Garfield? Again? Why are you running around with him? Isn't he busy teaching school?" The edge in her voice made me feel like I was fifteen and she caught me with the neighborhood graffiti tagger.

If I told her the truth, she'd blab to Dave, who'd call Nick, who'd probably crumble and turn in the spell book. "I don't know Nick's schedule, Mom, only that we're meeting later."

"I can't imagine what you have in common with him. It's not that I don't like Nick. You know I do. Remember, it was my idea to call him about the tarot cards. But really, Liz, he's so bookish. He's not right for you, not like Jarret."

"You're right. He's nothing like Jarret. I'll be home at one. Send Daddy over. Have fun with your card club tonight and good luck with the quiches. Got to go. Love you, Mom."

Chapter Twenty-six

I turned left onto Outpost Drive and headed south past the Spanish- and Mediterranean-style homes that edged the tree-lined street. A quarter mile down, I found Tawny's street and navigated my car through a lane cramped with parked cars. Between houses I caught glimpses of the canyon that swept down to the Hollywood Bowl at its base.

Tawny's address was posted on the mailbox in front of a Tudor-style stone mansion at the top of the lane. A blue Prius and an old Volkswagen Bug were side by side in front of the iron-gated portico connecting the four-car garage to the main house. I parked at the curb, grabbed the sweater, and walked to the gate.

I didn't see a doorbell. Tawny said she'd leave the delivery entrance unlocked, so I unlatched the iron gate and walked in. Ahead, an expanse of lawn stretched toward a small stone guesthouse. The panoramic view swept across the city from Mulholland Drive to downtown Los Angeles. A bank of clouds moved over the hills from Los Feliz toward the Cahuenga Pass.

The property felt like a park nestled on the roof of a skyscraper. Rose bushes bordered the edge and shielded the drop into the canyon beyond. A volleyball net was set up to the right, a fenced-in pool to my left. Droplets of water sparkled on the grass in the sun. My heel sank into the damp earth so I tiptoed across the lawn with my arms out for balance to avoid slipping or tripping. While I was providing morning entertainment for the people inside the house, I hoped Tawny would see me and come out. She didn't. I continued my tightrope act all the way to the terrace of the guesthouse.

I knocked on the glass-paneled door. There were voices inside, so I knocked again, harder, and then tried the door— it was unlocked. I poked my head in.

A basket of folded laundry was on the green-velvet sofa. Magazines littered the coffee table. I scanned the empty room through to the kitchen banquette on the back wall. The voices came from a cooking show on the television.

I stepped inside. "Tawny?"

No response. Two doors on the left opened to a bathroom and small bedroom. I checked both rooms, didn't find Tawny, and then crossed the great room to the kitchen area. Two clean mugs and a glass carafe of coffee sat on the counter near the sink. I left Sophie's sweater on the sofa and went outside to check if Tawny went to the main house.

The property was still. No barking dogs. No curious maids, peering out of the windows. Wind rustled leaves on the trees outside the garage. A lone caw echoed from the canyon behind me. I made my way back across the lawn and knocked on the French doors to the main house.

"Hello?" I strained to hear voices or the pad of steps inside.

Nothing. Maybe she went on an errand and forgot about me. I went back to the guesthouse and dialed Tawny. A phone started to ring in the bedroom. I followed the sound. Her cell phone was on the bedroom dresser, ringing. Her purse was there, too. Where was she? I hung up and wandered to the kitchen again. An empty vase sat on the counter. Okay, maybe she was in the back, cutting flowers, and didn't hear me. I went outside and circled the guesthouse and then began to walk the perimeter of rose bushes.

Cut red roses were piled on the ground near a broken rose bush at the edge of the canyon. A succession of loud caws from the hill below drew me closer. My heart began to pound.

I parted the bushes. The land at the edge had caved—chunks of soil and grass scattered down the embankment. Thirty feet below, Tawny lay crumpled in a heap, her back to me. Her red hair was tangled in the brush. Her powder-blue sweats were covered with dirt. Her leg was bent forward at a perverse angle. I recoiled in horror.

"Oh my God." Then I shouted down the slope. "Tawny!"

Her left hand moved, then fell limp into the dirt.

I vaulted back from the edge, pulled my cell phone from my purse, and dialed 911. "There's been an accident." I gave the operator details and the address. "I'm going down to help her."

The operator was polite but firm. "No, ma'am. Stay on the line with me. Do *not* go down there. Do you understand?"

I shoved the phone into my back pocket and tore off my coat, draping it over the rose bush for the paramedics to see. I got on my hands and knees and looked down the canyon to Tawny. Dried shrubbery covered the hillside. If I held the branches for leverage and support, I could climb down to her without falling.

I backed over the edge and got my footing on a rock four feet below. I turned, grabbed a sturdy branch, and eased my way down. I held my eyes on the ground in front of me. I knew if I looked out into the canyon, I'd get dizzy. I slid on my backside, going from shrub to shrub to slow my progress. Twigs clawed at my hands and face. Dust swirled around me and caught in my throat.

I heard sirens wailing.

As I inched toward Tawny, I talked, hoping she could hear me. "Hang on. I'm coming. It'll be okay. I called for help. Don't move. It's me, Liz."

My foot slipped on a rock. I began to tumble. I lashed my arms and grasped at a branch to stop myself. A trickle of blood rolled down my cheek. My hands burned from grasping the dried branches and twigs.

Then a loud male voice. "Ma'am, *stop*. Don't move. We're coming down to you."

Three firemen in yellow jackets and gear tied to their bodies dropped over the ledge into the canyon. Two men rappelled past me toward Tawny.

Another stopped at my side and took my arm. "Stay still, ma'am. Are you hurt?"

"No. I'm okay." I watched the men below with Tawny, and then looked up at the young man with me. "She fell."

"Let's make sure you're okay. I'm Kris. What's your name?"

"I'm Liz. And really, I'm okay. I'm more worried about her."

"Humor me, and let me check your limbs to be sure." He gently felt my arms, legs, and ribs. "Does this hurt?"

"No."

"This?"

"No." I looked up at his face, half hidden by a fireman's cap. When he turned to unhook his equipment, I saw the name on the back of his hat: Bage.

"We'll get that cut cleaned out after I take you up. First, we have to wait until my team transports your friend on a stretcher."

Kris Bage and I watched as the men below attended to Tawny. When they eased her over, I flinched. Shear handles protruded from her chest. Blood drenched the front of her clothing. One of the firemen swaddled bandages around the shears and over the wound. They lifted her onto a metal stretcher, secured her with straps, and then nodded to the team above. My stomach clenched as her form passed me on the stretcher. Her face was covered with an oxygen mask. She didn't move.

Kris strapped me into a body harness. He gave a signal, and I was raised up the hill. At the top, I pulled out of the gear and started toward Tawny.

The EMT at her side removed the oxygen mask and shook his head at his partner. "No BP. No pulse. Multiple rib fractures. The shears pierced through to her heart. She bled out."

My knees buckled.

Kris caught my elbow and steadied me. "I'm sorry, Liz. C'mon, let's get that wound on your cheek attended to."

An EMT checked me over again, then cleaned and bandaged my cheek. Two LAPD patrolmen led me to a patio table under the portico. They logged my identification and took a detailed statement. Although the coroner was responsible for determining if Tawny's death was an accident, the senior officer on scene decided not to hold me.

"You won't release my name on the scanner or to the press, will you?" I said when we finished.

The patrolmen glanced at each other, then back at me.

I realized how guilty I sounded. "I don't want my family to worry about me. I'd rather tell them myself," I said, in a half-truth covered by a hopeful grin. Real truth—I didn't want Dave to hear I found another body, pitch a fit, call Nick, and hinder our investigation.

"No, ma'am. We don't put witness names on the scanner," said the senior officer.

Captain Pinney, from the LAFD, stopped at the table and introduced himself to me. "You took a risk going down into the canyon, Miss Cooper. I admire your courage and compassion, but you were smart to call for help first."

I looked away, and the vision of Tawny alone in the canyon flashed through my mind. How could I think of myself when a life had been lost? Tears welled. "I wish I had found her sooner."

WHO DO, VOODOO?

As Tawny's body was loaded into the ambulance, a fifty-something couple in tennis gear entered the yard. They introduced themselves as the owners of the house. The woman buried her face in her hands when she learned what happened. Her husband gave the police contact information for Tawny's family. When I could leave, I walked with my head down through the gawking crowd outside. All I wanted was to get into my car, shut the door, and feel safe. My hands and face stung; my clothes were coated with dirt. I was nauseous from shock. I needed to be alone to get my bearings.

A crow, perched on the fence next to my car, flapped its wings and took flight, following the ambulance with Tawny's body down the lane. The caws from the canyon echoed in my head. I thought of the crow on Robin's lawn the day Josh died. The crow in the lot when we found Sophie. The murder of crows that woke me this morning. And Callia's curse. I vomited into the gutter.

I wiped my mouth with a handkerchief, started the car, and steered down the lane. When I got to Mulholland Drive, the canyon I had just crawled out of descended to my right. I fixed my eyes on the road ahead. Screw coincidence; screw logic. Tawny was another victim to Callia's curse. The thought terrified the hell out of me.

Clouds shifted over the sun. I stopped for the red light at Cahuenga Boulevard and looked at my face in the rearview mirror. A white bandage covered my cheekbone. My hair was dusty and disheveled. Then I looked at the dashboard clock: one o'clock.

I put on my headset and called Nick's cell phone. "I'm sorry," I said when he answered. "I'm on my way. Where are you?"

"Waiting on your front steps. Where are you?"

"North Hollywood. Nick—Tawny's dead." I described how I found her. "The ground beneath her literally crumbled—that damned curse . . ."

"Oh, man." He let out a long sigh. "I talked to Osaze this morning. He's waiting for us. He knows the legend of the curse and wants to see the spell book."

"Does he know how to stop the curse?"

"He wants to see the spell book. Your voice is shaking, Liz. Should I come and get you?"

"No. I'm fine. Just talk to me for a while. Tell me about the lore on crows. What do they mean?"

"Why do you ask?"

"A crow guided me to Tawny. Another crow followed her ambulance off. Robin believed crows trumpeted death after a crow waited on the lawn the night before Josh died. I heard a crow the night we found Sophie."

"I'll explain the whole mythology when you get here."

"Tell me now, please." I didn't want to be alone on the drive. If I could launch him into one of his lectures . . .

"Okay," he said. "First, let's acknowledge that cities are full of crows. There are two on a tree across the street from your townhouse right now. But, to give you a general answer on crow superstition, crows are mentioned in folklore from all over the world."

As Nick talked, I wove through traffic on Cahuenga and passed the studios and restaurants that lined Ventura Boulevard.

"Many cultures believe a single crow is a portent of death," he said. "Groups of crows can be lucky. Then again, there are those who believe a prediction of good luck can also be an omen of death. Crows are a link to the spirit world and, in that sense, could be alert to the increasing momentum of Callia's curse. The spirits she employed are vigilant."

His voice soothed me; the topic didn't. I was a mile from home when I interrupted. "Thanks, I get it. I'll be home in five minutes."

When I pulled up in front of my townhouse, Nick leaned on the railing outside my front door with his arms folded, studying the sky. Jarret sat on my top step, staring at the street.

What the hell was Jarret doing there? I parked in the garage, walked through the house, and opened my front door.

Jarret vaulted to his feet. "Hey, Lizzie Bear. Whoa, what happened to you?" He came forward to kiss me. His breath smelled like beer.

I backed away. "What are you doing here, Jarret?"

He brushed his sandy-brown hair back and grinned. "I talked to your mother this morning. She said your dad was picking up some plate, and I came instead so we could talk." Jarret looked back at Nick. "Privately."

Nick shrugged. "I was expected, pal."

The cut on my cheek throbbed as I seethed with anger. My mother knew damned well Nick would be here. "This is a bad time. I don't have time to talk."

Jarret rubbed the shoulder of his pitching arm, an old ploy for my attention. The shoulder triggered memories of him, wincing in an ice bath, downing pain pills while I worried about his state of mind and our future. Not anymore.

"Wait here," I said. "I'll get the plate."

My foot crunched on the "HELLO" welcome mat. I looked down. Oh, great. Madame Iyå's lust gris-gris that I dropped last night. Forty dollars' worth of guaranteed passion. Nick and Jarret both followed me, stepping over the gris-gris on the way in. Oh well.

I went to the kitchen and rifled through my cabinets.

In the living room, Jarret started in on Nick. "I want to talk to Lizzie alone. You can leave."

"I could, but I'm not going to. Don't you have a baseball game to be at? Oh, yeah, that's right," Nick said. "Your team fell out of the play-offs."

I looked behind the dishes on the top shelf. Where was the damn pie plate?

"Didn't know girls like you followed sports, Nickster. I'm here to talk to my wife."

"Your ex-wife."

"Lizzie must be bored silly without me if she's hanging out with you," Jarret said.

"My guess is she was bored silly with you. Hell, you always were a letdown. No wonder she left you."

"You think you have a shot with her now? You want someone to mess around with? I'll give you a few numbers. This afternoon, Lizzie and I are—"

I marched into the living room with Aunt Minnie's pie plate in hand. "Are doing what, Jarret? Arguing some more? If you forgot, while you were out collecting those phone numbers and making a fool out of me, I left you. Here." I held out the plate. "Take this and leave. Nick and I are busy."

Jarret wouldn't take the plate. His face cracked into a grin. "I miss you, Lizzie Bear. C'mon. Spend the afternoon with me. We can go to your favorite restaurant for crispy fries and beer."

Nick took the plate from me, shoved it at Jarret, and smiled. "I don't think you heard her. Liz and I are leaving. Together. Time for you to go."

"You just can't get out of that old habit of butting in and telling me what to do." Jarret took a step toward Nick.

"I should have broke your arm in college when I had the chance to. Maybe you'd have a real life by now." Nick edged forward until they were nose to nose.

Jarret rolled his shoulder. "Jealous?"

Nick smirked. "Considerate."

I had no patience to mediate whatever they were acting out. "Enough." I separated them and looked up at Nick. "We don't have time for this."

Jarret scowled at me, his mouth set. "I need to talk to you."

"I'm talked out." I took his arm and led him outside.

He held up Aunt Minnie's pie plate. "This was a wedding gift?"

I nodded.

Jarret raised the plate over his head with both hands and smashed it onto the concrete. Then got into his car and drove off.

I picked up the mat littered with Madame Iyá's lust gris-gris and shook it over the railing. A wind blew the gris-gris back, into my face. Damn it. I tried to brush myself off. Forget the gris-gris; I was covered with dirt from the canyon.

Nick and Jarret bickered over me anyway? Maybe Madame Iyå had some talent.

Nick watched me from the door. "Are you going to be okay?"

"I will be when Osaze puts an end to the damned curse."

Chapter Twenty-seven

I went upstairs to wash up and swap my dusty clothing for clean jeans and a T-shirt. I removed the bandage from my cheek and dabbed ointment on the cut. When I came back down, Nick was tossing the pieces of Aunt Minnie's pie plate into the trash.

He brushed off his hands and held the front door open. "Did you know Jarret would be here?"

I shot a look at him. "Of course I didn't know. Why the hell would I invite Jarret over?"

"Lunch?"

"Not funny."

Nick opened the car door for me, then got in the driver's seat. We drove in silence. I stared out the car window, my mind arcing from fury at my mother to worry about Robin to the mental image of Tawny's twisted body in the canyon.

"Want to talk about it?" Nick said.

"You mean Jarret?"

"No, I mean what happened this morning."

"No." But I did want to. Tears welled in my eyes, then rolled down my cheeks. I turned away and wiped my face. "I'm worried about the other people in the spell book. Robin freaked when I brought up the curse. I don't know what to believe. One death is a coincidence, but two? Within thirty-six hours?"

"I know." He stopped for a red light on Vineland. "A death each day since Sophie was murdered. The momentum of Callia's curse is intensifying."

"Nola told me Callia was adamant about protecting her secrets. The spell book belongs with Nola and the family."

"We have to give it to the police," Nick said. "I don't see how returning the spell book to the family would change the curse or help solve Sophie's murder. As time passes, the trail to the killer will go cold. Do you think Buzzy or Tawny killed Sophie?"

I shook my head. "Buzzy had an alibi. Tawny wasn't at the Greek that night. Why are you so intent on putting the spell book into evidence? Robin's initials will incriminate her even more. She's being arraigned on Monday—why stack the evidence against her?"

"You're certain she's innocent?"

"Yes." I snapped out the word. "We need to talk to Madame Iyå again, too."

"L. M. and H. M. have to be warned about the curse first."

"Linda and Henry," I said. "When I tell them Osaze reversed the curse, maybe they'll open up. I need information to give to Barnes. The police have blood evidence and an alleged witness. We have nothing but a spell book. We're losing."

"Have faith, Liz," Nick said. "Let your intuition guide you. Thinking and plotting cloud your instincts."

"Now I know the world is upside down—I'm talking about spell books and you're playing psychologist."

Nick turned onto the freeway ramp toward Hollywood. "Just making conversation."

"You want conversation? Okay," I said. "I know you and Jarret weren't friends in college, but why did you want to break his arm? What was that about?"

"It doesn't matter. It was a long time ago." Nick put the radio on.

I turned the radio off. "Catch me up."

"It was nothing."

"A nothing that came up again today."

Nick adjusted his rearview mirror, clicked on the turn signal, and changed lanes toward the Vine Street exit.

"Damn it, Nick. Tell me what happened."

He paused. "I caught him in bed with a girl at a frat party."

An unexpected pang pinched my heart. I thought Jarret's affairs started when our marriage soured. Asshole. "What did you do?"

"I told him if I ever caught him cheating on you again, I'd break his pitching arm," Nick said.

"Why didn't you tell me? Did you tell Dave?"

"No. You seemed so happy at the time. I didn't think you'd appreciate me butting in. Would you have believed me?"

"Probably not." I remembered how infatuated I was with Jarret in college. So proud of my engagement to the star college baseball pitcher, so excited about our future together, so blinded to his faults. I knew he drank, but I thought it was a phase. I didn't know about the girls. "Thanks for telling me. No more secrets—okay, Nick?"

"Okay, Liz."

I caught the flash of his grin. "Is there anything else you want to share?"

"I don't think so."

"Are you sure? What about your engagement over the summer?"

Nick laughed.

"That's funny?" I said.

"Yeah, it is. Where'd you hear that?"

"Dave."

"You misunderstood." He stopped for a red light on Hollywood Boulevard.

"He said *engagement*. Hard to misunderstand one big word," I said.

"One word is not the whole story. The engagement story was a fabrication, not my idea. Last summer I did research in Playa Del Alma, a village in Costa Rica. I met a family whose daughter, Isabella, was keen on attending college here in the states. Her grandfather forbade her to leave the village unless she was married. So, Isabella told him we were engaged."

"And you brought her here?" I leaned against the car door. My mind spun visions of Nick and a Latin beauty. Why did I ask?

"Isabella came here on her own to attend UCLA. Her parents always knew the truth. I talk to her on occasion. But I'm very happy with the company I'm keeping right now." Nick reached for my chin and leaned over to kiss me. A horn blasted behind us. Monty's Glass Repair's fist-waving driver was not a romantic, and I slid away, unconvinced.

"I want you to meet Isabella," Nick said. "I think you will like each other. I'll explain to Dave again. My fault for not being clear with him."

"Maybe he didn't want me to steal away his best friend," I said. "Dave's not good at sharing."

"Is that what you're planning? Sharing my friendship with Dave? I had something more romantic in mind."

"Like sweeping me off my feet by getting my best friend convicted?"

We turned onto Osaze's street. A white sedan with an open trunk was parked in his driveway. Boxes were stacked on the asphalt. A young woman with jet-black hair was picking up one of the boxes. She looked up as Nick backed into a parking space.

I did a double take. "Nick—I think that's Sophie's cousin Nola."

He looked in the driveway. "Nola? That's Osaze's daughter, Noemi."

"Hold it." I stopped him before he opened the car door. "Nola is Osaze's daughter?"

"That's who you call Nola?"

"Yes. Didn't you recognize her at the party?"

"I didn't see her. That's definitely Noemi. I gave her that Mardi Gras sweatshirt she's wearing as a sixteenth birthday present."

"Do you know what this means?" I said. "Sophie was Osaze's niece. Callia's spell book belongs to his family."

Nick cocked his head, his brow wrinkled.

"Uncle Nick?" Nola tapped at Nick's window. Her smile dropped into a frown when she saw me in the passenger's seat. Nick got out of the car and hugged her. I tucked the spell book under my arm and joined them in street.

"You two know each other?" Nola looked from me to Nick.

"We're old friends," Nick said.

Osaze came out onto his porch and held the door open for a beautiful Latino woman. The top of her wavy black hair stopped beneath Osaze's chin. A silver crucifix hung from a chain above the green V-necked sweater covering her ample bosom. Nick waved, and the woman broke into a wide smile. We started toward them—Nick with his arm around Nola's shoulders, and me, close behind.

Nick said to Nola as we walked, "Where did this Nola moniker come from? Did you change your name?"

She grinned up at him. "When I graduated beauty school, I wanted to name my business 'Noemi of Los Angeles' or 'Noemi of LA.' My friend Linda decided it should be called 'NoLA.' Capital *N*, small *o*, and capital *L-A*." Nola scribbled it out in the air. "Linda started calling me Nola, and it stuck. You can keep calling me Noemi, Uncle Nick."

"Which do you prefer?" he said.

"I like Nola if you can get used to it. It's been so long since I've seen you. Why are you here?"

"We came to show this to your father." I held up the spell book.

Nola stopped. "Amazing. You found it. Where?"

"Sophie left it at Collins Talent," I said.

When we got to the porch, Nick shook Osaze's hand and kissed the woman's cheek.

Osaze smiled at me. "Ah, the beautiful Elizabeth." He turned to the woman. "This is my wife, Ivalisse. Ivalisse, this is our new friend, Elizabeth."

Ivalisse greeted me with a radiant, dignified smile. "It's nice to meet you. Please, come in. I made lunch."

She led us inside. Nick and Osaze went into the living room. Ivalisse started toward the back of the house. As I lingered in the foyer to talk to Nola, I saw Madame Iyå's son, Jimmy, coming down the hall toward us.

"It's the sexy lady from last night," he said to me. "Hello again." His eyes shifted to the spell book.

"Hello again." I tensed, then forced a smile. After Osaze's condemnation of Madame Iyå the other day, I didn't expect to see Jimmy here. I clutched the spell book to my chest.

Nola tugged at Jimmy's sleeve. "Do you mind bringing the rest of Sophie's boxes inside for me? I'll meet you and Linda at the apartment later. I want to talk to my father about something."

"Yeah," Jimmy said. "No problem. I'll finish up and then I'll see you back there."

Nick called from the living room, "Liz, come in here—I want Osaze to see the spell book."

I joined him on the beige Victorian sofa and set the spell book on the coffee table. Sheer white curtains beneath claret jacquard drapery covered the bay window behind us. Osaze was on a straight-backed Queen Anne chair across the room. Nola sat cross-legged on the floor at Osaze's feet.

"You didn't tell me that the spell book belonged to your family," Nick said to Osaze.

Osaze folded his hands and bowed his head. Then he looked at Nick and me. "I had to see it to be certain. The less we speak of its existence and the less known of my family's connection to it, the better. Callia placed powerful protections on her work. She was very specific with her instructions to the spirits, and they've been obedient to her for over a century."

"Those protections are in motion now," Nick said. "Since you and I talked this morning, another of Sophie's spell customers who defied the curse died. That makes two of the five Sophie listed. The others are at risk, including a close friend of Liz's. We need to know if you can stop the curse."

"I warned Sophie about using the spell book." Osaze rubbed a hand across his forehead. "It was rightfully hers, but she was young, too impatient to wait for her initiation as a Vodoun priestess. She didn't yet understand the extent of the power Callia bestowed on female descendants or the force of the curse. She'll never know now."

I saw the pain in his face. "I'm sorry for your loss. Sophie was a beautiful young woman."

"Thank you. Our hearts are broken," he said. "I have to consult my spirit guides for instructions from Callia. The spell book was empowered to obey direct female descendants. Now that Sophie is gone, the daughter-to-daughter lineage is finished."

"Who controls the spell book now?" Nick said.

"What about me?" Nola said, looking up at her father.

"You are the daughter of a son, dear one, and loved deeply," Osaze said, quietly. "But Callia's power cannot be passed on to you. You must create your own mastery with spirit. When it's time, I will teach you."

"We have to put Callia's voodoo to rest." Nick leaned forward with his fingers laced between his knees.

"You are correct to worry, Nicolas," Osaze said. "What was put into action cannot be stopped. Anyone who bought a spell and defied the curse remains under the absolute threat of the spirits who protected Callia. We can't call off the spirits once a curse is in action. And if you try to stop them, they will turn on you."

"You have to find a way to end it," Nick said.

Ivalisse came into the room, wiping her hands. "Lunch is ready."

We followed her into the kitchen. A glass pitcher of lemonade sat in the middle of the table next to a large platter of tuna-salad sandwiches on toast.

I was halfway into my chair, then remembered the spell book sitting on the coffee table. Jimmy had come back into the house with more boxes while we were in the living room, but I didn't see him leave. I got up and excused myself. A taupe kitten scampered past me in the hall and darted into the living room.

I heard a hiss, then Jimmy's voice. "Scram, you rodent."

When I entered the room, Jimmy was tucking the spell book into his jacket.

"What are you doing?" I said.

I glanced down the hall to call for Nick and Osaze. Then I heard a click. Jimmy grabbed my arm and pushed me into the hall against the front door.

He put the tip of his switchblade to my throat. "Scream and I'll cut you."

My heart pounded. I lifted my chin to pull away from the sharp metal. He pinned me to the door. Seconds passed. Jimmy didn't know what to do with me. He couldn't get out without moving me somewhere.

I knew this kid. He was a momma's boy. He followed instructions. Madame Iyå wasn't there to tell him what to do.

"Stealing won't help your mother." My pulse raced. "The spell book is cursed. Remember how Callia's spirit slammed the door at the séance? Imagine what Callia would do if you stole her secrets. Leave the spell book, Jimmy."

He kept his eyes on me, shaking his head no.

Jimmy was a knife wielder; Sophie was beaten to death. Jimmy couldn't have been her killer.

"The police will be looking for the spell book," I said, my voice soothing. "I won't say anything. But they will figure out you took it. The police will go to your mother. It won't look good. You'll both be under suspicion for Sophie's murder. That would be wrong. It would break your mother's heart, wouldn't it, Jimmy?"

He moved the knife off my throat. "My mother didn't kill Sophie."

"I know," I said. "And neither did you. Leave the spell book here, Jimmy. You have to protect your mother."

"I . . ." Jimmy backed away. He touched the spell book under his jacket.

"What's taking you so long?" Nick's voice came from the kitchen door.

The blade in Jimmy's hand glinted; sweat beaded his forehead. He slid the knife up his sleeve as Nick came down the hall.

"I forgot where I left the spell book. Jimmy helped me find it. Thanks so much." I took the spell book from Jimmy and nodded. "If I don't see you again, please send your mother my best."

Jimmy bolted out the front door.

I leaned against the doorjamb to steady my wobbly knees. When I found my breath I said to Nick, "One more person off the suspect list."

"What does that mean?"

I explained my thinking.

"You figured he wasn't the killer because he had a knife and Sophie was beaten?" Nick's face was red, his voice strident. "Where did you come up with that? I'm no cop, but I never heard a theory like that. You could have been killed."

"Nick, I knew. Everything inside of me said he wasn't the killer."

"I buy your reasoning only because he didn't knife you. If he did kill Sophie in an attempt to get the spell book away from her, then he wouldn't hesitate to kill you to keep it." Nick pulled his phone from his pocket.

"What are you doing?"

"I'm calling Dave to have Jimmy picked up."

"No." I took his hand and stopped him from dialing. "Then you'll have to tell Dave about the book. And swear you won't say anything to Osaze and the others. Let it go. I want the time you promised me."

Nick hesitated, looking from me to his phone to the street and then back to me. He blew out a frustrated breath and shoved the phone back into his pocket. "Fine. But that's it. You're not leaving my sight."

"Fine with me," I said. "I could use the backup."

We walked to the kitchen. Ivalisse, Nola, and Osaze were already eating.

Nick sat down and reached for a tuna sandwich. "Liz, tell Osaze what happened at the séance."

I looked at Nola. "Didn't you tell him yet?"

She stopped midbite, furrowed her brow, and shook her head.

"What séance?" Osaze reached for the lemonade.

"A few of us gathered at Sophie's apartment last night: Me. Nola. Sophie's roommate, Linda. A neighbor, and some friends. Madame Iyå led the . . ." The words came out before I remembered Osaze's disgust with the woman.

Osaze slammed his glass, spilling lemonade onto the tablecloth. "Madame Iyå?" He glared at Nola. "You let a con artist use Sophie's memory for personal profit? I thought you had better sense than that, Noemi. Then you invite her worthless son to my house today? I told you to stay away from that pair. What's wrong with you?"

Nola shot me a thanks-a-lot look, then said to Osaze, "The séance wasn't my idea. Linda made all the arrangements. I had to be there—to make sure Madame Iyå treated Sophie with respect, Father. I can't stop Linda from hanging out with Madame Iyå or Jimmy. It was Linda's idea for him to carry the boxes here, too."

Ivalisse lifted an eyebrow. "That's a first—you taking orders from your friends."

Nola shrugged and bit into her sandwich.

"Something occurred at the séance that Madame Iyå had no control of." I described Linda's outburst.

Osaze sat back with his arms folded. "I'm not surprised. Callia wanted the spell book returned to the family."

"But why choose me for the task?" I scooped a bit of tuna on my finger and dropped my hand to the side of my chair. The taupe kitten, next to my chair, licked it off.

"She trusted you," Ivalisse said.

Chapter Twenty-eight

Osaze rose from his chair at the table. "If you'll excuse me, I want to spend a few moments alone in the sanctuary to seek guidance." He picked up the spell book and walked out the back door, the taupe kitten trotting behind him.

Ivalisse and Nola started the dishes. Nick and I cleared the table, navigating around each other in the small kitchen until Nick gave up and leaned against the yellow tiled counter. Ivalisse washed. I dried. Nola stacked clean plates in the white overhead cabinets.

"Is Linda at the apartment today?" I said, handing Nola a glass. "I want to talk to her."

"Yeah, I'm meeting her as soon as we finish here," Nola said. "What about?"

I hesitated, unfamiliar with the conventions of voodoo curses. Does the curse make a judgment on a gray area like a third-party mention? I already danced around the curse with Robin; did it matter how many other people I talked to? I shrugged.

"Well, hell, if you don't want to say, then never mind," Nola said. "I'll tell Linda to wait for you."

"Watch your mouth, Noemi." Ivalisse dried her hands on a dishtowel. She gave Nick the pitcher of lemonade to put in the refrigerator. "Osaze is ready for you."

I glanced out the kitchen window. The door to the sanctuary was ajar. Ivalisse shooed the three of us out of the kitchen. Nola left for the apartment. Nick and I crossed the backyard.

Candlelight flickered behind skulls on the shelves inside the sanctuary. Osaze, eyes closed and palms tented to his lips, sat on the velvet throne at the far end of the room. Nick slipped into the chair next to him. I took a bench to the side.

Osaze began to speak. "There is disruptive energy from spirits safeguarding Callia's secrets. Sophie's death stirred anger and revenge. Time is running out. Each new moon heightens the momentum of the curse in its obedience to Callia's mandate. The threat to those who breached their promise is imminent." He looked over to me. "Callia is grateful the spell book has returned to our family. I have her sanction to destroy it and release the curse."

The tension in my shoulders relaxed. "Can you release it now?"

"Tonight," Osaze said. "I will burn the spell book under the waning moon. The curse will dissipate in the ashes."

"And anyone under the influence of the curse will be safe?" I said.

"Yes."

"Osaze." Nick leaned forward in his chair. "We can't burn the book. What about a reversal spell?"

"A reversal spell turns the voodoo back at my family," Osaze said. "The curse is attached to the spell book. Why don't you want it destroyed, Nicolas?"

"The spell book is evidence in Sophie's murder," Nick said. "I have to give it to the police."

Osaze's brow creased. "How is it evidence?"

"Burn it." I tapped my foot.

Nick turned to me. "Robin's lawyer will want to see it, too."

I winced.

"Who is Robin?" Osaze said.

"She's my friend," I started carefully, searching for a way to explain.

Nick didn't seem to mind explaining for me. "Robin is a suspect in Sophie's murder. Robin and Sophie argued the night Sophie died."

Osaze frowned.

"I'm sorry, Osaze," I said. "I should have told you sooner. The police used their argument as a motive to link Robin to the crime."

"But they can also use the spell book to broaden their investigation," Nick said.

"To whom?" I snapped back. "Henry and Linda? More likely that they'll see Robin's initials and stop there."

"What was their argument about?" Osaze said to me.

"The tarot cards we showed you were used to harass Robin," I said. "Madame Iyå told me she gave the only copy of the deck to Sophie. Because of that, we assumed Sophie left the cards on Robin's door."

"Proof by assumption?" Osaze said.

I shifted on the bench, unwilling to discredit Sophie to Osaze. "It was foolish of Robin to accuse Sophie without more proof. But I promise you that Robin didn't hurt her. I've known Robin my whole life. She's not a killer."

"Do the police have evidence against the woman?" Osaze said.

"Evidence that was planted," I said. "Robin is innocent."

"Innocent because she's your friend or because you have proof? You judged Sophie without confirmation but you can acquit the accused because you think you know her well? We see the best sides of our friends and loved ones, Elizabeth, absolving them from blame."

"All the more reason to turn the spell book over to the police," Nick said. "Let them pore through it and find a clue to the killer."

"They won't." I stood in front of Nick and crossed my arms. Maybe a kick in the shins would keep him quiet. "Putting the spell book in evidence will exacerbate the problem."

"Enough. The woman purchased a spell?" Osaze looked at me, his eyes cold and piercing. "Explain how you had the audacity to come here and ask me to help someone accused of killing my niece. The truth."

I put my hand to my heart. "I'm sorry if I offended you. Despite the evidence, I believe in Robin. When she's arraigned on Monday, her life will be turned upside down, and the person who really murdered Sophie will go free. We weren't aware that Sophie was your niece, Osaze. We came, hoping you could end the curse. Two of Sophie's clients are dead. I'm frightened for the other three."

Osaze tented his hands under his chin. "Those three bought spells with their own free will, advised and aware of the consequences of the curse. Are you truly so frightened for them? Or are you eager for me to burn the spell book based on a desire to destroy it as evidence? If the spell book will help bring my niece's killer to justice, then Nicolas is right. It must be turned over to the police. Why should I help my niece's alleged killer? Let her choices direct her fate."

"What about the other two?" Nick said.

Osaze shrugged.

"Henry's an elderly man, an innocent. Linda was Sophie's roommate and close friend." I brushed a bead of sweat from my forehead. "Surely you wouldn't let them stand in harm's way."

Osaze paused. "I can create a hex breaker to protect them, but it requires the presence of the cursed. The initiation is complex—bathing in oils, talismans, and daily incantations. Bring the old man and the girl here tonight. I'll take their presence as proof of your altruism, Elizabeth. Tomorrow I will call the detectives and give them the spell book."

Nick paced between the shelves of skulls. "The DA is up for reelection next month. A quick prosecution on a sensational case would look good."

Osaze threw his head back and laughed at Nick's last sentence. Curious, I waited for an explanation.

Instead, he said to Nick, "Do you believe in the woman's innocence?"

"Liz is passionate about it. I believe in her."

I was warmed by Nick's confidence in me but still angry with him. If it weren't for his big mouth, the spell book would be burned.

"We'll make certain the two come tonight," Nick said.

"What about Robin?" I said. "The police will question her about her initials in the spell book. She'll be forced to explain, and she'll unleash the curse."

"When you can prove her innocence, I will help her," Osaze said. "Until then, Callia will decide how the curse plays out."

"There are others." I picked up the spell book and flipped through the pages until I found the "Safety Spell." I held the page in front of Osaze. "Look."

Osaze studied the entries. Nick read over his shoulder. There were lines of initialed signatures, each dated 2005 in the same wobbly penmanship.

"That's my mother's handwriting." Osaze set the spell book on his lap, and his eyes drifted to the floor. "She must have shared spells with evacuees in Houston after the hurricane. So many lost everything."

"Your mother tried to help them," I said, kneeling in front of him. "They should be protected, too. We can't track all these people down for you to perform a hex-breaker. The only way to keep everyone safe is to burn the book."

The sanctuary was silent. Nick stared at the floor. Osaze gazed across the room to the lantern lit above the altar. I looked from one to the other and waited.

Osaze opened his hands on his lap, palms up. "It pains me to allow the curse to menace so many when I know how to end it. But I want the killer brought to justice. And if the spell book aids a conviction, it must go to the police. This afternoon I will pray to the Iwa to guide the two of you to a suitable resolution. Then I will prepare for the ceremony and your return."

Osaze began to walk through the sanctuary, blowing out candles until he reached the door. Nick and I followed and we walked to the main house together.

Before we entered the back door, Osaze took me aside. "I will pray for the spirits to accompany you, Elizabeth. Pay attention. If your friend is indeed innocent, they will guide you."

Oh, great. More voices.

Inside, Ivalisse was at the stove. The kitchen was filled with the scent of garlic and onion, coming from the pot she stirred.

"Ivalisse," Osaze said. "Gather the group. We're performing a ritual tonight."

She lowered the gas flame to simmer and set down the spoon. "Everyone?"

"Yes," Osaze said. "The energy must be powerful. Prepare food and music to please the spirits. I am breaking Callia's curse."

Ivalisse raised her eyebrows, then smiled. She looked from Osaze to Nick to me, opened a drawer, and took out a notebook. We left her at the phone, making calls.

At the front door, Osaze shook Nick's hand and kissed mine. He said, "The ritual will be at midnight. Go in peace."

Nick and I crossed the street to his car. The late afternoon sun glistened behind pink and gray clouds. A cool breeze rustled through the trees. I pulled my jacket closed and lowered my head.

Nick wrapped an arm around my shoulder. "Don't worry, Liz. We're doing what we can."

"I am worried. How does any of this hoodoo help Robin? We need someone to give us a lead, not a ritual." I slid into the passenger seat. My cell phone rang.

My mother. "Is Jarret on the way with the pie plate or are you two still busy talking?"

I bit my lip to hold back my fury. "Find another pie plate. Jarret left hours ago without it. I'm in Hollywood with Nick."

"Oh."

"Don't ever send Jarret to my house again, Mom. Let go. I did."

"I don't want you to be lonely," she said.

"I'm not. I'm happy with the company I'm keeping." I glanced at Nick as he steered the car into the street.

"What are you two doing?" my mother said.

"We're trying to help Robin," I said.

"Put Nick on the phone."

"I can't. He's driving."

"Just put him on the phone."

I tapped Nick's sleeve and handed him the phone.

He drove with his left hand and held the phone to his ear with his right. "Hi, Vivian." His eyes stayed on traffic; his head bobbed as she talked. "Okay . . . Okay . . . I see . . . Thanks, yes, good-bye."

He hung up and handed me the phone.

My cheeks burned with embarrassment. "What did she say?"

Nick smiled. "She threatened to have your father and brother beat the crap out of me if I took advantage of you."

I burst into laughter, then sobered. My mother has said worse. "Did she really?"

"I'm kidding." He chuckled. "Your mother wants to help

Robin, too. She pulled a tarot card on Sophie's killer this afternoon. She wanted to tell me because she knew I'd believe her."

Of course she'd think that. "And?"

"And she pulled the Page of Pentacles, reversed." Nick turned right onto Melrose Avenue. "The Page of Pentacles is someone young, could be female, and opportunistic, but the card reversed makes her lazy, a saboteur, or a rebel. Sound familiar?"

"No. Maybe Linda will know." I stared out the window. The neon lights from the shops on Melrose glared at me. "Tell me again why turning the spell book in to the police will help Robin? I can't think of a reason."

"It keeps you and me out of jail. It's better for Osaze to hand it in. Robin, Nola, and Ivalisse knew we had it—and Jimmy, which means Madame Iyå knows, too. If any one of them told the authorities, we could be charged with concealing evidence."

"I see."

"And the police would assume we held back the spell book to aid and abet Robin. Now, if asked, we tell them we saw it belonged to the family and returned it to Osaze without reading it."

"I understand," I said. "Now explain what was so funny about the DA's reelection. Why did Osaze laugh?"

"I brought the DA up for a reason." Nick turned onto Henry and Linda's street. "Osaze went to college in Haiti to avoid the draft. While he lived there, two significant events occurred—he met Ivalisse, and he joined the Haitian resistance to overthrow the dictatorship. He still funds the rebels down there. Osaze doesn't trust authority."

"But he's turning over the spell book."

"Maybe."

I whispered, "I hope you're right. I hate this."

Nick backed into a parking spot in front of Henry's building. "We're not giving up yet."

Chapter Twenty-nine

The curtain in Henry's front window parted and his delighted smile caught my heart as Nick and I walked up the front steps. He buzzed us in and was waiting outside his apartment door when we entered the foyer.

"Two days in a row." He grinned.

"Can't get enough of you." I kissed Henry's cheek and stepped aside. "This is Nick Garfield."

"Your boyfriend?" Henry reached to shake Nick's hand. "You're a lucky man. Maybe you two want to rent an apartment from me? No vacancy, but I'll put you first in line."

I held up a hand to stop Henry before he had us married. "No. Thanks. Do you have a few minutes to talk?"

"Sure," Henry said. "Come inside. I'm cooking dinner."

Henry's apartment smelled like a cherry tobacco–glazed pork roast. On his television, a photo of Sophie flashed above a "Suspect in Custody" caption. I moved in front of the TV so Henry wouldn't see.

Nick strolled across the living room to the china cabinet on the far wall. Henry followed and pointed with enthusiasm at the logo-embedded china on the shelves. "Are you familiar with the Super Chief, Nick?"

"I am," Nick said. "My grandfather was a machinist in the Chicago rail yards. Great stories."

"I rode the Super Chief. Let me show you something." Henry reached for his scrapbook.

I stopped behind them. "Maybe you two could swap railroad stories tonight at Osaze's."

Henry set down the scrapbook. "Tonight?"

"Yes," Nick said. "We came to invite you to a—"

"Get-together," I said.

"Not another séance, I hope." Henry laughed. "One a year is my limit."

"It's not a séance, but . . . Let's sit for a minute, okay?" I settled onto the couch.

Henry shut off the TV and sat in his armchair. He studied me; his eyes creased, his brows furrowed. "What's this about?"

"Before she died, Sophie sold voodoo spells with a curse. Sophie's uncle Osaze is gathering some of her friends at his home tonight to break that curse."

"It has nothing to do with me," Henry said.

"We saw your initials, H. M., in her spell book, beneath a spell for 'Home Safety.' You may be in danger," Nick said.

Henry reached for his scrapbook. He pushed the side of it with his finger, straightening the edge to align it with the table corner. "Why do you think the initials belong to me? H. M. could be a lot of people."

"Could be, but I thought of you first," I said.

"You could be wrong." He looked away.

"But if I'm not . . ."

Nick sat forward. "Here's the deal, Henry. We know Sophie's spells came with a warning and a curse. Unfortunately, two of Sophie's clients ignored the warning. They died in accidents."

"What's he saying, Liz?" Henry's hand quivered on his knee. "Who died?"

I left the couch and crouched down at Henry's side. With my hand resting on his, I said, gently, "One was a publicist Sophie knew and the other was Tawny—the girl you met last night."

Henry dropped his head and sighed. "You think I ignore warnings? I don't. Enough said."

"I know you're cautious, Henry. When Osaze ends the curse, no one will have to worry about what they say. But to be protected, the spell buyers have to be at the ritual. I want you there. I know you and Sophie were close, shared secrets. Please say you'll come." I squeezed his hand, not willing to let go until he said yes.

"Maybe I'll drop by to give my respects to Sophie's family but I'm not saying H. M. is me. Leave the uncle's address, and I'll think about it. When is it?"

"Tonight, at midnight," Nick said.

"Midnight?" Henry laughed and waved me away. "I'll be in bed."

Oh, great. I pressed my lips together and looked at Nick.

"Liz told me you're a good sport," Nick said. "Even if you're not the H. M. in the spell book, her uncle asked us to gather the folks dear to Sophie. The spells she sold were more powerful than she knew. Spirits were stirred up, and they're targeting people and places closest to her. You'd be doing all of her friends a favor by being there. Linda will be there. So will Nola. Will you help us out and attend?"

Henry rubbed his chin, then nodded. "But you should tell every H. M. you know. I'm not the only one in this city."

"We will," Nick said. "We'll explain more after the ritual is over."

"Not necessary," Henry said. "The less I know, the better."

I pulled a notebook from my purse, wrote out Osaze's address along with my phone number, and gave the paper to Henry. "We'll be there at eleven."

He led us to the door. "So late. I hope I can stay awake until then."

I stopped on the threshold. "Henry, Sophie needs you there. Do you want us to drive you?"

"No, no. I'll be there." Henry saluted me and closed the door.

"'Sophie needs you there'? That's odd, coming from you," Nick said as we walked down the hall together.

"Whatever works. She popped into my mind. But damn, I forgot to ask Henry about Sophie's visitors."

"You can quiz him tonight. After the ritual, Henry will be free to tell you whatever you ask," Nick said.

"I just don't know if we're on the right track. Robin is sitting in jail while we do invites to a hex-breaker. We should be looking for suspects."

Nick took me by the arm. "By the way, did Robin admit she bought a spell when you talked to her?"

"She didn't deny it, but we were careful." I searched his

face. "Did I do something wrong? You told me the terms of the curse were literal."

"No. You did nothing wrong. But one of the draws of voodoo is the effect on the mind. If Robin thinks she broke the covenant, the worry could torment her, make her unstable, open to harm."

"Thanks for planting that in my mind. If you had let Osaze burn the damn spell book, everyone involved would be safe . . . and sane." I twisted out of Nick's grasp and knocked on Linda's door.

"Where the hell have you been? It's open." The voice sounded like Nola.

We walked in. Nola and Linda were across the room, lifting the sofa. Linda's face was bright red. The sofa tilted as she struggled to hold up her side.

"We stopped to talk to Henry," I said.

"Liz." Linda panted. "We thought you were Jimmy. He never showed up to help us move the furniture."

Nola looked at us over her shoulder. "Hey, Uncle Nick. Can you lend a hand here? Linda's out of gas, and I can't move this thing myself."

"Both of you—put the sofa down. Let me do that." Nick darted past me toward the girls.

While he moved one side of the sofa, and then the other, to the center of the room, Nola said, "Linda, this is my uncle Nick. He and the shrink are pals."

"You came in the *nick* of time." Linda moved a strand of sweaty hair from her forehead and giggled.

"Will you help me lift the entertainment unit, too?" Nola said.

"Hold it," I said. "We need to talk to you first."

"Can we talk while we work?" Linda said. "The painters will be here in the morning. We need to finish packing Sophie's bedroom."

I released a breath to keep from screaming in frustration. "No. I need your attention. I have disturbing news."

Linda and Nola plopped onto the sofa.

"Nola already told me about Buzzy and Tawny," Linda said. "It's horrible, so sad."

"There's more to it. Buzzy and Tawny bought cursed voodoo spells from Sophie, and the curse turned on them." I looked at Nola. "Your father created a hex-breaker to protect the rest of her clients. He's doing the ritual tonight."

"You have to be there, Linda. The hex-breaker will protect you," Nick said.

Linda fingered a small cross hanging around her neck. She looked confused. "Protect me? I don't practice the occult. I'm a Christian. I had nothing to do with Sophie's voodoo."

"But you lived together . . ." I searched Linda's face.

"Sophie and I agreed to keep beliefs out of our friendship. The only voodoo I know about is the spell Sophie used on Sam," Linda said.

My mind swam. "If you don't believe in the occult, why did you host the séance?"

"The séance was Jimmy's idea," Linda said. "I agreed to host it for Sophie's friends. I thought gathering everyone to connect with her spirit would bring us all comfort. I'm glad we did. I felt meditative, closer to Sophie last night."

Meditative? Linda had scared the crap out of me when she was in her trance.

"But I saw your initials in Sophie's spell book," I said.

Linda cocked her head. "In a spell book?"

"Beneath a 'Fame' spell," Nick said.

"It wasn't me. I don't believe in the occult. The initials belong to someone else."

Nick stood over Linda and Nola. His eyes drilled into them. "You both know Sophie's friends. Who could L. M. be? Think."

Linda flinched. "Um, L, okay. L-A, Laura? L-I, Lisa?"

"Oh, for crap's sake," Nola interrupted. "It's probably Lulu."

"Of course," Linda said. "I totally forgot about her."

Yes. The whisper brushed through my mind. "What's Lulu's last name?"

"Don't have a clue." Nola shrugged and looked at Linda.

Linda shook her head.

"You're friends," I said.

"Not me," Linda said. "Sophie and I met Lulu in Hissy's class."

"We barely talked until Lulu intro'd Sophie to Sam at a video shoot I worked on for a Collins client," Nola said. "After that, Lulu and Sophie became chummy. Lulu's a goofy chick. Always claimed she'd be famous one day and would need my services for her hair and makeup. As if."

I looked at Nick. "The 'Fame' spell."

Nick nodded, then said to the girls, "We need Lulu's last name now. If she is the L. M. in the spell book, Lulu's at risk until Osaze conducts the hex-breaker."

"The receptionist at Hissy Fit will know." Nola bounded across the room for the phone. When Nola finished the call, she said, "Manchester. Her name is Lulu Manchester."

I pulled out my cell phone and dialed Collins Talent. The call went to voice mail.

"This is Liz Cooper, I'm calling for Lulu Manchester. Lulu, if you get this message, please call me. It's important." I left my number, hung up, and checked my watch—close to five. "Nick, we have to get over to Collins now to warn Lulu and get her to the ritual."

Before I slid my cell back in my pocket, Nick was at the door, keys in hand, "Let's go."

We rushed outside and got in the car. I redialed Collins Talent again. Voice mail.

"Call Nola. See if Hissy Fit will give her Lulu's home number," Nick said.

We were in the thick of West Hollywood traffic when Nola called me back. "No go. Confidential, blah, blah. She wouldn't even call Lulu and leave a message for me. Sorry."

I put my phone in my pocket. "Damn."

"What if the office is empty? Then what?"

"I'll see if I can get up there. Robin keeps a card file of numbers on her desk. Lulu's number must be in it."

Nick sped up.

Chapter Thirty

Beverly Hills was strained with street and sidewalk traffic. Streams of Mercedes-Benz sedans, BMW convertibles, and Range Rovers nudged ahead of us up Camden Drive. When we passed the "Guest Parking Full" sign at the entrance to the Collins Talent garage, Nick winced.

"Drop me off and circle the block," I said. "There's a public lot across the street. You can park there or wait in front. If Lulu's not here, it won't take me long to search Robin's file for her home number."

Nick pulled to the curb and rubbed my shoulder. "Call me when you get upstairs."

I left him and ran up the rose marble steps, then through the glass doors. A silver-haired old man in a blue security uniform was reading a newspaper behind the security desk. He looked up as I crossed the lobby.

"Hi. I'm Liz Cooper. I'm here to see Lulu Manchester at Collins Talent." I signed the guest register.

"We already locked the elevators. Is she expecting you?"

I straightened my shoulders and raised my chin. "Yes."

"Let me call up there. I'm not supposed to let visitors up unannounced." He dialed, then said, "This is security. There's a visitor waiting in the lobby for Miss Manchester." The guard looked at me. "I left a message. No answer."

I bit my lip. Now what? I slipped a hand into my pocket, pulled out my cell phone, and held it up. "Sam Collins left his cell phone at my office today. He's waiting for me to return it. He needs it tonight."

"You said you're here for Miss Manchester."

"She's his assistant. Maybe they're in a meeting. I'm sorry, but my friend is waiting for me out front in his car. Can you possibly escort me up?"

The guard looked me over. "I can't leave my post. But you look honest, and I don't want Mr. Collins to get angry. I'll unlock the elevator for you." He ambled to the bank of elevators near the back of the lobby and turned a key next to the fifth-floor button in the waiting car. "Call me on extension three-four-three when you're done. I'll send the car back for you. Or you can take the stairs if you want some exercise. Have a good evening, miss."

The elevator opened on the fifth floor. The overhead lights were dimmed, the corridor was empty, but the lava lamp on Lulu's desk was still on. I heard someone talking and followed the sound, coughing to announce myself.

The voice came from Robin's office. Robin's family photos and her favorite Bodega vase lay on top of a box of colored files outside the door. I peeked in. Lulu was on the phone, sitting behind the desk in a faded "Lou Reed" T-shirt; her sneaker-clad feet rested on the desktop. Her hair was wild, her lips painted a deathly gray-mauve. An array of laminated passes on multicolored lanyards hung from the corner of the computer screen. A vintage Janis Joplin poster was taped to the back wall. Empty paper cups were piled in the wastebasket. The office looked like the backroom office of a repair shop.

"I'm positive, Sam. You told me six o'clock, not five. I'll call the messenger back and make it a rush. I'll fix it . . . shit." Lulu moved her feet to the floor, hung up, and buried her head in her arms on a stack of papers.

I wanted to hug her out of sheer joy at the sight of her. A pile of boxes and files on the floor blocked my path. "Thank God."

Lulu looked up and grimaced. "What are you doing here?" She pulled Robin's Rolodex file toward her and rifled through it. "Wait, one sec. I have to call the damned messenger service before . . . Crap. Why doesn't she keep her numbers in the computer like everyone else in the world does?"

The phone rang. Lulu peered at the number on the screen, then picked up. "Hello?" She held up a finger for me to wait as she talked. "Sound check is at eight. I go on at ten. Okay, cool. Make sure the engineer has my new set list. See ya then. Bye." She hung up and raised an eyebrow at me. "Hi?"

"I thought you weren't here. I called several times. Didn't you get my messages?"

"Messages?" She glanced at the blinking red message light on the phone. "Noooo. I've been too busy. I've been trapped in this room all day, moving my stuff in. It's been nuts since Robin's been, um, gone. Not that I'm not happy to see you, but why are you here again? You're looking for me?" She played with a frame on top of the desk, sliding it back and forth until she was satisfied with the placement.

"I have to talk to you," I said. "But weren't you about to make a call? I can wait."

"Damn. The messenger." Lulu jerked out a card from the Rolodex and dialed.

I went into the hall and called Nick. "Lulu's here. I'll tell her about Osaze's and then I'll be right down. Where are you?"

"Near the Collins driveway, in a red zone," Nick said. "Do you want me to come up?"

"No. You'll get a parking ticket. I won't be long. I hope," I said. "Wish me luck."

"You don't need luck, Liz. You need faith. You can convince her to go to Osaze's. I know you can. Call me if you need me," Nick said.

Lulu was still on the phone. Her face was a splash of red. Not a good look with the gray-mauve lipstick. She flung a box of pens against the wall. She pleaded, then shouted at the caller about a pickup.

"I'm in charge of the Collins account now and if you can't do what I want, then I'll find another messenger service to handle Collins Talent business." Lulu waited for the dispatcher's response. "Good." She slammed the receiver. The phone rang again.

Lulu checked the number on the screen before picking up. "Dude." Her mood switched from raging to coquettish. She grinned; her tone was a singsong tease. "Will you record me off the board tonight? I need a DAT to play for Sam Collins next week. This show will convince him to put me in the studio—I know it will. Make sure there's not too much echo on my voice and keep my guitar in the background, okay?"

As she chatted, I watched the message light flashing red at the top of the phone. My calls went unanswered along with anyone else whose numbers Lulu didn't recognize. Robin would never be that unprofessional.

Lulu laughed and cleaned her fingernails with the tip of a letter opener as she talked. "I'm not worried. I told you— I have guaranteed good luck now. It's like winning the freaking lottery, dude."

"Lulu." I wanted to stop her from saying anything more. If she was talking about the "Fame" spell, she was making a huge mistake.

She turned her back to me and lowered her voice. "I have to hang up. Someone is here. I can't talk. I'll see you tonight."

Lulu set the receiver in its cradle, then dumped the contents of a carton onto the pile on Robin's desk. "I gotta finish moving my stuff so I'm ready for Sam on Monday."

With the empty carton in hand, she brushed past me into the hall. I followed.

"Lulu, wait. We need to talk. It's important." I took her arm. "You could get hurt."

"Are you threatening me?" She jerked out of my grasp. Her eyes flashed.

"No." I raised my palms. "I'm sorry. I'm trying to help you."

"Help me with what? What do you want to tell me? I'm busy." She spun away and moved down the hall toward her desk with me trailing behind. She stopped at her desk in reception.

I sat on the beige-leather visitor's couch, facing her. "I have bad news."

"Did they charge Robin?"

"No."

"Then what's the news?" Lulu fiddled with files on her desk.

"Tawny Dalton is dead."

Lulu continued to pull files and read without looking at me. "Who's Tawny Dalton?"

"She was a friend of Sophie's who bought a voodoo spell. I thought you might know her."

"Nope," she said with a shrug. "Is that why you were calling me? To tell me that?" She opened a drawer and emptied its contents into the box.

I shook my head and took a breath. "No. It's about Sophie's voodoo spells."

"I know . . ." Lulu smiled. "They work."

"Please, wait until I'm finished before you say anything else. It's important. Okay?"

"Okay, but . . ."

"I know about the curse on the spells. Buzzy and Tawny both bought spells and died because they triggered the curse," I said.

Lulu circled her hand like a bored teenager, urging me to go on.

"There's a spell for 'Fame' in the spell book with the initials L. M. next to it." I leaned forward. "Lulu, if you bought that spell from Sophie, I'm warning you—don't talk to anyone about it. If you already have, the curse is in motion, and you're in serious danger."

"That's not true. I'm fine." She swept her hand through her hair. "In fact, I just told someone how the spell was working out exactly the way Sophie told me—"

"You already told someone about the spell?"

"Sure I did," she said. "That spell turned everything around for me as soon as I used it. First I got a club booking, and now I'm Sam's assistant. All of the artists *and* Sam's important friends will know me now."

Nice of her to write Robin off so easily.

"You don't understand about the curse, Lulu. Didn't Sophie tell you to keep the spell to yourself?"

"I remember Sophie telling me not to tell Robin. Sophie couldn't stand her."

"You weren't supposed to tell *anyone*," I said. "Sophie's uncle can protect you if you come to his house tonight. He's performing a hex-breaker."

Lulu twirled a purple pen on her desktop. She looked up at me and smiled. "Nope. I'm singing at the Troubadour tonight. Isn't that cool? You should come there instead. Don't stress about the stupid curse. Sophie's dead. It can't hurt me. Come and see my show."

I buried my head in my hands and then looked up. "No. I want you to come with me."

She fidgeted and glanced at the computer screen. She picked at her nails. Then she began loading the box again.

"Lulu, you can't sing tonight," I said.

Lulu stiffened. "Yes, I can, and I'm going to. You can't stop me. Nobody can stop me." She threw a stapler into the box, then stood with her hands on her hips. "That bitch Robin sent you here to scare me, didn't she? I know she doesn't want me to have her job. Just like she didn't want Sophie and Sam together, either. She's jealous of me. Sam will see how talented I am, and he's going to help me. Robin's pissed because I told the police I saw her coming out of the parking lot, isn't she? Well, tell her it's not my fault she's going to prison."

How could Lulu see Robin in the parking lot unless she was there, too?

Lulu opened her bottom drawer and took out a deck of cards so familiar I held my breath. The last time I saw those beige skeletons, they were spread on the counter at Botanica Mystica: Madame Iyå's homemade tarot deck that was used to harass Robin.

I walked to the side of Lulu's desk.

Lulu held the tarot deck in her hand. "I deserve my shot working for Sam. I do everything around here and more, especially this week. You don't know half of the crazy stuff that happened. Lawyers, police, the press, and they all want to talk to Sam. And I'm the one who is protecting him. I'm the only one who knows what to do around here. He's going to reward me, too. He owes me. Even Sophie told me that Sam likes me better than Robin."

"I know this deck." I took the tarot deck out of her hand, unwrapped the rubber band, and began to fan the cards.

Lulu reached for the deck. "Give me that."

"You believe in the occult, don't you?" I sat on the couch with the cards. "Do you know how to read these?"

"No, I don't."

"Oh, come on, Lulu. We both know what these are." I fanned the cards again. "This deck was designed by a very powerful voodoo queen. You really should respect their potency. Maybe you already know what kind of trouble they can create for someone. Do you know the tarot employs the same theory as the *I-Ching*? The cards will speak to the moment if you lay them out a certain way." I was inventing as I went along. "I'll tell you what. If you don't believe me about the curse, what if we ask the cards if you're in danger? Will you come with me to Osaze's if the cards say you're threatened?"

Lulu sat still, her wary eyes fixed on the tarot cards. She didn't know what the cards meant. I needed her to believe that I did.

"I'll lay out all the cards for the answer. The deck inherited your energy by sitting in your desk. It will use your energy to unveil your destiny," I said.

I dealt the tarot cards on the floor facedown. A row of eleven cards spread in front of me. Then I counted the remaining cards on top, solitaire style, until the deck was exhausted. Three of the seventy-eight cards were missing.

Lulu bent forward in her chair. "Do you really think the cards can read my future? Will they tell me when I'll be a star?"

"Oh, absolutely."

Chapter Thirty-one

"We'll use the top eleven cards for your reading," I said to Lulu, pointing to the tarot deck spread on the floor in front of me.

The waning moon shone through the window at the end of the hall. I picked up the eleven cards and swept the rest aside. Applying the same grand gestures my mother used at her readings, I closed my eyes and took a deep breath. I tapped the first card and held it up.

"Let's see what we have here." If I got one card that looked like danger, I could run with a story that would get her to Osaze's. Simple enough.

A female skeleton with flowing auburn hair sat on a throne: "EEIPRSSST." I concentrated to allow the anagram to unfold. The first letters that jumped out were the three *S*s and the *P-I-E*. Sophie. No, that wasn't what I wanted. I looked again and I saw it: *priestess*.

Lulu got out of her chair to see the card. "That looks like Sophie. Well, except for the bony face." She giggled, then caught herself. "Oops, didn't mean . . ."

"It's okay, Lulu. I think you're right on." Strangely right on. "The skeletons on the cards are symbols that feed on our thoughts. Let's keep reading."

"But I'm not thinking about Sophie." Lulu sat down, her elbows on her knees. She flipped a pen against her palm. "Except that she gave me that . . ."

Tarot deck. With Sophie's cards in my hand, their scheme began to unfold. Sophie drafted her little ally, Lulu, to harass Robin.

"Sophie was the source of the spell. We're on the right track."

Lulu tapped the pen faster. "What's the next card?"

I turned it over: "GIIJNNO CEFORS." Two skeletons in skirts, three coins drawn over their heads. I took a minute to unlock the anagram: *joining forces*. That was weird. The card confirmed my suspicion: Sophie and Lulu were in league with each other.

"It's a pact," I said. "Did you and Sophie make a pact when she gave you the spell?"

Lulu shook her head quickly. "No."

I couldn't call Lulu on her lie. I had to get her to Osaze's first—even if I was furious with her. When Lulu planted the tarot cards at Robin's door, the chain of events leading to Sophie's murder began.

I held the next card up. "ABGIILNOOT": *obligation*. Ten coins, no skeletons.

"Are you sure there wasn't a pact, Lulu? Because this card shows its result: coins, money, fame. But they're attached to an obligation. A trade maybe? Did you do something for Sophie?"

"What is it? Let me see." Lulu took the card from my hand. "Aha. Look—it's lots of money. The spell was for fame, and fame brings money. I'm gonna be rich. It worked. I'm not in danger. I told you so."

The shadows from the lava lamp danced along the walls. I sensed a presence in the hall. I felt energy in the cards I held. I couldn't erase Sophie from my mind.

"You're not in danger *yet*," I said to Lulu. A whisper—Sophie's voice?—urged me to turn the next card: "AEEIL-NORTV."

Skeletons fled an arched, gray-stone structure. I closed my eyes and saw two people leaving the Greek Theater. One was Sophie.

"They're fans going wild at my stadium concerts," Lulu said. "That's so cool."

"AEEILNORTV": *revelation*. Something about Sophie, a pact, the Greek. But, damn it—what the hell did Lulu have to do with Sophie that night? My stomach went sour.

"Turn over another one. Am I going to be super-super famous?" Lulu circled her hand again at me to move on. Her knee jerked up and down while her sneakered foot tapped the floor. "Come on, what's the next card?"

The next card was "MNOO": *moon*. A full moon with the face of a skeleton floated in the center of a starless night sky. The moon was full the night Sophie died.

I looked down the hall through the window. A thin cloud veiled the waning moon. I held up the card. "It's the moon, Lulu. This one is your warning. Osaze told me he has to perform the hex-breaker before the waning of the full moon the night Sophie died."

I heard the whisper again. *There's more.*

"I think it means I'll be famous by the next full moon." Lulu ruffled her hand through her hair. "After Sam puts me in the studio. This is so exciting. Turn over one more card. C'mon. This is fun."

Fun? My nerves jangled. The reading wasn't getting Lulu to Osaze's. I closed my jacket tight to my chest. The scent of roses: my scent, Sophie's scent, drifted into my nostrils. I thought about the night of the party. Lulu was next to Robin when Sophie spat out her warning. Was Sophie directing the message at Lulu?

"Come on." Lulu poked my arm, shaking me from my thoughts. "What's the next card?"

I flipped it over. Neither one of us spoke. "ADEHT": *death*. The skeleton lying dead in the woods held a white rose. Sophie's favorite flower.

"The curse." Lulu bolted back. She stood, pushing the chair away from her desk. "I'm done. I don't want to see anymore."

I did. Lulu had watched me as the cards unfolded. She wouldn't look at me now.

"We have to finish the reading. The cards are telling a story. Look." I laid the cards on the sofa next to me for her to see, pointing at each card as I read. "The priestess joined forces with someone and made a pact. There was an obligation, maybe a favor, then a revelation, maybe a betrayal. A full moon, and a death."

I revealed the next card. Nine vertical swords hung over a skeleton on a bed. "GILTU": *guilt*.

Lulu pulled a large black purse from under the desk, sliding its strap over her shoulder. She picked up her keys, then stopped, drawn to the card. "What is that one?"

"Guilt. The cards are telling us who Sophie's killer was." My heart was pounding.

"Bullshit."

I looked up. "Don't you want to see if the cards get it right?"

"It was Robin." Lulu looked away.

"Then the next card will confirm that. Ready?"

"I'm leaving." Lulu circled her desk.

"One more, Lulu, one more." I snapped the card with my thumb.

She hesitated, watching my hand. I turned the card over.

The dancing, black-haired, and skirted skeleton played a guitar. The anagram scrawled beneath read "FLOO": *fool*. The voice whispered, *Lulu*.

"It's you, Lulu. It's everything about you." I looked up at her. "Tell me what happened between you and Sophie that night. It's time to tell the truth. I can help you."

Lulu backed away, clutching her purse to her chest. I waited. She stared at the card. Then she looked straight at me.

"I don't need your help. The voodoo worked. Don't you see? It was meant to be. Even Sophie was surprised when I told her about my booking. She told me I owed her. Sophie was obsessed with Sam. She hated how close he was to Robin so she made up a plan to make Robin quit. She said if I didn't help her, she'd reverse the fame spell I bought. She made me scare Robin with the tarot cards her dead husband got and with Robin's messed-up photo. When Robin guessed it was her that night, Sophie turned on *me*." Lulu spat out her words. "Sophie put the voodoo on me, but I made her pay, the bitch. I have to go do my show now. My audience is waiting for me."

"No, Lulu. It's too late. We have to tell the police the truth." I blocked her path. Lulu tried to push past me. I grabbed her arm. "Don't."

Lulu's eyes flashed like a cornered animal. She wrenched out of my grip and shoved me to the side. I lost my balance and fell backward on her desk, the sharp edge jamming into my back.

She grabbed a glass paperweight off the desk and cocked her arm. "Let me leave now, or I'll kill you, too."

I gripped the side of the desk and shoved Lulu away with my foot. The paperweight flew from her hand and shattered the lamp. Lulu lunged at me, knocking me into the wall. She swung her purse and hit the side of my face. I touched my cheekbone. Blood dampened my fingers. I wobbled and tripped over the desk chair onto my knees.

Lulu fled toward the stairwell. I pulled myself up and followed, yanking my phone out of my pocket as she dashed through the door.

"Nick—Lulu killed Sophie. She's coming down the stairs. I'm right behind her. Stop her. Get the police." My words fell out in gasps. I clomped down the stairs.

"How did . . ."

I hung up to get a grip on the railing. Then I took the steps, two at a time. My back and side burned with pain; the cut on my face throbbed.

Lulu was a flight below me. The glare of the fluorescent lights in the stairwell stung my eyes.

She wore sneakers; I was in heeled boots. Damn heels,

useless. I catapulted down, following the sound of her steps and the jangle of her purse. By the time I passed the third floor, Lulu was two sections below me, nearing the lobby. I wouldn't catch her in the stairwell.

I filled my lungs and shouted, "Security. Somebody. Stop her." My voice bounced against the gray concrete bricks and echoed above me. I was a flight above the lobby. Lulu bounded through a door to the parking lot. My heel caught. I slipped and twirled around. I grabbed the rail; my knee slammed on the step. I yelped. I pulled myself up and hopped down, pain shooting from my knee to my hip.

The lobby door nearly smacked me in the face when it flew open. The guard came halfway into the stairwell, and then Nick pushed him aside.

"I told you something was wrong up there," Nick said to the guard. Then he started up the stairs toward me. "Liz, are you—"

"Not me, Nick. Lulu. Stop her. Garage." I pointed to the door Lulu had disappeared through. "Don't let her get away."

"Don't worry," Nick said to me. He turned to the guard. "Get an ambulance. She's hurt."

The guard disappeared into the lobby, talking into the static of his walkie-talkie. "This is station twelve."

"Nick. We have to catch Lulu." Didn't he get the urgency here? Clearly, he was not an action hero or fast thinker. "She killed Sophie."

"I heard you on the phone. How do you know?"

"Nick, stop talking and go get her." I pointed toward the door to the garage.

Instead of obeying my demand, Nick tucked his arm

under my good leg, wrapped my arm around his neck, and picked me up.

"Nick, are you insane? She's getting away," I said, trying to push myself out of his grasp.

He opened the lobby door. "Yeah, I don't think so." He carried me across the lobby toward the glass front doors. "Barney Fife back there didn't believe me so I left the old guy to his newspaper and improvised. The police should be outside just about . . . now."

A loud crash, breaking glass, and the sound of crushing metal coincided with our exit through the doors and the blare of police sirens in front of the building.

Lulu had sped out of the garage and slammed her car head-on into Nick's old sedan blocking the exit.

Nick looked at me and smiled. "Parking in Beverly Hills was a nightmare."

"Put me down," I said. "I told you to park in the public lot."

A fire truck and an ambulance pulled up in front. One of the firemen took a dazed Lulu out of her car and led her to the EMT and waiting patrolmen.

A young Beverly Hills patrolman came up the marble steps toward us. "Can either of you tell me what happened here?"

Nick pointed to Lulu. "I want you to arrest that girl for battery. We'll explain after the EMT checks my girlfriend's leg."

Nick called me his girlfriend. In public.

"What happens to Lulu now?" I said.

"Look." Nick pointed to the cameraman and reporter unloading equipment on the curb. "The local media are always the third responders to a Beverly Hills crime scene. Lulu will get her headlines. But the fame she bought came in the wrong flavor. I want to get you looked at, then we make a statement and get Lulu charged."

A female EMT bandaged my bruised, not broken, knee and I signed a medical release. Nick called Dave and I called Ralph Barnes, requesting both to meet us at the Beverly Hills police station. While we waited for the tow truck and a cab, I laid out my theory to Nick.

"Sophie had Lulu leave the tarot cards at Robin's door. When Robin confronted Sophie, Sophie thought Lulu had confessed their plan. Then, when Sophie was thrown out of the party, she cursed Lulu, not Robin."

"So Lulu followed Sophie to the parking lot . . ." Nick said.

"Yep, fearing Robin or Sam would learn the truth and fire her. If she lost her job at the agency, she would lose her industry connections, too. Her big plans for fame go into the toilet. Lulu's temper, which I can testify to, got out of control. She bludgeoned Sophie, left her alone to die. Then Lulu spotted Robin, walking in the lot with Orchid. If Robin were arrested for Sophie's murder, the path would be cleared for Lulu to take Robin's place at Collins. Sam was Lulu's ticket to a singing career. Lulu followed Robin out of the parking lot into the ladies' room and wiped Sophie's' blood on Robin's purse."

"You saw all of that in the tarot cards?" Nick said.

I shivered a little, remembering the whispers in the hallway on the fifth floor. "It's the damnedest thing. I let go of logic and let my imagination guide me. The tarot cards laid out the basics and the story fell into place."

Nick put his arm around me. "That's how it works, Liz."

Chapter Thirty-two

Nick and I left Dave, Carla, and Ralph Barnes behind at the Beverly Hills police station. Lulu would be transferred to jail and questioned about Sophie's death. Monday she'd be arraigned for criminal battery on me. Carla arranged for a warrant to search Lulu's apartment for traces of Sophie's blood and a murder weapon. Barnes had enough in contention to release Robin into his custody.

Nick and I took a cab to my townhouse, then drove my car back into Hollywood. It was close to midnight when we parked outside Osaze's home.

"Am I dressed appropriately for the occasion?" I looked down at my jacket and jeans. Would we be huddled inside the skull-filled sanctuary?

"After everything that happened today, do you still need a dress code and a plan, Liz?" Nick helped me out of the car. "You look beautiful."

I smiled. "What do you think Osaze will do with the spell book now?"

"As far as I'm concerned, the spell book had nothing to do with the murder, it was all about the tarot cards. The police have the tarot deck, along with the cards left at Robin's, in evidence. I'll explain, and Osaze will decide what he wants to do with the spell book."

The soothing hollow timbre of a wooden flute drifted over the rhythm of steel drums and floated through the trees from the backyard. A small group of people sat on the porch steps. They nodded at us as Nick escorted me to the backyard.

Torches circled the perimeter of the yard. In the far corner, next to the sanctuary cabin, a bonfire blazed in the pit of a massive granite table. The flames flicked embers into the night sky. The yard was alive with guests talking, laughing, and drinking. Teens wore sweaters and jeans; older adults were dressed in multicolored African tunics. Henry was across the yard on a folding chair with a plate of food perched on his knees and his hat in hand. He was showing his Super Chief pins to the man at his side. Outside the back door to the house, three young men in bright flowered shirts played instruments. One beat a steel drum in a slow rhythm; another blew lightly into a wooden flute. The third man kept time, scratching on a long painted tube while he sang a bewitching African chant in a baritone voice. On the grass in front of them, men and women swayed their shoulders and hips to the beat.

A cloth-draped altar, laden with an assemblage of candles, fruit, and vegetables, was behind the fire pit. A framed photo of a stunning woman of color stood in the center of the altar. The woman's small lips were curled in a serene smile; her delicate cheekbones and slicked wavy hair framed piercing black eyes—the same face I had seen framed in Sophie's room. Callia.

A large, oval-shaped, tin tub filled with water and lemon and orange slices was positioned in front of the fire pit.

Food tables bordered both fences. Aluminum platters with mounds of ribs and burgers, salads, cut fruits and corn bread were spread out. A man in an apron turned slabs of ribs on a barbeque, filling the air with the aromatic scent of roasting meat. My stomach panged with hunger.

Osaze made his way through the crowd to Nick and me. "Welcome. Eat, drink, and dance. It pleases the Iwa. We must entice them to bless the ritual."

"First, we talk. I have news, my friend," Nick said.

Osaze smiled. "I had a feeling. Tell me."

A round African American woman in an orange-and-red-print caftan and a ponytail of gray hair interrupted our little group with a smile. She reached out to me. "You come with me into the house, honey, and I will prepare you for the bath."

Bath? Okay, I suspected I looked bad—it was quite the day—but I thought I was at least presentable and certain I didn't smell. Or might I be the sacrificial near virgin? I turned to Nick and touched the cut on my cheek.

"No, Makena, this is Elizabeth. There is no cleansing bath for her tonight." Osaze glanced at Henry across the yard, then said to us, laughing. "Mr. Marx wouldn't let Makena bathe him until you got here. And where is Sophie's friend—the woman cursed? Did you bring her?"

"No, we didn't. Let's talk," Nick said. He turned toward me and rubbed my arm. "Would you mind if I speak with Osaze alone?"

"Of course not," I said. "I'll go get something to eat."

"Yes, come, come." Makena took my hand. "I'll make you a plate."

As Makena guided me through the crowd, I looked back at Nick and Osaze. The news that Sophie's killer was in jail would be bittersweet to her uncle. Nick led Osaze to the side of the yard and put a hand on his shoulder, facing him. Osaze nodded, then stopped to look up to the sky as Nick talked. Ivalisse joined them. Osaze said something to her, and she put a hand to her mouth. Nick wrapped his arms around her. I lost sight as the dancers crossed in front of them.

Makena pulled me along toward the food tables. "Come on, Elizabeth, you skinny thing. The spirits will be insulted if you don't join in and eat."

The last thing I wanted to do was insult any spirits. I eyed the tub across the yard, grateful I was curse free and wouldn't be dipped. My mouth watered from the sight and smell of food. I stacked a plate with ribs and corn bread and ate while Makena introduced me to some of the folks standing nearby. All were Vodouns who came to participate in the ritual.

"I thought the spell book was an old wives' tale," said Michael, a tall, elegant man of about fifty, with cocoa skin and a black goatee. "The book with a curse so powerful that just knowing about it could kill you."

His wife, Belinda, a striking beauty with a shaved head and a nose ring, smiled. "We were going to spend the night at home, but Osaze said Callia's spirit needed our encouragement and support. And when Osaze puts out the call, we answer."

"And Sophie's spirit, too." Michael shook his head. "We're here to help Sophie find peace in the other world."

I saw a shock of jet-black hair over Michael's shoulder.

"Shrink." Nola sidled in between Belinda and Makena. "You look like someone beat the crap out of you again. What happened?"

I lowered my voice and leaned in, away from Makena's searching stare. "I ran into a flying purse, a runaway chair, and a steep stairwell. I'm fine. How did the move go?"

"All of Sophie's things are here, in the spare room. But that punk Jimmy up and disappeared. Linda and I had to finish the whole damn cleanup alone," Nola said.

"I had the impression that your father didn't . . ."

"Like Jimmy?" Nola broke into a mischievous grin. "My father hates him. But we needed the extra help. Jerk bailed on me anyway. Did you bring Lulu?"

Something brushed against my leg. I looked down. The taupe kitten peered up at me. I waved at it with two fingers and winked, and she wove a figure eight through my legs. Michael, Belinda, and Makena drifted back into the crowd. I steered Nola behind the table for privacy. "Lulu's in jail. She confessed to Sophie's murder. It's over."

Nola glanced across the yard toward Osaze, then to the altar. I expected shock, but Nola's face opened in a broad smile. In the moonlight, standing tall in a silk tunic of turquoise and black, a silver pendant at her throat, Nola looked regal.

"Wow," Nola said. "So Robin is innocent after all. I knew

I felt Sophie's presence when you came in. I don't know why her spirit is hanging around with you, but you brought her here tonight."

I thought about the presence I had felt and grinned. The kitten at my feet let out a tiny howl. I reached down to pick her up. She looked at me and howled again. I patted her little head and cupped her to my chest. She began to purr.

"See? Erzulie knows." Nola gave the kitten a scratch behind her ear.

"Erzulie?"

"Yeah. Sophie named her Erzulie when she was born," Nola said. "That's her little darling. Sophie was going to take her home as soon as the kitten could leave her mother. Check out her eyes."

I looked at the little kitten nestled in the crook of my elbow. Erzulie stared up at me. Her left eye was a light crystal blue; her right eye was golden amber. She opened her mouth and yawned and then jumped out of my arm and ran through the crowd.

"Cats are sensitive to spirits and demons. They're very aware," Nola said as Erzulie darted away. "But I guarantee you that if Callia's spell book is around, you won't see any dogs. They don't trust spirits."

The band stopped playing. Nick joined us at the side of the yard. "Osaze's ready to begin."

Conversations subsided. All eyes followed Osaze as he walked toward the altar. His gold ankle-length robe, threaded with black embroidery, swished from side to side as he moved.

I grasped Nick's arm—Osaze held the spell book pressed

against his chest, both hands crossed over it. Nick smiled at me, his eyes twinkling.

As Osaze passed, the crowd casually sat on the grass in front of the fire. Nick and I found an open spot between the sanctuary wall and the altar. Henry joined us.

"Thank you for coming." I hugged him hard.

"You didn't tell me about the bath," he said, eyeing Makena across the yard. "I'm not taking my clothes off in front of her."

I smiled. "You won't have to. Just watch and listen."

The crackle and smell of fire filled the air. Osaze placed the spell book in front of Callia's picture on the altar and circled it with burning black candles. He rang a small bell.

"To summon the spirits," Nick whispered.

Osaze sprinkled liquid to each of the altar's four corners, then faced the crowd. "Tonight we are here to honor and celebrate the *mo* of my revered ancestor Callia. Her legacy, the book of her spells, is on the altar charged with Callia's memories and the memories of all the women who carried on her bloodline: her daughters, Marie and Renee. Her granddaughters Luce and Laure. My mother, Florence, my half sister Juliette, and dear young Sophie. All tutored to cast and protect the power that Callia brought from the mountains in Haiti. Now that the female-to-female lineage has ended"—Osaze locked eyes with Nola, who was sitting in front of him—"a new generation of women will honor Callia's spirit with their own power. It is a new day for Callia's family. Her book of spells will be released to the fire, and we respectfully ask the Iwa to remove the curse Callia enlisted for protection."

Osaze spread open his arms and ceremonially embraced the crowd, and then he looked up to the waning moon. "We honor the Iwa with offerings of food and drink to please them."

I leaned close to whisper to Nick. "Who are the Iwa again?"

He cupped his hand to my ear. "The spirits who carry the power in the other world. Callia is an ancestral spirit, *mo*. Her powers are different."

Osaze turned to the altar and held up a small bag. Candlelight reflected in the sequins as he circled the satin bag above the leather-covered spell book. Then he put the bag aside and picked up the spell book. "Callia, honored ancestor, with your permission and the blessings of the Iwa, I will send this spell book and the curse that it carries to the flame."

Osaze stood in front of the blazing fire pit. My body pulsed with anticipation. A breeze, drifting above us, wrestled the rose bushes and filled the air with the scent of burning wood and roses. A crow landed on the block concrete wall behind the altar and cawed.

Little Erzulie jumped into my lap and settled in with her head up and ears alert.

Nick was right. Some things are beyond science or logic. He put his arm around me and squeezed. I rested my head on Nick's shoulder, hypnotized by the flames and Osaze's slow, melodic chant.

Osaze tore the spell book into the fire, page by page. Embers of burning paper floated into the sky. The crowd picked up the chant in a language I could neither make out nor follow. Nick and I swayed to the rhythm. And then, with a final incantation, Osaze reached for the satin bag behind him and shook the contents onto the burning pages. The fire flashed into an enormous golden blaze that reflected onto Osaze's upturned face and arms. The crowd lifted their arms with him.

The spell book was in ashes and its curse along with it.

A slow drumbeat began. The rest of the band picked up the rhythm. Men and women rose to their feet to drink and dance again. Osaze, Ivalisse, and Nola came to the corner where Nick, Henry, and I sat.

"Thank you. My family is grateful." Osaze looked down at us and beamed. "And I see that Erzulie has found her charge."

I stroked the kitten, asleep in my lap. "She's adorable."

"Adorable? That hellfire?" Ivalisse laughed and rolled her eyes. "She only came out from chasing mice under the house for two people—you and Sophie. I think she's staked a claim on you. She'll be angry if you leave without her." Erzulie purred so hard she made my thigh vibrate.

"Do you think so? I love cats. I'd love to adopt her." I scratched the top of Erzulie's head.

It was settled. After we said our good-nights, Nick carried the empty cat carrier to the car. Erzulie insisted on riding in my arms on the way home. Or I insisted on holding her. Whichever it was, we agreed.

As Nick drove toward Studio City, my phone rang. "Hi, Liz, this is Ralph Barnes. I'm at the Van Nuys jail with someone who wants to talk to you."

Robin came on the line. "I'm going home. Barnes told me what you did. Thank you." She let out a long, shaky breath somewhere between a laugh and a sob. "Thank you so much for always being on my side and believing in me.

Since we were kids, when Josh died, and now this—I'd never have made it through without you. I owe you so much."

"You're my friend, Robin. That's what we do for each other." I smiled. "But no more lies, promise?"

"No more lies," Robin said.

"No more voodoo?"

"But the curse . . ."

"Osaze burned the curse with Sophie's spell book. No more magical shortcuts, right?"

"Right. I'll even bake you that pie to smash in my face."

"And waste a perfectly good freedom pie? Hell, no. We're eating it."

She laughed. "Thank you, and please thank Nick, too. I love you, Liz."

"Love you, too," I said.

Thirty minutes later, Nick and I walked into my townhouse. Erzulie jumped from my arms and disappeared to explore her new home, while I set up her food dishes and Nick filled the litter box we picked up at the all-night drugstore.

When all was put in order, I opened a bottle of wine and plopped down on the sofa next to Nick. Erzulie found the empty pouch from Madame Iyå's lust gris-gris and batted it across the rug.

"What's that she's playing with?" Nick said as I leaned back on his chest with my head on his shoulder.

The kitten tossed the pouch into the air, then scuttled after it.

Dilemma. I was either going to tell Nick the truth or tell him a more reasonable, less embarrassing lie. I respected him too much to lie. No, it was more than that; I liked him. Actually, I was falling for him. *Get real*, I thought, I had already fallen for him too hard to lie. "It's the pouch from a lust gris-gris Madame Iyå sold me," I said.

He put his chin on top of my head and stroked my cheek with the back of his hand. Then he kissed his way down the side of my head to my ear. "Did it work?"

His soft, warm lips at the crook of my neck sent a light, dizzy shiver through my body. "Not sure," I whispered, with my lips on his forehead.

We watched Erzulie nudge the pouch next to Nick's foot, where she sat straight up, waiting for attention.

"What do you want, kitten?" Nick said.

That little trollop answered by falling onto her back with her legs spread open and her chest exposed.

"I think the gris-gris may have worked for her," I said.

Nick shifted me around and lightly kissed me. Then he kissed me. Then he really, really kissed me with a hunger that shot a sweet bolt of heat through my body.

"What about you?" he said between kisses, brushing back my hair.

"The gris-gris was meant for you, not me." I could barely catch my breath. I tasted his lips on mine, pulling me in.

"Then you wasted your money."

"Did I?"

"I'm way past lust."

"You are?" My words barely made it out as he slid his warm hand under my T-shirt and up the flesh of my back. With a flick of his fingers, my bra was undone. Oh my. I pushed him back and sat up. My equilibrium was gone.

Nick folded his arms and watched me pull off my boots. I flung my socks across the room. Erzulie picked up the chase. I stood up.

"Come on," I said, holding my hand out to him.

"Where are we going?" Nick smiled.

"Upstairs."

"To dance?"

"Oh yes."

NEW FROM NATIONAL BESTSELLING AUTHOR

Madelyn Alt

Home for a Spell

Indiana's newest witch, Maggie O'Neill, needs a new apartment. But when she finally discovers a chic abode, Maggie's dream of new digs turns into a nightmare: The apartment manager is found dead before she can even sign the lease. And Maggie finds herself not only searching for a new home—but for a frightfully clever killer.

penguin.com

New York Times Bestselling Author

Charlaine Harris

introduces a southern librarian whose bookish
bent for murder gets her involved in a real-life
killing spree...

REAL MURDERS
The First Aurora Teagarden Mystery

"Charms and chills."
— Carolyn Hart

"Ingenious...an engrossing tale...a heroine
as capable and potentially complex as P.D.
James's Cordelia Gray."
— *Publishers Weekly*

"One of the most original premises I've ever
come across in a mystery, and the whole
book is great bloody fun."
— Barbara Paul

penguin.com

Discover the Aurora Teagarden
Mysteries from

Charlaine Harris

the author of the Sookie Stackhouse,
Harper Connelly, and Lily Bard series

Real Murders

A Bone to Pick

Three Bedrooms, One Corpse

The Julius House

Dead Over Heels

A Fool and His Honey

Last Scene Alive

Poppy Done to Death

M335AS1208